FELIX GREY

and the

Descendant

FELIX GREY

and the

Descendant

Mario Theodorou

Neem Tree
Press

This is a work of fiction. Names, characters, businesses, places, events and incidents are either the products of the author's imagination or used in a fictitious manner. Any resemblance to actual persons, living or dead, or actual events is purely coincidental.

Published by Neem Tree Press Limited, 2025

Copyright © Mario Theodorou, 2025

1 3 5 7 9 10 8 6 4 2

Neem Tree Press
An imprint of Unbound
c/o TC Group, 6th Floor King's House, 9–10 Haymarket,
London SW1Y 4BP, UK

www.neemtreepress.com
www.unbound.com

A catalogue record for this book is available from the British Library

ISBN 978-1-915584-83-0 Paperback
ISBN 978-1-915584-84-7 Ebook UK
ISBN 978-1-915584-85-4 Ebook US

All rights reserved. No part of this publication may be reproduced, distributed, or transmitted in any form or by any means, including photocopying, recording, or other electronic or mechanical methods, without the prior written permission of the publisher, except in the case of brief quotations embodied in critical reviews and certain other non-commercial uses permitted by copyright law. For permission requests, write to the publisher at the address above.

Printed and bound in Great Britain by Clays Ltd, Elcograf S.p.A.

For Ελένη and Άβα

Dreams come true when you dare to believe in them.

Characters in Alphabetical Order

Agnes Lock, TUC representative
Alfred, Mr Houlston's apprentice
Amelia Woodruff, Oxford Professor
Arthur Jenkins, young miner
Charles Joyce, Lord Privy Seal
Clement Morris, poker player
Commissioner Thompson, Metropolitan Police
Ernest Booth, TUC representative
Ezra Fox, Docklands villain
Felix Grey, Prime Minister
Francis Banks, Tower of London curator
Francis Wood, Secretary of State for Foreign Affairs
Henry Coleridge, poker player
Humphrey, Steward
James Coleridge, poker player
James Creswell, Speaker of the House
James Henry, Chancellor

Jonathan Burbage, poker player
King Edward VII
Lord Cecil, House of Lords member
Lord Monteagle, House of Lords member
Mason, crow mask
Mason, eagle mask
Mason, goat mask
Mason, lion mask
Mason, monkey mask
Mason, owl mask
Mr Houlston, owner of Houlston & Sons
Mr. G Pulleyn, mysterious benefactor
Mrs. Hughes, Head Cook
Philip Masters, Oxford Professor and mathematician
Seema Sharma, Hostess at the East India Club
Thomas Percy, Home Secretary
Tom Fellows, owner of The George Inn
William Foster, miner and union man

– September 12th, 1904 –

East India Club

"East India Club," announced a porter, opening the carriage door.

Lord Monteagle stirred and slowly opened his eyes. He was feeling the ill effects of an afternoon spent drinking fine wine and brandy with his associates in Fitzrovia. He heaved himself up from his seat and gingerly stepped out of the carriage onto the busy pavement.

St. James's Square had a reputation for its bustling nightlife but was exceptionally crowded during the long winter months. The constant rain did little to dampen the spirits of those gentlemen who frequented the many clubs in the area. They stretched from the corner of Pall Mall and Waterloo Place to St James's Street and Piccadilly, boasting some of the most beautiful buildings in the city; great Georgian houses spread over five floors of marble and stone.

Monteagle had barely straightened his top hat and tie when an elegant, brown-skinned woman approached. She wore a sheer patterned tea gown, and her piercing green eyes shone brightly against her oil-black hair.

"Welcome, my Lord," she said, in a mild Indian accent. "My name is Seema Sharma. I am a hostess at the East India Club. Mr. Burbage has been anticipating your arrival."

"Very well," slurred Monteagle, his breath emanating a strong smell of alcohol. "Lead the way."

Seema Sharma led Monteagle up the wide marble stairs towards the double oak doors and the club's reception hall. In the centre of the room, framed by ornate vases overflowing with wildflowers from the Indian subcontinent, stood a towering sculpture of the goddess Durga sitting on a ferocious Bengal tiger. A symbol of the club's past as a base for workers of the East India Company.

Monteagle took a moment to study the paintings hanging from the walls, large portraits of past maharajas and British governors of India, all equal in size and splendour.

"Does it surprise you to see Indian maharajas on the walls of a London club?" asked Seema Sharma, reading his indignant expression.

"Nothing surprises me anymore," sneered Monteagle.

"These pictures are a representation of our combined wealth and power," continued the hostess. "They depict what can be achieved by the coming together of our two great nations."

"Ha!" scoffed Monteagle. "You would speak of India in the same breath as England?"

"Do you not invest your English wealth in our Indian resources?"

"You forget yourself!" barked Monteagle, clearly affronted by the hostess's familiarity.

"My humble apologies," replied Seema Sharma, her tone measured. "I meant no offence. Please, let us continue."

At the top of the staircase, the hallway split in two directions. Seema Sharma led Monteagle along the west corridor with its vibrant red-and-gold carpet towards a wooden door adorned with a carving of the elephant god, Ganesh.

"They are just through here, my Lord," she said, opening the door and inviting Monteagle to enter.

Inside, a group of gentlemen sat around an oval-shaped cards table with neatly stacked banknotes piled in front of them.

Jonathan Burbage, a well-turned-out greying man with warm blue eyes, rose to greet Monteagle.

"We were about to start without you, my Lord," he jested.

"I was held up," replied Monteagle bluntly.

"Well, no bother, you are here now, and the night is still young. Allow me to introduce James and Henry Coleridge," said Burbage, motioning towards two finely dressed brothers. "They have just returned from a spell in India where they have established a very successful tea plantation."

"My Lord," bowed James Coleridge, followed by his brother, Henry.

"And here on my right," continued Burbage, "is Mr. Clement Morris, one of London's premier insurers and a notorious cardsharp."

"Nonsense!" protested Morris, a middle-aged man with sharp features and cold, calculating eyes. "Although, I should be happy to cover your losses, for a small premium, of course."

"Pay him no attention," warned Burbage. "He likes to gain a psychological advantage before the game has even begun."

"Is there anything to drink?" asked Monteagle, cutting across Burbage's introductions.

"Yes, of course, what would you like?" asked Burbage.

"Whiskey," replied Monteagle.

"Good idea, whiskeys all round!" called Burbage, waving his hand theatrically at Seema Sharma.

The hostess poured five measures from a tall crystal decanter, then added a single ice cube to each glass before handing them out to the guests.

Monteagle took his seat alongside the house dealer, removing a large pile of banknotes from inside his pocket and placed them on the table for all to see.

"I was just regaling these gentlemen with stories of our time together in India, setting up your plantations," continued Burbage, taking his seat. "What days they were."

"You are a sentimentalist, Jonathan," replied Monteagle, gulping down his whiskey. "You cling too tightly to the past."

"A man's memories are worth their weight in gold," protested Burbage, "and I know you still reminisce on that time as fondly as I do, even if you do not care to admit it."

"I certainly do not. I find the Indian heat unbearable, as I do the people, the food and the roads."

"Tell me, my Lord, how do you find working with the locals?" asked James Coleridge.

"We have a straightforward understanding. They are employed to work our lands and if we are unhappy with their day's efforts, they are sent home without pay."

"That's rather old-fashioned, wouldn't you say?" replied Henry Coleridge.

Monteagle held up his empty glass and motioned towards Seema Sharma to refill it. "It guarantees efficiency and ensures a satisfactory return on our investment."

"Yes, but what about your relationship with your workers?" asked James Coleridge. "Surely, they can't be overly enthused with such an arrangement?"

"If they do not like the conditions of their employment, then they are free to leave. There are thousands more who would readily take their place."

"That I can account for," agreed Burbage. "I have never seen so many people in one place. It's like a giant colony of ants."

"Such an abundance of labour must have a positive effect on your insurance premiums," added Clement Morris.

"We can always guarantee production, if that's what you mean," replied Monteagle, taking hold of his newly filled glass from an indignant Seema Sharma, who had been listening to their conversation in silent fury.

"Gentlemen," called the dealer, taking advantage of a small break in the conversation, "shall we begin?"

"Yes, I think so," replied Burbage, adjusting his banknotes. "We are all sufficiently acquainted."

The dealer shuffled the pack and began to deal the cards.

"The game, sirs, is three-card poker, with a starting bet of two shillings," he announced, placing the remaining stack by his side.

A businesslike hush fell over the table as the men placed their starting bets in the centre and gathered their cards, taking a moment to arrange them and consider their strategies.

"The bet is with you, my Lord," said the dealer, motioning towards Monteagle.

Monteagle took a second to scan the table and his opponents.

"Raise, one pound," he declared, placing a banknote in the centre of the table.

"That is quite a substantial bet, my Lord," replied Burbage, tossing his cards towards the dealer. "Too rich for my blood."

"And mine," agreed Clement Morris, placing his cards to one side.

"I should like to test your mettle, sir," announced Henry Coleridge, placing a banknote on the table alongside Monteagle's.

"I'm afraid I am out too," said James Coleridge, reluctantly throwing his cards down.

"Two players remaining," called the dealer, motioning towards Monteagle and Henry Coleridge.

Monteagle swiftly drained his whiskey, setting the glass down before turning to address his opponent.

"I am unfamiliar with your estates in India; are they in the north?" he asked.

"They are," replied Henry Coleridge, "although we cannot call them our own. They are leased."

"That is most interesting," said Monteagle, throwing down two cards to be replaced by the dealer.

"Do you still have many interests in India, sir?" asked Henry Coleridge, replacing a single card.

"Some. Although, I own them all, lock, stock and barrel."

"Then you are fortunate indeed."

"Your choice, my Lord," prompted the dealer, refocussing their attention on the game.

"Five pounds," declared Monteagle, sliding his banknotes across the table.

"Five pounds?" repeated Burbage, shocked by the size of Monteagle's bet.

"Indeed," replied Monteagle, suddenly feeling a hot flush come over him. He wiped a bead of sweat from his brow and leaned forward arrogantly. "It's five pounds if you wish to continue."

Henry Coleridge took a moment to consider Monteagle's bet, before reluctantly placing his cards face down on the table. "Not on this occasion, my Lord," he conceded. "I fear my cards are not quite strong enough to test if you're bluffing."

"Bravo!" clapped Clement Morris. "Very clever, my Lord. Your questions were merely a ruse to ascertain how much money it would take to scare off your opponent. Fortunately for you, Henry unwittingly gave you all the information you needed."

"Naturally," said Monteagle, rising from his seat to collect his winnings. "One must always play the man and not the cards."

As he reached across the table for his money, a sudden wave of dizziness overcame Monteagle. He swayed, clutching the table leg for support.

"Are you alright, sir?" asked Henry Coleridge, observing Monteagle with concern.

"I am quite…well," replied Monteagle, his speech becoming slow and laboured. "I just…need…to…" he trailed off, unable to finish his sentence.

Suddenly, his legs buckled beneath him, and Monteagle collapsed to his knees, his eyes vacant.

"My Lord!" exclaimed Burbage, rushing to Monteagle's side to assist him. "What's happening to him?" he asked, alarmed by Monteagle's limp frame.

"It appears his lordship has had too much to drink," replied James Coleridge, taking hold of Monteagle's other arm.

"I shall summon his carriage at once," said Seema Sharma, hurrying out of the room.

The men carried Monteagle's unconscious body out of the card room and down the long, winding staircase towards the club's reception. Hearing the commotion, members began to appear from their rooms, eager to catch a glimpse of the stricken peer.

Outside, a waiting carriage stood ready to receive Lord Monteagle. The men carefully placed him on the long wooden bench inside, draping a blanket over him before shutting the door.

"Take him home and give him something to sober up," called Burbage to the driver, who promptly took hold of the reins and guided the horses forward into the pale early-morning light.

It was some time before Lord Monteagle finally began to regain consciousness. He could feel thin rays of sunlight on his face as he lay stretched out on the carriage bench.

He pulled himself up, his head still hazy from his sudden turn, and wiped the long beads of sweat from his forehead. Outside, he could feel the horses running at full tilt and the carriage rocking wildly from side to side.

"Slow down, Jacob!" he called out, mustering what little strength he had. But the carriage only seemed to accelerate further, hurtling through the cobbled streets at a frenetic pace.

Monteagle reached for the window, trying to pull it open and alert his driver, but the latch was jammed.

"I'm quite alright, Jacob. Slow the pace!" he yelled, his voice lacking its usual punch.

Outside, Monteagle could see the London streets passing quickly by the window. The broad pavements and ostentatious Georgian houses that marked out the affluent area around St James's Square had been replaced by the rough cobbled alleyways and tall warehouses of the London Docklands. Monteagle gaped at the unfamiliar surroundings. Why were they here of all places?

Memories of his evening at the East India Club began to form in his mind. He recalled the card room, the game of poker with Burbage and his associates, his winnings…then, nothing. Just a feeling of utter helplessness. His last recollection was of faces looming over him as he knelt on the poker room floor, unable to move. Had he been poisoned?

Monteagle glanced around the carriage in shock. He hadn't noticed at first, but the vehicle he was travelling in was not his own. It was far less spacious, with narrow, hard wooden benches replacing the luxurious, cushioned leather seats he was accustomed to. His eyes returned to the windows, noting that they were smaller than his and covered with a thin black material that allowed the passenger to see out, while completely blocking any view of the carriage's occupants from the outside. There were no handles on the doors, only a bar to rest one's arm.

Monteagle pressed his body against the door and looked up through the gap in the window cover towards the driver. He could not see the man's face, but his frame was larger than Jacob's, with broad shoulders and a thickset neck covered in tattoos. Monteagle pulled at the carriage door, but it would not move. It was locked from the outside.

"What is the meaning of this?" he shouted, banging on the carriage roof.

Exhausted from his futile efforts and still feeling the effects of the poison, Monteagle sank back in his seat, gasping for breath. Suddenly, the horses began to slow, bringing the carriage to a halt. Through the window, Monteagle watched as the driver dismounted. He scanned the compartment looking for anything he could use as a weapon, but the small carriage had been expertly stripped and prepared for his abduction.

Within moments the driver was at the carriage door, his sinister gaze piercing through the shaded window. A sardonic smile played across his lips, revealing his black and yellow teeth. He looked like the type of ruffian one would expect to frequent the Docklands' notorious drinking holes and opium dens. The driver removed a key from his pocket and used it to unlock the door, slowly opening it to reveal a gun levelled at Monteagle's stomach.

"My Lord," he bowed mockingly.

"Why have you brought me here?" asked Monteagle.

"My employer desires an audience."

"Whatever he is paying you, I will treble it. Just take me back to my club," demanded Monteagle.

"Ha! You men of title think everything has a price."

"Does it not?"

"Some things are worth far more than money," replied the driver, pulling Monteagle out of the carriage and thrusting the gun into his back. "Now, walk!"

Reluctantly, Monteagle obeyed.

After weaving their way through a series of narrow side streets and cobbled walkways they emerged at one of the river's many docks. Passing groups of workers loading supplies, Monteagle hoped to catch someone's attention and alert them to his situation. But these were casual labourers, hired that morning and given a chance to earn a wage, something they were unlikely to jeopardize by noticing anything out of the ordinary.

Monteagle took a deep breath, noticing that the air was thick with the sweet scent of sugar mixed with the sickly smell of burning rubber. He suspected they were somewhere between Tower Hill and Wapping, where such products were known to be stored in recent years. The area had been renowned for handling the trade in luxury items like wool, wine, ivory and even ostrich feathers. But the small waterways couldn't cope with the rapid increase in vessel size and the lack of railway access saw a sudden decline in the viability of such trade, and with it a sharp rise in the flow of illegal goods and criminality. It wasn't uncommon for people to disappear off one of the many piers and jetties that lined the docks around the area, never to be seen again, a fact that wasn't lost on Monteagle.

As they neared the river, the driver directed Monteagle towards a menacing black barge, moored on the bank with a narrow gangway leading to its deck.

"On you go then," he said, pointing his gun towards the vessel.

"And if I refuse?" asked Monteagle.

"Then I'm to put a bullet in your back and send you to the bottom of the river."

Monteagle hesitated. He knew that once inside the barge, the possibility of escape, or discovery by the authorities, was limited.

"Get a move on!" snarled the driver, prodding Monteagle viciously in the ribs with his weapon.

With little choice but to proceed, Monteagle reluctantly stepped onto the rickety gangway. He could still feel the weakness in his legs as the bridge swayed and wobbled beneath him, almost causing him to lose his balance. He finally made it across, relieved to feel solid ground under his feet once more.

At the end of the walkway stood a door with a dimly lit entrance. Monteagle cautiously stepped inside, allowing his eyes a moment to adjust to the change in light. As the shadows sharpened, he made out a long, narrow room with a low ceiling, its timbers creaking softly with the river's movement. There were several mismatched pieces of furniture scattered about, and a worn oilskin coat hung from a hook near the doorway. The air was thick with the smell of damp wood and stale tobacco, undercut by a faint trace of engine oil. Monteagle's attention was suddenly drawn to a tall, shadowy figure at the far end of the room, silhouetted against the faint light seeping through a grimy porthole.

"Welcome," called the figure in a rasping voice.

"What do you want with me?" asked Monteagle, a hint of authority returning to his voice.

"Only what's owed, my Lord."

"I have no debt with you," declared Monteagle.

"Oh, but you do, sir. You have a very substantial debt indeed."

The shadowy figure struck a match and lit his pipe, revealing a red leather patch over his left eye.

10 Downing Street

Heavy raindrops dappled the black gates surrounding 10 Downing Street. It had been a wet start to autumn, and the slow march of feet usually heard outside had disappeared along with the summer sun.

Inside, Humphrey set about lighting a fire for his master, Felix Grey. He placed the heavy logs on top of the tiny embers and fanned the gathering until flames appeared, filling the study instantly with heat.

Humphrey stood up, straightening his stiff back. The cold weather had brought on his arthritis earlier than usual, and he was thankful for the fire's warm relief.

Felix had offered to bring in some help, but Humphrey refused. He'd been with the Grey family for over four decades and had practically raised the young prime minister, ever since the early passing of Felix's mother, Leonora Grey, to cholera. A strong-willed petitioner for women's rights, Leonora had made Humphrey promise to always remain by Felix's side, and he was not prepared to break his oath or see his life's work handed over to a stranger. Besides, he liked to stay active. It was hard work, but Humphrey had seen first-hand what happened to people in semi-retirement; their joints began to seize up, and their muscles wither away, bringing on old age quickly. No, he would continue in his role and keep his strength while he could.

He circled the room, checking everything was in place before allowing himself a moment's rest. He'd barely taken a seat and closed his tired eyes when he heard the door to Number 10 open and the house staff spring into action.

Humphrey let out a long sigh. He was used to the furore that usually accompanied Felix's return from Parliament. It was as though the house itself had awoken from a long rest, with every room and all its staff readied and waiting to receive the prime minister.

Humphrey slowly pushed himself up from his warm seat and straightened out his suit. Within moments, the door sprang open, and Felix bounded in, accompanied by his friend and the Home Secretary, Thomas Percy.

Percy was a rotund man, heavily built, with flushed cheeks and a loose suit that made him appear older than his forty-four years. In contrast, at only thirty-four, Felix was young for a prime minister, with an athletic figure and the odd speck of grey in his neatly combed black hair. He wore a cleanly pressed suit with polished shoes, and a handkerchief rested on the brim of his chest pocket.

"Afternoon, old man," he said, approaching his steward.

"I am beyond your cajoling, Felix," replied Humphrey. "The fire is lit, and I am content. How was Parliament?"

"In an uproar, as always."

"And what, pray tell, do they have to moan about today?"

"The list is both long and infuriating," replied Felix, pouring himself a large scotch.

Over the past few months, he had become accustomed to the taste of scotch whiskey and enjoyed a stiff measure or two to wash away the day's cobwebs.

"They have no stomach for reform," declared Percy, lowering his plump frame into one of the seats facing the fire. "They like to cling to their outdated traditions."

"There is nothing wrong with tradition, Home Secretary," countered Humphrey, "only its application. Greedy men will find advantage in any idea, old or new. Now, will you be staying for dinner?"

"Unfortunately not. I have a mountain of work that requires my immediate attention."

"I won't hear of it, Thomas," protested Felix. "There is nothing that can't wait until you are properly fed and watered. Humphrey, have another place set for dinner, will you please? And let Mrs. Hughes know that she will be feeding an extra mouth."

"Very well," replied Humphrey, setting off to coordinate matters.

"You do realise that he's wasted here," said Percy, when the study door had closed behind him. "He should be in the backbenches, whipping the members into shape."

"He'd have them running for cover," agreed Felix, amused by the thought. "He's been with the family ever since I was a young boy. I don't know what I would do without him."

Felix crossed the room and held his hands over the fire for warmth. It had been a short journey back from Parliament but a cold one. On the mantelpiece sat a picture of Felix, taken on the night of the general election. Crowds had gathered outside Downing Street to welcome their new prime minister. It was a night he would never forget; the clapping and cheering, the warmth and optimism he had felt from the British people.

Having been parachuted into office at the tender age of thirty-two, Felix had become the second youngest prime minister in British history, with only William Pitt the Younger having been more junior. With little experience to draw on and few alliances in either Parliament or his coalition government, he'd found the first two years in office difficult. Many of his reforms had been blocked in the Commons, and Felix was finding it impossible to effect any meaningful change, let alone live up to the public's inflated expectations of him.

Had he known how easily people's opinions could change, how quickly the dissenting voices would appear, he may have held back a little, detached himself from the euphoria that would inevitably fade with time, instead of standing on the steps to Number 10, smiling broadly and waving.

Hindsight would make an excellent companion for any man, but particularly a prime minister.

Felix's thoughts were interrupted by a knock at the study door.

"Come in," he called out.

A young footman, dressed in full livery, entered the room.

"Sorry to disturb you, sir," he began, "but Police Commissioner Thompson is here to see you."

Felix exchanged a surprised glance with Percy. The commissioner had never visited Downing Street without prior arrangement. He would usually send an officer ahead to make enquiries before arriving in person.

"This is most unorthodox," said Percy. "Shall I ask him to come back at a more suitable time?"

"No need," replied Felix, preferring to confront the unknown head-on. "Send him in," he instructed the footman.

"Good evening, gentlemen," began the commissioner, entering the room. He was a short man in his late fifties, with greying hair and a tightly cropped moustache, and his perfectly polished boots and precisely pressed creases bore the mark of a former British army officer. "Apologies for the abruptness of my visit, but I come with grave news. I thought it best to inform you directly before you heard the undoubted whispers in Parliament."

"Go on," replied Felix, his interest piqued.

"In the early hours of this morning, Lord Monteagle was abducted from the East India Club while engaged in a game of poker with his associates. The perpetrators drugged him with an organic compound known as ether, a common anaesthetic, colourless and easy to mask when poured into a person's drink. They then switched Monteagle's carriage with their own, ensuring his lordship's associates unwittingly delivered the stricken man directly into their clutches, swiftly disappearing with him into the night."

"What cowards!" exclaimed Percy.

"Indeed, sir. The men were clearly organised and had been planning the abduction for some time. They knew of his lordship's arrival and had made the necessary arrangements to extract him swiftly and with minimal fuss."

"Military men?" asked Felix.

"It's a possibility, Prime Minister."

"Have they issued any demands?" asked Percy.

"No," replied Thompson, producing a small envelope from his pocket. "They did leave this, however," he said, handing the envelope to Felix. "We found it in one of the backstreets, lying on the cobbles alongside Monteagle's driver, Jacob Moore."

Felix opened the envelope and took out a small rectangular card, no bigger than a half-pound note. It was light in weight but rigid to the touch and had a series of strange markings on both sides. He turned the card over in his hands, noting the odd shapes and symbols.

The first, an image of a common five-pointed star, had been crudely drawn and was faded and out of shape. Felix had seen many like it in the history books and encyclopaedias at Number 10, and on the walls and paintings of his Mayfair club. The second image, however, was less obvious to him. It seemed to depict a giant goat's head with four horns pointing in opposite directions, surrounded by a cluster of stars with fire and smoke swirling around them. The goat's face was strikingly human, and its black, marbled eyes seemed to stare back at Felix from the paper.

"Are you familiar with these signs, Prime Minister?" asked Thompson.

"No, unfortunately not," replied Felix, placing the card back inside the envelope. "I've only a basic knowledge of semiotics, and this is way above my limited understanding."

"Pity," said Thompson. "No one at the station can make head nor tail of it."

"How is your questioning coming along?" asked Percy.

"We've interviewed the club staff, but no one seems to have seen or heard a thing prior to his lordship's sudden turn, and the hostess has sworn on record that the whiskey bottle Monteagle had drunk out of that evening was opened in the room and could not have been tampered with. We've taken statements from each of the guests in attendance, all of whom were dismayed to hear that Lord Monteagle had been poisoned. We also took the liberty of looking into their whereabouts immediately before and after the abduction, and their alibis appear to hold water."

"And his family?" pressed Percy.

"They are just as bewildered as we are," replied Thompson.

"And what of his driver, this Jacob Moore fellow?" asked Felix.

"According to Mr. Moore, he'd been on the carriage awaiting his master's return when he decided to rest his eyes. That was the last thing he remembered. Our officers found him some hours later, curled up on the wet cobbles with a bloodied scalp and the envelope resting beside him."

"And do you believe his account?" asked Felix.

"His injuries are consistent with his explanation."

Felix took a moment to ponder the information. It had been a clean and well-planned abduction, but it had been carried out in plain view of the public and inside one of London's most famous and busiest members' clubs. How was it possible that no one knew anything about it?

"Have the press been made aware?" asked Percy nervously.

"Not yet," replied Thompson. "I'm confident that the matter is still contained, although stories of this nature tend to have a short lifespan before they are leaked out. I would say twenty-four to forty-eight hours at most."

"Then time is of the essence, Commissioner," said Percy. "Have your teams interview the East India Club staff again. If they had been planning this abduction for months, then there is a strong chance there was someone on the inside. We need to find the cracks in their stories. Also, look into Monteagle's affairs, his business associates, his finances, his mistresses. There must be a reason why he was the target."

"We are doing everything we can and more," replied Thompson, a hint of irritation in his voice. "We have experts engaged in all manner of modern scientific and forensic analysis, including our new Fingerprint Bureau at Scotland Yard who are looking for any unexplained fingerprints on either the whiskey bottle or the players' glasses. We also have officers checking the rivers and backstreets for any sign of his lordship's…"

Thompson suddenly stopped, reluctant to say the word *body* and tempt fate.

"Understood, Commissioner," said Felix, reading Thompson's thoughts. "Do keep us informed of any developments. I should like to know how things progress."

"Very well, sir," replied Thompson, turning to take his leave. "Oh, I almost forgot," he said, spinning around to face Felix. "The evidence, if you will, Prime Minister."

"Ah, yes, the card."

Felix looked around his desk for the envelope, but it was nowhere to be seen. He glanced over at Percy, who shrugged his shoulders, equally bewildered. Felix checked his pockets, only to find that he had inadvertently slotted the envelope, with the card inside, into his suit jacket.

"My apologies," he said, embarrassed. "I must have placed it in there without realising."

Felix held out the envelope, ready to return the evidence, when, without warning, he snapped his hand back before Thompson could take hold of it. Something about this case had piqued his interest and made Felix suddenly reluctant to part company with the mysterious card.

Before trying his hand at politics, Felix had carved out a successful career as a lawyer, following in the footsteps of his father and grandfather before him. It was this instinct, this need to scrutinise a piece of evidence and unravel the case, that had been suddenly reignited in him.

"Prime Minister?" questioned Thompson, pointing at the envelope in Felix's hand.

"If your team is having trouble identifying the marks, perhaps I could be of assistance?" offered Felix.

"How so?" asked Thompson, confused.

"I have a close acquaintance at Oxford University, an ex-collegemate who is somewhat of an expert in semiotics. I would be happy to present the card to Professor Woodruff for review."

Thompson took a moment to study Felix. It was most unusual for a prime minister to offer his assistance in police matters, but how could he refuse?

"Very well," he said, "but I must insist that the card is dispatched to Scotland Yard immediately on your return. It is, after all, the only evidence we have."

"Naturally," agreed Felix, slowly feeding the envelope back into his jacket pocket.

Having concluded his business, Commissioner Thompson departed for Scotland Yard, leaving the men to their thoughts, and the warm fire.

"What do you know of Lord Monteagle, Thomas?" asked Felix, his mind alive with questions.

"Not a great deal," replied Percy. "He likes a drink or two, and clearly likes to gamble. Perhaps he'd become indebted to someone? There are some very unsavoury people around these poker tables, you know."

"Yes, but why abduct him in such a manner? Why not wait until he was in his home or somewhere less public? And the card…" continued Felix, rubbing the small paper object in his pocket. "Clearly, they wanted people to know what they were doing."

"Best to leave it to the authorities, Felix," warned Percy. "You've got enough on your plate."

Felix nodded, trying to reassure his colleague, even though he'd already begun making plans for the trip to Oxford in his mind.

The men were disturbed by another knock at the study door. Felix barely had time to answer when the door swung open and Mrs. Hughes, a stout woman in her mid-fifties and wearing a cook's uniform, burst into the room, followed by a distressed-looking Humphrey.

"Prime Minister—" she began, clearly annoyed.

"Apologies for the interruption," interjected Humphrey, "but Mrs. Hughes was insistent on speaking with you directly."

"What is it, Mrs. Hughes?" asked Felix.

"This old buzzard," she replied, giving Humphrey a sharp look, "has just informed me that we will be entertaining the Home Secretary this evening."

"That's correct," replied Felix.

"But, as usual, he's neglected to ask our guest the pertinent questions that would enable me to fulfil my duties to the best of my ability and to the standard this house has come to expect."

"Has he indeed?" asked Felix, casting an amused glance at Humphrey.

"Indeed, he has," confirmed Mrs. Hughes. "We have a little saying up north, *Tha meks a better door than a winder.*"

"And what in heaven's name does that mean?" asked Humphrey, his patience waning.

"It means that you're always getting in the way," replied Mrs. Hughes turning to address Felix directly. "If I could just have a minute or two with our esteemed visitor, Prime Minister, I'll be able to get all the information I need."

"Please, be my guest," said Felix, motioning towards a nervous-looking Percy.

"If you would kindly follow me, sir," began Mrs. Hughes, leading the Home Secretary towards the study door. "The kitchens are just this way. We can discuss what you would care to eat as we walk. You might also wish to wash your hands before dinner…"

With the strong-willed head cook marching Percy out of the room, and Humphrey departing to continue with his dinner preparations, Felix turned his attention to the study window, peering out at the world on his doorstep. As the Autumn daylight faded rapidly, the new electric street lamps buzzed into life, illuminating the usually dark streets outside. He could see that the heavy rain had finally ended, and people were beginning to reappear on the streets. How quickly life returned to normal, he thought. Life, however, had been anything but normal for him ever since he'd won the general election and become the British prime minister. Perhaps it would never return to normal for Lord Monteagle either; not unless the peer was found soon and in one piece.

Corpus Christi

It took all of Felix's considerable willpower to sleep that evening. Thompson's visit had filled him with a nagging curiosity, and he could think of nothing else as he prepared to settle in for the night. He paced the large room, recounting every detail of their conversation, hoping to uncover even the slightest clue he may have missed or overlooked. As with any crime of this nature, there would have to be a strong motive, a compelling reason behind the action, and Felix was determined to uncover it. However, having turned over the facts in his mind for hours and exasperated by his lack of progress, Felix finally retired to his bed, determined to renew his efforts the following day.

The next morning, Felix arose to the sound of activity. Under Humphrey's close supervision, the house staff were busy preparing Number 10 for a parliamentary dinner and had overwhelmed the building with their enterprise. It was a rare chance to see the house put to its full use and the staff wasted little time dressing the state rooms and polishing the fine silver. Felix made his way through the hustle and bustle towards the dining room. He had decided the previous evening to make enquiries into the symbols on the card and was keen to make an early start.

After a quick breakfast of eggs and spinach, Humphrey summoned the car for their short journey to Paddington Station, where the necessary arrangements had been made for their safe but surreptitious journey to Oxford and an audience with Professor Woodruff at Corpus Christi.

The train carriage was small but agreeable. The staff had fitted the long wooden benches with comfortable leather cushions and had placed a large pot of tea alongside the day's broadsheets. Humphrey poured the tea while Felix took the opportunity to catch up on the morning headlines. He had always considered the newspapers a sound measure of public opinion. He flicked through the tall pages, folding each neatly as he passed, moving from one article to another in search of anything that might grasp his attention and distract from his obsession with the Monteagle case.

At first glance, there seemed to be little to hold his interest. The pages were full of the usual stale political and economic commentary, including a detailed account of the rapid growth of German manufacturing alongside a list of Britain's largest factories, to give readers a like-for-like comparison. The top spot, noted Felix, was held by Bryant & May, a matchmaker based in the East End of London, which employed a particularly high number of women and girls.

There was some light relief, however, in the form of Captain Scott's expedition to the Antarctic and a report on his time with the emperor penguin colony at Cape Crozier and the dizzying effects of snow blindness. But any feelings of contentment were short-lived as Felix turned the page to reveal a most concerning headline.

"Tragic accident or avoidable manslaughter?" he muttered under his breath.

Felix sat up a little straighter, focusing his attention on the article in front of him.

> Tragic accident or avoidable manslaughter? These are the questions surrounding the death of Arthur Jenkins, a young miner from the Rotherham district of South Yorkshire. Mr. Jenkins, 22 years of age, had worked in the Silverwood Colliery for more than five years and witnessed first-hand the site's old and malfunctioning machinery. As a union man, he endlessly petitioned the company directors about the need for investment, often warning against inevitable accidents and possible deaths.
>
> It is, then, with a sense of heavy irony that on the day of our Lord, Friday, September 10th, 1904, Mr. Jenkins met with his tragic and untimely end at the hands of the faulty

equipment he had so feared during his time at Silverwood, crushed under the weight of a collapsed rig. In memory of Mr. Jenkins' death, the miners of Silverwood have sworn to strike until the company directors agree to make significant assurances on investment.

The Right Honourable Milton Cavendish, the Leader of the Opposition, has called on miners of all counties to petition the government on what he has described as "a systematic failure to protect the great working people of this country." The enquiry into the death at Silverwood continues.

Felix set the newspaper aside. He knew that despite the tragic nature of this young miner's story, it would likely be exploited and used as a weapon against him. Arthur Jenkins' sudden and avoidable death represented everything that was wrong with a system that favoured a privileged few over the masses, a narrative his opponents would undoubtedly twist and manipulate for their political gain. There was no such thing as "off-limits" in politics, no moral code when it came to Westminster. Every story held value, and this unfortunate miner's tale was worth its weight in gold.

Felix contemplated returning to London, but with the police already investigating the incident, and the train now Oxford-bound, there seemed little point in changing course. Instead, he penned a letter of condolence to the Jenkins family in Rotherham and prepared a short statement for Parliament calling for an enquiry into the events at Silverwood. Felix tried to reassure himself that his actions stemmed from a genuine sense of moral duty rather than mere political obligation, but in truth, it was increasingly difficult to distinguish between the two since coming into office. For now, his letter would bring the family some small comfort and give him a little time to find out what he could about the abduction and the symbols on the card.

It was late morning when the train pulled into Oxford Station. Felix and Humphrey disembarked onto the platform, when Felix caught sight of a tall, gangly figure dressed in a leather pilot's jacket and pastel trousers, complete with a driving hat and smoke-covered goggles.

"Professor Woodruff!" he called out.

The professor's appearance hadn't gone unnoticed among the passengers waiting on the platform, who quietly whispered to one another as the gawky scholar bounded past them to greet Felix.

"My dear Felix, how long it has been!" said the professor, removing the hat and driving goggles to reveal a tangle of braided auburn hair and bright green eyes.

"A female professor at Oxford?" exclaimed Humphrey, taken aback.

"Yes, it did come as quite a shock to people at first. You know how worked up those stuffy old newspapers can get," replied the professor, the slightest hint of Texan in her accent. "They're clearly not that impressed with our ability to birth all human life on this planet, including their own. But thankfully, the furore seems to have settled down of late."

"Amelia, allow me to introduce my rather tactless and old-fashioned steward, Humphrey," said Felix, shooting Humphrey a hard look.

"Ah, Humphrey, yes, of course!" replied Amelia, taking Humphrey's hand. "I've heard so much about you. The roots beneath the great oak."

"We do what we must," replied Humphrey, averse to her brash American manner, and mindful of the gawking public.

"Never mind the locals," said Amelia, sensing Humphrey's uneasiness. "They like a good old stare. It reminds me of a visit I once had from a young sultan. He travelled with an incredibly large entourage, including several servants, a menagerie and his harem. It caused quite a stir, I can assure you."

"Nevertheless, I think it would be a good idea for us to leave, before we attract any more unwanted attention," pressed Humphrey.

"Fear not. I have my car waiting outside. It might be a touch overcrowded, but it will see us to our destination," said Amelia.

"I'm sure it will be adequate," replied Humphrey, prompting them forward.

Outside, the town was blanketed by a thin layer of frost. Amelia led the men to her waiting car, a cast aluminium vehicle in British racing green with a two-person cushioned bench, a small steering wheel, and a soft retractable roof.

"The Rover 8," she announced proudly. "A great feat of British engineering. Although, not quite a Ford, but hey ho, it'll do."

Felix helped Humphrey into the car. His arthritis had been fine on the train, but he'd felt its presence the moment they stepped out into the cold Oxford air. Thankfully, Amelia carried a large flask of hot tea with her on journeys, and she poured Humphrey a small cup with a nip of whiskey for good measure. With her guests seated, Amelia wound the vehicle crankshaft, firing up the engine. As it coughed and spluttered into life, the exhaust kicked out a plume of black smoke for the station onlookers to see, much to Humphrey's annoyance. Undeterred, Amelia hopped into the car and took hold of the steering wheel.

"All snug?" she asked cheerfully, crunching the car into gear, causing even more disturbance. "Then let's be off," she concluded, finally pulling the vehicle away from the station.

The journey to Corpus Christi was largely uneventful. Humphrey found solace in the quiet streets and gentle melodic hum of the town, a welcome departure from the bustling, cacophonous exuberance of London. Meanwhile, Felix and Amelia took the opportunity to reminisce on their time together at Oxford University. They had first met in the Bodleian Library, where Amelia worked as a cleaner, while secretly pursuing her degree under a male pseudonym. One evening, Felix stumbled upon her pouring over the same course text as his, prompting him to gently coax a confession out of her. Moved by her determination and incensed by the injustice, he committed himself to helping her navigate the logistical challenges of being a woman in a male-only university. Amelia went on to pass with flying colours, top of her class, even outperforming Felix, a fact she often delighted in reminding him of.

Corpus Christi College was small by Oxford standards. The beautiful main quad with its central tower, dining hall, library and adjoining chapel had stood for nearly four hundred years and showed few signs of ageing. The famous Pelican Sundial stood in the centre of an open court with its majestic golden bird looking out over the grounds and beyond.

Amelia guided the car through a large stone archway and into the cobbled square. As she brought the vehicle to a standstill, the engine let out a loud bang, announcing their arrival to the entire campus. Suddenly, several young faces appeared in the line of windows above them, curious to see the identity of the professor's latest visitors.

"Nothing to see here!" shouted Amelia, as they climbed out of the car. She'd witnessed first-hand how quickly news could travel around college and did not want a repeat of the furore that had accompanied the young sultan's visit. The timid prince had barely set foot in her office when hordes of students filtered in to get a look at their exotic visitor, inadvertently blocking the exits and trapping the sultan inside for hours.

Amelia hurried Felix and Humphrey through the square and into a warren of charming lesser buildings, stopping outside an old cottage with a thatched roof and an antique oak door.

"We have landed," she breathed, taking hold of the brass knocker, and hammering it.

Within moments, the door creaked open to reveal a diminutive, grey-haired woman dressed in a dusty steward's uniform, straining to focus on the people in front of her.

"One second," she called, fumbling in her pockets for her spectacles. "My glasses are here somewhere. I was just using them."

"No need, Hopkins. It's only me," said Amelia, stepping past her steward and leading the men through the main hall.

"Righto, Professor," replied Hopkins, finally locating the glasses on the top of her head. "Would you like me to prepare some tea and sandwiches?" she asked, placing them on the bridge of her nose, only to see that the professor and her guests had disappeared.

The professor's office was small and cramped, with several bookshelves overflowing with novels and encyclopaedias. At first glance, Humphrey mistook it for a poorly kept library, but the messy desk in the centre of the room littered with the professor's papers quickly revealed its true identity.

"Please, do make yourselves comfortable," said Amelia, rummaging through a small box of odds and ends, looking for something.

Felix and Humphrey surveyed the room for a place to sit down, but even the chairs were covered in the professor's files.

"Ah, there you are!" announced Amelia, emerging from the mess with a brass magnifying glass in her hand. "Now, let's take a look at this card of yours."

Felix reached into his pocket and removed the envelope, handing it to Amelia.

"This is our only scrap of evidence. I would like to take it back to London in one piece."

"You have nothing to fear, I assure you," said Amelia, removing the card from the envelope and holding it up to examine the symbols. "And you say it was found at the scene of the crime?"

"Yes, in a cobbled alleyway, along with Monteagle's unconscious driver."

"How interesting."

"What do the symbols mean?" asked Felix.

"Well, they could mean any number of things, depending on who you are and what you choose to believe."

"No speaking in riddles," cautioned Felix.

"Very well. For the laypeople in the room, there are many organisations, past and present, mythical and actual, who would lay claim, or not, to the symbols on this card."

"Professor…"

"Sodalitas!" exclaimed Amelia, holding up her magnifying glass to emphasise the point. "Secret societies to the outside world. Men and women, but mostly men, with fancy rings and clever handshakes. But to those who know, groups and fellowships of very powerful and very dangerous people. Although, I confess, I have never seen these symbols appear together in such a manner."

"Do you think Monteagle was involved with one of these secret societies?" asked Humphrey.

"It is possible. He is, in many ways, just the kind of man you would associate with these types of organisations. Wealthy and powerful. It would not be unrealistic to assume his involvement or even membership with one of them."

"But what would make an organisation turn on one of their own in this way? What possible offence could he have committed that would lead to such a reaction?" asked Felix.

"It is hard to say. Codes of conduct vary significantly between each group and are as secretive as the organisations themselves. However, what is clear is that trust is essential to their existence. It's their very lifeblood. If one link were to break, it could have far-reaching consequences for the entire chain. These organisations have been known to deal with weaker links swiftly and with a savage brutality to preserve the group's integrity."

"Perhaps Monteagle was on the verge of breaking rank and exposing the organisation?" suggested Felix.

"That would account for his abduction," replied Amelia.

"And the card?" asked Felix.

"A show of force, perhaps. A message to their members that they had dealt with the situation. The card was clearly left to serve a purpose."

"But by which group?" asked Felix.

"The key is in the combination of the symbols," replied Amelia, placing the card on the table for Felix and Humphrey to see.

"Let us start at the very beginning. The five-pointed star, or the pentagram, as it's more commonly known, represents the five elements of nature: earth, fire, water, air and the spirit. It is pagan, but also a prominent emblem within freemasonry. Though its significance, like most, is concealed behind a smokescreen of secret society ambiguity."

"Good heavens," said Humphrey, taken aback by Amelia's revelations. He had known several masons over the years, including members of his own family, and had seen the organisation as nothing more than a social club for gentlemen. He'd never have imagined it being associated with such dark and shadowy affairs.

"There are many faces to these organisations, not merely the common ones you may be familiar with," said Amelia, observing Humphrey's reaction. "Think of them as icebergs. Only a small fraction is visible above the water, but there are entire mountains beneath, hidden from view."

"I had no idea," said Humphrey.

"And what of the other symbols?" asked Felix.

"Well, they are altogether more revealing, particularly the goat's head."

"I was certain I'd seen it before," said Felix.

"You will have come across it, no doubt, in relation to the medieval knights. You may remember the deity more clearly by his name, Baphomet?"

Felix took a second to think about the name. It was familiar, but he had not read much on the Knights Templar since leaving Oxford, just the odd piece here and there in the rare moments he'd found time to pick up a book.

"The knights were accused by Pope Clement V and King Philip IV of France of worshipping Baphomet during their trials. Many were executed for their supposed offences. The knights have a long and shadowy association with freemasonry and Baphomet, who interestingly appears in many of their rituals and initiations."

"So, you believe there is a credible link to the masons?" asked Felix.

"It's certainly a thread worth pulling on," replied Amelia. "But this is no ordinary branch of freemasonry. In all my years of study, I have never come across these symbols displayed as they appear on your card. I think an audience with the masons may set us on the right track."

"Do what you can, Amelia, but I don't want you placing yourself in any unnecessary danger. This is a matter for the police; we are merely trying to assist where we can. We're certainly not trying to be heroes of any kind."

"You worry too much, Prime Minister," replied Amelia, trying to mask her excitement.

But Felix recognised the mischievous look in his friend's eyes. He'd seen it many times before. The impetuous Texan had a reputation for bumbling her way in and out of perilous situations, and this case had undeniably captured her interest.

Electric Sparks

"Go on then, give it a try," urged Lord Cecil, observing his son William's reluctance with growing impatience.

The young boy had been staring at the newly fitted light switch for some time with no hint or suggestion of any action. Since hearing about his family's conversion to electricity, William's classmates had teased him daily about the effects of electric sparks, and he had grown fearful of this strange new power source.

"It really is very safe. You will feel no ill effects," pressed Cecil, urging his son forward.

William peered up at his father's stern face, searching the deep lines and weathered skin for any signs of uncertainty.

"You are sure, Father?" he asked, hesitant yet eager to prove his courage.

If William's classmates' stories were to be believed, the merest touch of one's skin against the metal switch would be enough to send a lethal surge of electricity through the body, causing a person to blackout or, even worse, die.

Cecil rested a reassuring hand on the boy's shoulder. William reluctantly reached out and took hold of the small brass toggle, pinching his fingers around its smoothly curved head. To his amazement, there was no shock, no surge of electricity or anything else; he was still standing upright and in one piece. He took a deep breath, swallowing back his fear, and flicked the switch, casting a brilliant light throughout the large study. The effect was intoxicating. William watched as the light's energy danced around the room, reflecting off the ivory walls and crystal chandeliers into the tight corners and tiny nooks that had only ever known shadow and darkness. He'd never seen a room so brightly illuminated; it was as though someone had lit a thousand candles all at once.

"You must never allow fear to be your master," said Cecil, crouching down to meet his son's eye. "It is only an excuse for those who lack heart."

William felt a burst of pride swell in his chest. He had overcome his fears and his friends' apish warnings.

Cecil studied his son. He remembered when he was a boy, unsure of himself and his position, desperate to prove himself. He wanted to hug William, to tell the boy how proud he was of him, but as a father, he'd learnt to hide his emotions, barricade them behind a wall of conduct and protocol. He'd seen too many boys of privilege growing up with dark pride and arrogance in their hearts and was determined to raise his sons to be men of substance, even at the expense of his own feelings.

"We had better get washed up for dinner," he said, slowly rising to his feet, "or your mother will give us both something to fear."

The dining room was enormous, with an elaborately carved wooden ceiling and freshly papered white walls that added to the brightening effect of the new lights. Beneath the hanging chandeliers sat a long dining table covered in ornate china plates overflowing with vegetables and roasted game.

The staff placed the remaining garnishes and condiments on the table before charging the family glasses with wine. It had been a longstanding tradition for the head of the house to make a toast before dinner, and Cecil was not a man to challenge family customs.

Lady Cecil kept a close eye on her two sons. At fifteen, Peter had been permitted to taste wine at the house toast before, but this was William's first time, and she was determined to keep his consumption in check.

"Wait for your father, please," she said as the boys reached excitedly for their glasses.

"Just a sip, Mother," appealed Peter, "so that William can become accustomed to the taste."

"That is precisely my worry, that either of you should ever become too accustomed to its taste," replied Lady Cecil, waving the boys back into their seats.

After what had seemed like an eternity to the boys, Cecil finally rose to deliver a few words, allowing them to take hold of their glasses.

"We have much to be thankful for," he began, holding his glass with purpose. "Land, wealth, security. All the luxuries afforded to a family of our position and status. But it is all for nothing if we allow ourselves to fear the unknown. We must always remain tall in the face of adversity."

Cecil paused for a moment, fixing his eyes on William.

"I would like to toast to our courage, fortitude and indomitability, for those are the qualities that make us who we are today."

"A fine speech!" called a rasping voice, cutting through the warm atmosphere.

Cecil turned to see a large, hooded figure standing in the shadow of the dining room doorway.

"Who are you?" he asked.

The man stood upright, revealing his broad shoulders and full intimidating height.

"Just a messenger," he replied.

Suddenly, a gang of similarly hooded figures entered the room, spreading out to cover its full width. Cecil looked from the dark figures to his family. He could sense the fear and anxiety building around the table.

"What is the meaning of this?" he asked, trying to mask the concern in his voice.

"Afraid, my Lord?" mocked the man still hovering near the door.

"I am not the one who hides in shadows," replied Cecil.

"Ha! You have spirit. I'll give you that," said the figure, "but I am tempted to strip you of that foolish high-born pride of yours."

"If it is money you seek, none is kept here on the premises. Take whatever else you desire and leave."

The figure stepped forward, his dark frame seeming to grow with every stride until it felt like he would consume the entire room with his presence.

"My employer requests an audience," he said, finally moving into the light, revealing his scar-ridden face and a red eye patch covering his left eye.

"And if I refuse?"

"Then you shall be removed against your will."

Cecil's gaze drifted away from the intruder back to his family. He was tempted to test this criminal's mettle but would never forgive himself if any harm were to befall his wife and children, not while he could prevent it. His eyes suddenly caught the glimmer of light reflecting on metal. He turned to face William, noticing his son's hand wrapped tightly around the table knife and a wildfire burning in his eyes. Cecil placed a gentle hand on the boy's, feeling the calm return and his grip on the knife slowly release.

"Then I shall come freely," he called out, embracing his sons. "Look after your mother," he whispered to them, his eyes gleaming with pride.

Cat and Mouse

It was early evening when Felix and Humphrey returned to Downing Street. The journey back from Oxford had been slow, and neither man had managed to get much rest on the train.

Humphrey set straight to work. It was the middle of September and, as was the custom, the doors to Number 10 were to be opened to Felix's fellow politicians for an evening of food, fine wine and forced conversation.

Buoyed by Amelia's revelations, Felix made his way to the study to document his thoughts. As a lawyer, he'd learnt to make detailed notes on all of his cases, on the off-chance he'd need to reference a small detail or recall a name some months or even years later. It had been a worthwhile exercise and a skill that had proved beneficial during his time in office. The human brain could only commit so much information to memory, and there was a limit to the amount Felix could heap on Humphrey's sharp but ageing mind.

The study was warm and well-lit. On his desk, Felix found a copy of *The Times* newspaper opened on the centre pages, with a handwritten letter placed on top. Curious, he unfolded the note and read its contents.

> *Felix, I've managed to obtain an early edition of tomorrow's newspaper. Unfortunately, news of Lord Monteagle's abduction has reached the press. The miner's story is also gathering pace. We must do what we can to appease the workers, or we may see widespread striking. Cavendish has the look of a cat that has just eaten all the cream. Percy*

Felix placed the note to one side and picked up the newspaper. There was a small article detailing Monteagle's abduction, but, to his surprise, most of the space was dedicated to the young miner's death at Silverwood. The bold headline, *Murder in the First Degree*, sat in large type above a grainy black-and-white photograph of Arthur Jenkins, with his dark, ink-blotched eyes staring hauntingly back at Felix from the page.

Felix took a moment to consider the image. The poor quality made it hard to take in the scene, but he could make out a pier in the background and a young woman standing beside Arthur, holding a single rose. It was the sort of scene that could soften even the hardest and most unsympathetic of hearts; a young couple with their whole lives ahead of them, the promise of adventure in their eyes. There was something innately British about it.

The more Felix studied the picture, the more he realised just how far and wide the impact of this young miner's untimely death could spread. Percy was right; the situation needed addressing urgently.

Glancing at his pocket watch, Felix noted the time. It was close to nine o'clock in the evening, and soon Downing Street would be overwhelmed with politicians and their parliamentary staff, all bursting to discuss Monteagle's abduction and the miner's death. His eyes followed the mechanical hands as they marched around the watch face, willing them to stop. But even the prime minister could not control time, however much he longed to.

The state dining room was as grand as any you might find in the political houses of Europe. The staff arranged the guests' places at the long table, each with a set of silver cutlery and two large crystal glasses for wine and sherry.

Felix took the opportunity to greet his colleagues as they arrived. The men looked smart in their dinner suits, bow ties and finely polished shoes, and the ladies wore gowns of all colours and styles from notable French, Italian and American designers. The competition to be considered best-dressed was as fierce as the clamour for Number 10, with the competitors communicating their contempt for one another through a series of subtle looks and veiled gestures, mainly curt smiles and faux-friendly nods.

Thomas Percy made his way through the dining hall towards the smoking room, where several men had gathered to discuss their affairs out of earshot of the women. Among them were Barnaby Shaw, the pompous Shadow Chancellor and Old Etonian, and the leader of the Conservative Party, Milton Cavendish, a tall, middle-aged man with sharp features and cold, calculating eyes that gave off a weasel-like appearance.

The men were familiar and at ease in each other's company, but as with any gathering of close rivals, there was a dangerous edge in the air that could be felt by all.

"What is on the menu for this evening, Humphrey?" asked Percy, rubbing his heavy hands in anticipation.

"Always thinking with your stomach," mocked Shaw in his thick Yorkshire accent.

"A large appetite in life is no bad thing. Perhaps if your appetite were more considerable, you'd know how it feels to be in government rather than continuously sitting on the periphery."

"I believe the main course this evening is duck, Home Secretary," replied Humphrey, stopping Shaw from responding.

"A fine choice," replied Percy.

"And how does the prime minister's mood fare after the day's big revelations?" asked Cavendish.

"To which revelations are you referring?" questioned Percy.

"Why, the abduction, of course. Surely the news has reached him by now?"

Percy looked around the room at the amused faces.

"Well, I would say his mood is…"

"Much the same as yours, Milton," replied Felix, entering the room. "Saddened, but determined to see the guilty parties brought to justice."

"I am sure you are making every possible enquiry."

"Indeed, we are," replied Percy, "and when we find the culprits, I will ensure they feel the full force of the law."

"Do you have many leads?" asked Cavendish.

"It's still early in the investigation, but we've had one or two developments," replied Percy, embarrassed to admit that there had been little to follow up on since the abduction.

"Rumour has it, Monteagle had some very significant gambling debts. I should start your enquiries at some of the members' clubs he liked to frequent," suggested Shaw.

"I wouldn't pay too much attention to rumours," replied Percy.

"There is no smoke without fire, Home Secretary."

"And not all fires are lit with malicious intent."

Felix observed his opponents' interest in the case with growing uneasiness. The abductors, whoever they were, had been clever enough not to leave any trace, aside from the card, and even that morsel of evidence was shrouded in ambiguity. Percy's subtle remonstrations would not hold his questioners at bay for much longer, not now that the story had reached the newspapers.

Felix's thoughts were disturbed by the sound of the house bell ringing. Humphrey waited for the chatter to subside before announcing dinner and directing the parliamentarians and their partners to the dining room.

Felix sat at the head of the table near Percy, who was eagerly anticipating the first course. It wasn't long before the conversations resumed, and Felix found himself engaged in several debates around the table at the same time. They ranged from global economics to simple housekeeping at Number 10. Rarely had he spoken to so many people in such a short space of time about so many things. Rather than feeling exhausted by the experience, however, the interactions left Felix feeling surprisingly upbeat; proud, even, to have presided over such a successful event.

"Prime Minister," said Percy in a low voice, leaning in close to Felix, "we must discuss this Arthur Jenkins affair. The miners at Silverwood have begun their strike, and there have been murmurs of strikes in other mines, up and down the country."

Although spoken quietly, Percy's words had not gone unheard by the alert ears of Milton Cavendish, who had expertly positioned himself a few places down the table: far enough to be overlooked, but still within earshot of their conversations.

"Yes, do tell us, Prime Minister," said Cavendish, directing the table's attention towards Felix. "What are you going to do about this miner's death, and the impending strikes?"

Felix took a moment to consider the question. With so many watching colleagues waiting to jump on his every word, he did not want to say the wrong thing.

"We'll speak with their union and reassure them that we're carrying out a full investigation into the death of Arthur Jenkins, alongside a review of the working conditions at Silverwood."

"Spoken like a true politician," mocked Shaw, raising his glass.

"Come now, Prime Minister," replied Cavendish. "We're not in Commons. I think your colleagues would be interested to hear your true feelings on the matter."

To most around the table, Cavendish's jibes could easily be mistaken for the customary horseplay between parties, but both men had been engaged in a game of political cat and mouse for some years now, and Felix had become well-accustomed to his opponent's subtle but calculated attacks.

"Very well," said Felix, observing the growing interest around the table. "I believe working people were fed up long before this tragedy occurred. Arthur Jenkins' death just made them realise it. I also believe they deserve a far greater say in how their communities and working environments are shaped. Those are not unreasonable requests."

"That's a very progressive stance. And how exactly do you propose we appease these dissenters?" asked Cavendish.

"Their discontent is the result of a system that only rewards those in power. There is very little chance to better oneself in modern society. It's a regrettable legacy of an old system, which needs reforming."

"Tosh. What nonsense!" barked Shaw. "There has always been a battleground upon which the gentleman has fought with the lesser classes. It is no different now than it has ever been. Of course, they will moan and kick up a fuss, but they'll soon fall back in line when they realise it could cost them their livelihoods. They always do. A firm hand is all that is required."

It was clear from the approving nods that many around the table agreed with Shaw's summation. Most politicians had a vested interest in the system and were against social reform of any kind. It was this deeply rooted unwillingness to change that Felix had encountered time and again since becoming prime minister.

"If you think this problem will simply disappear under the weight of a few veiled threats, then I'm afraid you have sorely misjudged the situation and the British people," said Felix.

Shaw opened his mouth to respond when he was stopped in his tracks for a second time by Humphrey appearing at Felix's side, holding a small white envelope.

"An urgent message, Prime Minister," said the old steward, ending the conversation.

Felix rose from his seat and made his apologies before departing for his study to read the note in private. Once inside, he broke the seal and opened the envelope, unfolding the letter. It didn't say much, and was as direct and to the point as Commissioner Thompson had been in person:

A second abduction. Lord Cecil. from his home. No damage or signs of a struggle. Another card left at the scene. Still no demands. Thompson

Felix felt his stomach jolt. A second peer abducted in less than twenty-four hours, and another card left at the scene of the crime. There was now no question of this being merely a personal matter between Monteagle and this group or organisation. It was something far more significant. But what did these peers have in common?

One thing Felix was sure of was that these abductors, whoever they were, must have influence at the highest level to orchestrate the abduction of two lords with such ease and precision. They would need to know the peers' daily routines, comings and goings, public duties and personal commitments. They would need to know someone close to them; someone they trusted.

Felix's head was swimming. He placed the note inside his desk drawer and returned to the dining room to see out the remainder of the evening. He circled the room looking for Percy, but instead came face to face with a stocky man in a miner's uniform and wearing the red sash of a labour unionist around his torso.

"I am here representing the working men of this country, who are sick to death of the exploitation that is so rife throughout this land," he bellowed in a thick Yorkshire accent, bringing the event to a standstill. "We are at the end of our tethers with this government and seeing as you have been so intent on ignoring our pleas, you've left us with no choice but to deliver this document to you in person."

The miner handed Felix a long scroll of paper covered in petition signatures.

"How did you get into my house?" asked Felix, brimming with anger.

"Ne'er you mind that, what are you going to do about our demands? We will strike, you know. All up and down this land. Don't test us. We're ready for it."

Felix stepped forward, occupying a small space of no more than five inches between himself and the miner, showing that he would not be intimidated.

"If you wish to speak to me, invite me to one of your meetings, and we can talk like civilised people. But do not break into my home like a common thief and embarrass me in front of my guests. Such actions are beneath us both."

Whereas men like Shaw had dismissed the workers' demands as nothing more than a passing gale, Felix had been greatly alarmed by their growing discontent. The sudden appearance of this unionist at Number 10 had proven that any house was accessible and any man reachable.

"Move aside! Coming through!" shouted Percy, burrowing his way through the watching crowd followed by two police officers. "Escort this man to the nearest police station and see that he is charged at once," he roared. "We will not tolerate this sort of open rebellion."

"That won't be necessary, Thomas," objected Felix, the calm returning to his voice. "Take him to the kitchens and see that he is well fed, then return him safely to his lodgings."

"Are you sure?" asked Percy.

"It was just an error of judgement," replied Felix, turning to face the miner. "There are ways to have one's voice heard, and this was not one of them."

Felix nodded to the officers, and they escorted the man out of the dining room.

With the commotion finally over, the guests slowly returned to their drinks and conversations. Felix was pouring himself a large scotch when his eyes caught the sharp, satisfied gaze of Milton Cavendish watching from across the room. Cavendish lifted his sherry glass, evidently thrilled with the dark shadow that had been cast over Felix's evening. Felix raised his glass in return, acknowledging his opponent's victory, yet suddenly suspicious of Cavendish's part in the disturbance.

Old Pye Street

A day is a long time in politics, or so it had seemed to Felix over the past twenty-four hours. If he had been winning the battle over dinner, he was most certainly losing the war by the time his guests left, and he returned to his study to brood on the night's events and his unfortunate encounter with the miner.

On the surface, it appeared harmless enough. A disagreement between a union representative and a politician was hardly uncommon. Barely had there been a time in their short history when the unions were not upset by one government policy or another. But something about this unionist's demeanour struck Felix as different; something in their short but heated exchange had made an impression on him. He tried to recall the man's words, but his mind was still overwhelmed by the day's revelations.

However, one thing Felix was now sure of was Cavendish's involvement in the miner's sudden appearance. Such acts were consistent with his opponent's single-minded desire to become prime minister. But how had Cavendish managed to gain the union's trust and convince them to carry out such an openly rebellious act? What had he promised them in return for their support?

Felix felt his stomach lurch for a second time; he could sense the political wind changing. How had things become so strained so quickly? Only as recently as a year ago, his cabinet had been widely praised for its far-reaching reforms and modern approach to government. They had passed a record number of Acts through the great houses, most of which they had fought tooth and nail to deliver. But if a day was a long time in politics, then a year was quite simply an eternity.

There was also the pressing matter of Lord Cecil's abduction to consider. Felix opened his desk drawer and removed the commissioner's note, scanning the words for anything he may have overlooked, some subtle clue or detail that could shed some light on the mystery.

"A second abduction. Lord Cecil, from his home."

Hearing the words out loud seemed strange, as though voicing them somehow made the event more real. But why Cecil? Felix had occasionally dealt with him in the House of Lords and found him to be a man of substance. Quite rare in the halls of Westminster, which usually teemed with ruthless ambition. Surely there was nothing sinister lurking behind his cordial and well-respected manner. But then, nothing was ever certain in politics, nothing entirely as it seemed in the corridors of power, where great careers were often forged on rickety foundations. The only constant was time, and time had a way of unveiling even the most expert of disguises. Perhaps there was more to Cecil than met the eye.

"No damage or signs of a struggle. Another card left at the scene. Still no demands," continued Felix, thinking on each word as he read them.

The lack of any criminal damage or even a struggle suggested to Felix that there might have been some level of familiarity between the abductors and Cecil. Could Cecil have been expecting them? Or perhaps, even more alarmingly, could he have welcomed them into his home with open arms? That would mean it could have been someone he knew or even trusted.

Felix's thoughts were wild with theory and speculation. Determined to quiet his mind, he crossed the room to pour himself another scotch. As he rushed past the open fireplace, Felix stepped awkwardly on the hearth, throwing himself off balance. He scrambled to regain his footing, but his body had passed the point of no return, and he tumbled headfirst towards the mantelpiece, striking his head on the hard marble and landing on the study floor with a heavy thud.

Sprawled out and barely conscious, Felix could feel his head throbbing violently. He lifted his hand to his temple to assess the damage. Fortunately, there was only a tiny lump and no sign of bleeding. He forced himself off the floor and back onto his feet, cursing himself for drinking too much and allowing himself to fall in such a manner. It was another hammer blow to his confidence and, despite being alone in his study, Felix felt a deep sense of personal humiliation wash over him. Perhaps he wasn't the right man for the job after all. Maybe it was finally time to cash in his chips and clear the way for a better man to take the reins.

Felix took a moment to allow his body to readjust. He was still dizzy from the heavy bang on his head and did not want to risk another fall. As he leaned against the mantelpiece for balance, he noticed something odd. One of the decorative corbels had been turned ninety degrees and was now vertical rather than horizontal like the others. He looked down, realising that the dark coal-stained panel that usually glimmered in the glow of one of Humphrey's large fires was no longer there; it had vanished, revealing what seemed to be a long tunnel, dimly lit by lamps hanging from either side of its narrow walls.

Felix felt his head again, wondering if he was concussed and seeing things. He reached both hands out towards the large fireplace, expecting to feel the missing panel at any moment and return to his senses, but instead slowly moved forward, one step at a time, without obstruction, until he passed through the fireplace entirely and was standing in the tunnel on the opposite side.

He looked around the thin walkway in disbelief. The tunnel's light pastel walls, with floral designs of freesias and lilies, were as beautiful and elegant as any he had seen, and a pristine green carpet ran the length of the floor. Felix was aware of the notorious secret passages and tunnels in Europe's great castles and palaces, but he'd never heard of anything like that at Number 10. He couldn't understand why it was here or what purpose it served.

Resting high on the tunnel wall beside the entrance was a curious-looking lever with the parliamentary crest on it. Felix pulled hard on the lever, and the fireplace's missing panel began to judder back into position, sealing off the path back to his study.

Felix turned and followed the tunnel, unsure whether he was awake or still on the study floor, unconscious and dreaming. As he moved forward, the path began to curve away slowly. Felix counted his paces, estimating that he had walked over half a mile by the time he saw another door coming into view ahead of him.

Felix cautiously opened the door and stepped into a crooked hallway. It was the type one would expect to find in an old cottage or workman's house. He followed the exposed floorboards through another entrance, eventually entering an oval-shaped room dimly lit by a few struggling wall lights.

Inside, Felix noticed a large oak desk with an array of documents, maps and charts splayed untidily across it. Beside the desk were rows of shelves overflowing with books and encyclopaedias covering all types of subjects, from *Human Anatomy* to *How to Change a Motorised Wheel*. On the walls, in gilt-edged frames, hung portraits of past prime ministers. Felix recognised the faces of Sir Robert Peel, Lord Palmerston, Benjamin Disraeli, William Pitt the Younger and Arthur Wellesley, the Duke of Wellington. Just below the Iron Duke's portrait sat a gold plaque with something inscribed on it. He crouched down to read the words.

"Old Pye Street. Built for only the most curious, benevolent and adventurous of prime ministers."

Felix ran his hand across the plaque in astonishment. He could feel his senses tingling. He began to think about the other past prime ministers who might have found this secret room during their time at Number 10 and all the meaningful moments in history they might have orchestrated from inside it. He thought about the many battles and treaties, the foiled plots and the high-profile arrests. Could they have planned Napoleon's exile to Elba here? Or uncovered the identity of Jack the Ripper? After all, the mysterious Ripper murders had ended very abruptly and without anyone being brought to justice. Not publicly anyway.

Drunk on adventure, Felix's thoughts suddenly turned to his mother, Leonora, and what she would have made of the room and the message on the gold plaque. This was a place where prime ministers served not for personal gain or to further their careers but simply out of a duty towards the people they represented. It alluded to the promise of something more meaningful, higher almost than the role of prime minister. He was sure Leonora would have approved.

Felix could feel his mood lightening. A giddy, almost childlike excitement had replaced the self-doubt he had been wrestling with in his study. He spun around to investigate the rest of the room. Standing proudly against one of the walls was an old, run-down telephone switchboard with hundreds of telephone lines, cords and jacks. Felix leant forward to study the connections. All the major towns and cities were listed and set out in alphabetic order: Bath, Birmingham, Bradford, Brighton and so on, followed by the notable cities of Europe and then the rest of the world.

Felix continued past the switchboard towards a large clothes rail laden with workers' uniforms, overalls and coats, all colours, shapes and sizes. Alongside the rail was a tall wooden stand covered in hats of various styles: flats, Derbies, fedoras, boaters, bowlers, trilbies and top hats. Beneath the hat stand sat an even more comprehensive collection of shoes, complemented by a selection of canes and umbrellas.

Felix removed a few hats, trying them on for size before placing them back on their pegs. He could barely concentrate on a single item for more than a few seconds before his eyes were drawn to something else in the room. This time it was the presence of a small electrical generator hidden in one of the room's dark corners. Felix approached the generator and curiously flicked the switch, turning it on. It took a few moments for the dusty old engine to turn over and for a cluster of bulbs in the centre of the room to finally come to life, emitting a dull light and revealing the most breathtaking sight of all.

In the centre of the room, beneath the struggling lights, sat a full-scale model of London. It stretched from Buckingham Palace through Westminster and the City of London to the Tower of London on one side of the river, and from Vauxhall through

Waterloo, London Bridge and Southwark into Bermondsey on the other. It was close to five metres long and three metres wide, with almost lifelike detail. Each building had been replicated with a deftness of touch that only an artist of the utmost skill could have created. St. Paul's Cathedral sat at eye level, dominating the London skyline, while beneath the palace at Westminster, even the narrow London sewers and back alleys had been included.

Felix found himself wondering how long it must have taken to complete, how many months or years of painstaking sittings to produce such a work of beauty. He was almost scared to touch it for fear of damaging any of its features.

As he leant over the towering masterpiece, taking in its majesty, Felix felt a cold draught kiss the back of his neck. He turned to see a small corridor leading away from the room in the opposite direction. Unlike the splendour of the tunnel leading to Number 10, this one was narrow and bleak, with crumbling walls.

Felix stepped inside the unwelcoming corridor. He could feel the cold breeze pouring in through its warped and cracked walls. At the far end was another door, prompting Felix to press forward, determined to see where it led.

He took hold of the handle and carefully swung the door open, stepping out onto a dark stretch of cobbled road. The air was thick with the smell of raw sewage and vermin, which filled Felix's nostrils as he took in the derelict terraced street set apart from the affluent city. Scarred by years of neglect and poverty, the street housed some of London's most destitute inhabitants, beggars, invalids and alcoholics, all kept hidden and out of sight of civilised society. Those who couldn't afford a roof over their heads slept rough, battling the cold and disease.

Felix saw a group of them lying in the gutters like mice, gathered for warmth and safety. Above them, in the fading light, he could barely make out the ageing street sign.

It read, *Old Pye Street*.

Freemasons' Hall

Freemasons' Hall was an imposing building on Great Queen Street, with Holborn to its east and Covent Garden to its west. It had been the central meeting place for the masons since the mid-eighteenth century. Attached to the Freemasons' Hall was the Freemasons' Tavern, a remnant of the original cluster of buildings and a social gathering place for its notorious membership.

Amelia looked up at the famous masonic buildings in awe. She had studied the organisation for years, first from her home in America and then from her base at Corpus Christi, but she had yet to see the secret society's London headquarters in person. It was everything she'd anticipated and more.

Freemasonry was said to have dated back to the Middle Ages and the stonemasons' guild. However, like most stories connected to the masons, even that tiny piece of history was open to debate. What was known, however, was how quickly the organisation had grown and how far its influence and power had spread. Its members comprised some of society's most influential people: judges, landowners, politicians, even royalty. It was said that George Washington was a mason and that Benjamin Franklin had served as the head of a fraternity in Pennsylvania before his death. This combination of power, mystery and notoriety had attracted Amelia to the masons' story as a young woman and still intoxicated her to this day.

Amelia allowed herself a moment to take the building in and reminisce on the excitement she had felt travelling to London from America as a young student, desperate to see such sights. She'd spent much of her childhood in the Texan countryside surrounded by cattle and bison, two of the state's major exports. Although academics, her parents had left the city to take over the family business, exporting hides and furs across the continent.

For a young woman brimming with adventure and aspiration, leaving the thriving metropolis was like forsaking life itself. She could never quite understand her parents' decision to leave, nor how they had managed to adapt to the monotony of life in the semi-wilderness.

To pass the time, Amelia lost herself in books. She spent days on end reading about the great cities of the world and the many adventures that awaited her outside the confines of their small farming community. At the centre of her dreams were the old European cities, pulsating with history, art, and culture. However, rising above them all like a colossus was the great city of London, the apotheosis of the civilised world. Amelia revelled in stories of its cobbled streets and crooked alleyways, its meandering rivers and towering castles, its ancient universities and renowned temples of law. She voraciously consumed tales of London's legendary scientists, philosophers, artists, and rogues, as well as its formidable politicians and bloodstained monarchs. Even the notorious printing houses, taverns, members' clubs and clandestine secret societies held a mystique that captivated her imagination.

However, Amelia reminded herself that she had not come to gawp at the city's famous architecture, nor had she come to fulfil a childhood affinity with London's opulent displays of history and power. She had come to question the masonic hierarchy on the strange cards left at the scenes of Lord Monteagle's and Lord Cecil's abductions.

As women were unwelcome in the Freemasons' Tavern, Amelia had no choice but to arrive at her destination disguised as a man. She used an old makeup trick to age her skin and give off the appearance of facial hair and replaced her usually colourful clothes with the masonic white bow tie and tails, hiding her long auburn hair under a top hat. She approached the main entrance, joining the steady stream of gentlemen flowing towards the Freemasons' Tavern, slipping into the throng with the rest of the members.

The tavern was a vast room, well presented with high ceilings and Tuscan columns running the length of its long walls. Thick wooden beams made up the serving area, and several tables and chairs filled the open space.

Amelia noted the sheer volume of masons present. It was as though the entire membership had decided to descend on the building on the same day. They were all immaculately dressed in white bow ties and top hats and had gathered in groups to discuss all manner of topics, from modern agriculture to the rise of automotive transportation and everything in between. It was said that some of the world's most remarkable feats and scandals had been hatched in the Freemasons' Tavern, and Amelia could not help but feel the touch of history on her shoulder.

She walked around, carefully listening to the members' conversations, trying to get a measure of their tone and how they addressed one another. If she wanted to fit in, she would need to act appropriately and be convincing as both a man and a fellow mason. The endeavour had a relatively low chance of success but was incredibly high in adventure.

Amelia took up a spot at the bar and ordered a pint of ale in her best male voice. As she listened to the cacophony of conversations, she began to make out several foreign accents among the crowd. It wasn't until she overheard a group of Dutch members discussing the annual masonic summit that she realised she had snuck into the organisation's yearly assemblage.

Like a lioness stalking her prey, Amelia scoured the room looking for lone masons on the periphery of a group she might target and engage in conversation, but it wasn't easy. The sheer number of members and their sea of white bow ties and top hats made it almost impossible to decipher where one group ended and another began.

Fortunately for Amelia, an older gentleman broke free from the herd and approached the bar beside her. Amelia noted his educated tone and grandiloquent manner as he engaged the barman.

"A bottle of your finest Italian wine."

"I'll have to go to the cellar," replied the barman.

"Very well," barked the mason.

With the barman departed and the mason waiting, Amelia seized her opportunity.

"What treasures must be stored in that cellar," she said, attempting to draw the mason into a conversation.

"Indeed," he replied, stealing a disgruntled glance at her.

"Abe Woodruff," she proclaimed, stepping forward to introduce herself.

The mason took a small step back, shocked at being addressed so informally.

"Oh, of course! My apologies," said Amelia, immediately realising her mistake.

She quickly grabbed the mason's hand, attempting an elaborate secret society handshake, only causing him to recoil further.

"I'm newly joined," she continued, in her most charming Texan drawl. "We do it a little differently back home, in the States."

Amelia smiled at the mason, who promptly gathered his wine from the returning bartender and hurried off back into the sea of gentlemen.

Annoyed with herself, Amelia returned to her ale when she felt a presence behind her. She quickly spun around to find another well-turned-out mason standing at her back. Only this one was tall, with broad shoulders and a thick neck.

"There's no need to get heavy." she warned, finishing her drink. "I was just leaving anyway,"

"Professor Woodruff?" asked the mason.

Amelia looked up, shocked. "Depends on who's asking."

"We've been expecting you."

"Who is we, exactly?" asked Amelia.

"Please, follow me."

The well-built mason turned and strode off through the busy tavern. Amelia hesitated, considering the risk, then placed her glass on the bar and quickly followed.

"Where are we going?" she asked, struggling to keep up.

"I shall be escorting you to one of our meeting rooms. Once inside, you'll sit at the table and wait to be addressed. You may only ask a question when invited to do so."

"Sounds fun," mocked Amelia.

The mason led Amelia through the tavern and into a long corridor. They paced through a collection of halls and up various staircases, burrowing deeper and deeper into the building's complex warren of floors.

Amelia took a mental note of her surroundings, hoping to sketch a map of the building in her mind. However, after following the mason for over 20 minutes, Amelia realised she'd been walking around in circles. A clever trick to confuse the mind and save the masons from having to put unwelcome blindfolds on all their guests.

At last her guide came to a halt.

"We have arrived," he said, facing a white door with the red-and-white St. George's Cross hanging from it.

Amelia looked at the cross curiously. She'd not seen it on any of the other doors they'd passed. Perhaps this was a new wing of the building, or had they just added the cross to one of the original doors to confuse her further? Either way, the tactic had worked. Amelia was no clearer as to the layout of the building or her whereabouts within it than when they'd first set off.

The mason opened the door and ushered Amelia inside. The room was small and dimly lit, and it took a few moments for Amelia's eyes to adjust to the low light. She could make out the silhouettes of five figures sitting around an oval table in complete stillness. An empty chair was already pulled out, welcomingly, in front of her.

"Please, do sit, Professor," called a voice.

Amelia stepped forward and slowly lowered herself into the seat. She scanned the room, trying to take in as much information about her surroundings as possible, but there was very little data available in the semi-darkness. Once her eyes had become accustomed to the room, Amelia could clearly make out the figures gathered around the table. To her surprise, they were all dressed in black hooded capes with intricately detailed animal masks covering their faces.

At the head of the table was a rotund figure wearing a male lion's mask. Amelia could deduce from the figure's drooping shoulders and poor posture that he was a man, probably in his late fifties. To his right were two more men, both somewhat younger and sturdier. One of the men was wearing a goat mask, not too dissimilar to the goat's face on the abduction card, while the other hid behind a far more sinister-looking mask depicting a crow. On the left of the lion, Amelia could make out the shape of a woman, probably in her late forties, wearing an eagle mask, next to another middle-aged man in a laughing monkey mask.

"Welcome, Professor," said a voice.

"Thank you for joining us," said another.

Amelia looked around the table, unsure from behind which mask the voices had come.

"How did you know I was coming?" she asked.

"Our eyes and ears are everywhere," replied a voice.

"In that case, an invitation would have been nice."

"We are not in the habit of drawing attention to ourselves," said the voice. "We prefer to work in the shadows."

"Evidently," replied Amelia.

"Do you have the card?" asked another voice, disorientating Amelia further.

Amelia looked around the group of masons, weighing up her options. She hadn't come this far to leave without any answers. She reached into her pocket and pulled out the card.

"One of yours?" she asked, placing it on the table.

There was silence as the man in the monkey mask reached down and picked up the card, studying it. He passed it to his female colleague in the eagle mask, who also considered it before passing it on again. The card eventually made its way around the table, finally returning to the space in front of Amelia.

"A rather interesting collection of symbols, don't you think?" asked Amelia, trying to invite a conversation despite the mason's warnings not to ask questions until invited.

"How well do you know your history, Professor?" asked one of the many voices.

"Ask my students."

"I don't mean the stuff you read in your books at Corpus Christi, nor am I referring to the watered-down narrative the establishment serves up to keep its students complicit with the system. What do you know about real history?"

"I know about Baphomet, your goat god. I also know a bit about the pentagram and its links to freemasonry."

"Then you will also be aware that we have fought off attacks of this kind many times throughout our history."

"Attacks?" scoffed Amelia.

"Of course," entered another voice. "Surely a scholar of your intellect can see that we are being deliberately implicated in this crime."

"Sounds like the kind of thing I would say if I wanted to distance myself from the card."

"Ask yourself this, Professor," said another voice. "Why would we go to the trouble of leaving a card?"

"Perhaps to let your enemies know the consequences of crossing your organisation?"

"We have more sophisticated ways of making a point, most of which do not implicate us in criminal activity. After all, how do you think we learned of the abductions and your impending visit?"

"You know people in high places," conceded Amelia.

"And how do you think those people would react if they believed we were involved in abducting two lords?"

"That depends on your motive. What if it was necessary? What if Monteagle and Cecil were masons and had put the organisation at risk? In that instance, these high-profile people you speak of may have approved, even ordered the abductions themselves."

"You're fishing for information, Professor," called another voice. "You know very well that we cannot confirm or deny the identity of our members."

"Then I cannot discount your motive."

"Then it seems we have arrived at an impasse," said another voice. "We thank you for your time."

Amelia felt the atmosphere in the room change immediately. Within seconds the figures had returned to facing forwards with their backs straight and chins held up high, a formidable display of discipline and control.

"Is that it?" she asked. "Surely there's more to discuss. If you are being falsely implicated, at least help me find the people who are framing you."

Amelia's words had no impact on the figures or their cold wall of silence. She was glaring at them in disbelief when she suddenly noticed the well-built man who had accompanied her from the bar speaking to something or someone in the darkness on the other side of the room. She squinted to get a better look. She could make out the form of a sixth figure sitting in the shadows. She watched as the mason crouched down low, close enough for the other figure to lean forward, revealing his owl mask as he whispered something into the younger man's ear and slipped a piece of paper into his pocket.

The figure quickly returned to the shadows, and Amelia's guide made his way towards her.

"This way, Professor," he said, motioning towards the door.

Amelia slowly rose from her seat, her eyes fixed on the silhouette of the sixth figure in the corner of the room. There was still so much she wanted to know, so many unanswered questions. If anything, this brief encounter had presented more complications than solutions. Amelia looked back over her shoulder at the silent figures sitting like statues around the table. She contemplated asking a parting question but knew it was pointless. They had offered only the tiniest morsels of information, things they had wanted her to know; nothing more.

Once outside the room, the mason led Amelia on another maze-like journey up and down flights of stairs and through various corridors until they arrived back at the Freemasons' Tavern. Frustrated by her lack of progress, Amelia was about to take her leave when her guide pulled her to one side.

"One final thing, Professor," he began. "The type of paper your card is printed on is called bleached hemp with rag fibres."

"Excuse me?" said Amelia, taken aback.

"I am reliably informed that bleached hemp is an old printing material from India, rarely used on the presses nowadays. Only one remaining printer in London still has a stockpile."

The mason held out a slip of paper and handed it to Amelia.

"And why should I trust a man who sits in the shadows? He didn't even get to touch the card. I watched it the whole time, and it never left the table."

"He didn't need to touch the card, Professor. Let's just say his family are very well acquainted with the printing trade," replied the mason, before turning and departing.

Amelia stepped out of the Freemasons' Tavern and onto the bustling streets of Covent Garden. She walked for some time, crossing through Charing Cross and onto Piccadilly, before allowing herself to stop and look at the slip of paper. If her meeting with the masons had taught her anything, it was that you never knew who might be watching you at any given time. Slowly unfolding the note, she quietly read its contents to herself, her eyes shining with the promise of further adventure.

House of Commons

The early morning dew had begun to lift from the famous walls and arches lining the River Thames along the Embankment. The streets, although quiet, were starting to show signs of life, and it would not be long until the calm serenity was replaced by throngs of Londoners on their busy morning commute.

Inside Parliament, the Commons was preparing for an early start. There had been much to fill the newspapers of late, and the members were determined to cover it all before the short autumn recess. The doors opened promptly at seven o'clock, allowing the members to filter into the chamber. It was the usual hustle and bustle of rushing feet and clashing elbows as ministers hurried to secure a seat on the famous green benches before the start of the morning session. Those arriving after the rush were forced to gather by the doors or in the gangways hoping to hear all that was said and debated without the luxury of viewing their counterparts as they spoke. It was one of Westminster's remarkable peculiarities, to have a members' chamber with too few seats to accommodate its members.

Fortunately for Felix, he did not have to compete for his seat. As prime minister, his place on the front bench was always assured.

Felix made his way through the throng towards the centre of the House. Rarely had he seen it so busy. The benches were full, and members were already crowding the standing spaces, eager to secure an unrestricted view.

As the crowds continued to build, so did the anticipation. Felix felt a little flutter of nerves twist in his stomach. It was common for politicians to feel nervous before the start of a parliamentary session, particularly the last before a recess. There was always so much to be said, and many voices desperate to be heard and elevated. The scales were finely balanced, and for every person who managed to claw their way up a few rungs of the political ladder, there was always someone else haplessly slipping down to fill their void. Success was never assured in politics: it was fickle, and a politician required broad shoulders to withstand the constant slings and arrows.

"It's a full house, Prime Minister," said Percy, rising to greet Felix.

"So it seems," replied Felix.

He could feel his heart racing and the sweat building on the palms of his hands.

Across the dispatch box, Felix watched Cavendish holding court with his colleagues. He moved from one member to another, whispering instructions to each and patting them reassuringly on their backs. There was an easy confidence between them. They didn't look like men about to engage in a bruising political battle but instead seemed like spectators at the theatre or a football match, preparing for some form of sport or entertainment. The newspapers had once described the House of Commons as a modern-day Colosseum. As Felix nervously watched his opponents, he couldn't help but feel like the gladiator, standing in the great arena, waiting for the gates to open and the lions to be released.

With the ministers finally seated, the Speaker entered the house, followed by the clerks and the Serjeant at Arms, who laid the mace down on its perch to symbolise the King's authority over proceedings.

"Questions will be taken," began the Speaker, bringing the low murmur of conversations to a prompt silence, "but I would ask that the honourable members keep to one question and that replies be of a reasonable length. I am determined that we make good progress through the Order Paper today before we break for a well-earned autumn recess. Mr. Edward Stanley…"

The Speaker pointed to a large man with a round face and a bulging waistline.

"Prime Minister," bellowed Stanley, in a thick West Country accent, "it had been well documented, long before Arthur Jenkins' death, that the conditions in many of the mines, factories and plants up and down the country were below working standards, and you've done nothing about it. Even now, with this young man's blood on the chamber's hands, nothing is being done. So, I ask you, how many more young men will have to die before you act?"

"We are working on several reforms that we are readying for the House. We are also assessing some of the conditions at first hand to publish a report on the matter," replied Felix, rising from his bench to answer the question.

"A report?" repeated Stanley. "The need is an immediate one, sir. These company directors have been banking their profits for years while running as lean an operation as humanly possible."

Loud jeers greeted Stanley's words. Many of the members were the very same directors he was referring to.

"As a consequence," continued Stanley over the clamour, "much of their equipment is unsuitable for work, and there is a very real danger that unless this is addressed, there will be more tragic events like those that occurred at Silverwood. You mark my words."

Stanley returned to his seat to a chorus of boos.

"The Honourable Member for Taunton! Mr. Henry Huffington!" called out the Speaker, pointing to an elderly politician sitting on the upper backbenches and wearing a dark suit with a collection of military honours hanging from the breast of his jacket.

"Nonsense!" shouted Huffington, rising to his feet, assisted by members on either side of him. "The people are work-shy; they only want reform to satisfy their idle malingering. If we don't keep the collieries and plants running at full tilt, we'll fall behind the emerging German and American economies. What does the Prime Minister plan to do about that?"

A wave of cheers from both sides of the chamber greeted Huffington's question. Felix waited for the members to settle before addressing the House. It was clear which side of the debate held favour, and he used the time to think of an effective response.

"What is the benefit of having the world's largest economy if we cannot use it to better the lot of our people?" he asked defiantly.

"This House's primary duty is to maintain the strength and endurance of His Majesty's Empire!" called out Huffington to a second round of approving grunts and nods.

"I cannot agree, sir!" said Felix. "This House's primary duty is to its people, and we must strive to provide them with a better standard of living, both at home and at work."

"What standard of living will we have when we are forced out of our own Empire?" called a member from the backbenches, causing a further eruption of approval.

"Order! Order!" called the Speaker. "The leader of the opposition, the Right Honourable, Mr. Milton Cavendish."

A silent anticipation fell over the chamber as Cavendish rose from his bench to address the House.

"It should come as no surprise to this House to see our Prime Minister once again hide behind the plight of the British people. Our Empire is under attack, our rivals continue to build their capabilities, and a new power rises out of the ashes of our old colony across the Atlantic. But still, our Prime Minister does not have the backbone to compete. Rather, his reformist nature and lack of steel are further opening the door to our enemies."

"Here, here!" yelled members, waving their Order Papers with approval.

"It is not a case of backbone or steel," replied Felix. "How can we compete with our rivals if we cannot solve the growing problems we face here in our own back garden?"

"You see," growled Cavendish, "he is not fit for the fight! These new powers will take control of our seas and cut into our trade. It is little surprise that the workers are restless. We need a firm response. We need firm leadership!"

A cacophony of noise and paper-waving filled the chamber for a second time.

"Order!" bellowed the Speaker. "Order!"

After what seemed like an eternity to Felix, the noise finally subsided, and the members grudgingly began to settle back into their benches.

"We are in a dog fight, Prime Minister," observed Percy, wriggling in his seat.

It had been this way ever since Felix's government had come to power: the constant struggle for change, the battle lines formed between maintaining the old and paving the way for the new. To Felix, the mandate from the British people had been clear: reform those institutions that needed reforming; bring the cost of living down to an acceptable level and do your utmost to improve the lives of ordinary people. But for most in the House, these goals were secondary to the constant improvement of the Empire and Britain's standing in the world.

Felix took a moment to gather his thoughts. He knew that Cavendish would have prepared his attack meticulously and that, like a well-trained conductor, he would be driving his audience towards the big crescendo. But what could he do to stop him? Cavendish had the ear of the chamber.

Felix stepped up to the Table of the House. He looked around the room at the many dissenting faces staring back at him, each ready to jump on his every word. He thought about the missing lords and their families, Old Pye Street with its portraits of previous leaders, that inspiring plaque on the wall, and his mother, Leonora, and everything she had endured in her brief but purposeful life. He felt a surge of energy rush through his body. This was the Colosseum and, like a gladiator, he wouldn't go down without a fight.

He stood tall, about to speak, when he noticed something seesawing in the corner of his eye. Felix turned to see the Speaker waving his arm in the air, trying to get the chamber's attention. He was holding a white slip of paper aloft, which his clerk had handed him moments earlier.

"The prime minister has been called to attend to an urgent matter," he began, still waving the slip of paper in the air. "We shall reconvene after the autumn recess."

Roars of disapproval met the Speaker's announcement, members reluctant to let Felix off the hook. But there was little they could do. Felix returned to his seat, thankful for the reprieve. He quickly gathered his papers and departed for the Speaker's room.

The Speaker's room was a small box shape, richly decorated with high, oak-panelled ceilings and large portraits of past incumbents. In the centre of the room sat two red armchairs on either side of a charcoal grey fireplace with gilded roses running along the top.

"Mr. Speaker?" called Felix, entering the room.

He looked around, but the Speaker was nowhere to be seen. "How bizarre," he whispered.

"Isn't it just?" replied a voice from behind him.

Felix spun around to see Amelia sitting in the Speaker's chair with her feet on the desk.

"What on earth are you doing here?" asked Felix in astonishment.

"Saving your hide, by the looks of things. It was turning into a massacre in there."

"The wolves are well and truly baying for blood. But where is the Speaker?"

"You mean, the Right Honourable James Creswell?" said Amelia in a mock British accent. "Don't mind him. We're old friends. I simply slipped him a note asking him to bring proceedings to an end so that we could talk in private."

"Amelia, you can't just call an end to Parliament."

"I've been to see the masons…"

Felix stopped. He took a seat at the desk alongside his former college mate. "And?"

"And the plot, it appears, thickens greatly. Of course, they had been expecting me. They knew all about the abductions and the cards. In truth, there was little they did not know. Their people are everywhere, in the palaces, the courts, the police, even in there!" said Amelia, nodding back towards the House of Commons.

"What did they say?"

"They're claiming a case of misdirection."

"Misdirection?"

"They are concerned that whoever is behind these abductions is trying to frame them. They quickly reminded me that they had suffered these attacks before, from the knights, the French nobility, even the Pope. Let's just say they are more than familiar with the pattern."

"And did you believe them?"

"It's hard to say. It's possible they were telling the truth. On the other hand, it's just as possible they were saying whatever they needed to in order to throw me off the scent."

"But they knew of your arrival, which means they must have been watching you."

"Either that or someone in Oxford spotted us and reported back to them. Most of my students come from the types of families you'd imagine have ties with the masons. I wouldn't be surprised if some keen young tattletale followed us."

Felix took a moment to process the information.

"Well, if not the masons, then who?"

"I got the sense they weren't entirely sure themselves. The symbols on the cards are masonic but they were arranged in a way that I don't think even they had seen before."

"So, we're no closer?"

"I wouldn't say that, exactly. The meeting did produce something of interest."

Amelia reached into her pocket and removed the scrap of paper the mason had given her.

"What is it?" asked Felix.

"There was an elderly gentleman present at the meeting with a comprehensive knowledge of the printing industry and its varied materials. By all accounts, his family were rather big in the trade. As fortune would have it, he was able to spot bleached hemp with rag fibres from across a large and dark masonic room."

"What are you talking about?"

"This chap was very intrigued by your little card. Apparently, the bleached hemp paper it's printed on is produced in a little place called India. Only a handful of printers in the city still work with bleached hemp, and only one still stockpiles it."

Amelia handed Felix the folded slip. "I suspect they chose this type of paper as they knew it would be hard to trace. Near on impossible, in fact."

Felix unfolded the paper to reveal a name scrawled inside in pencil.

"Houlston and Sons of Fleet Street," he read.

"A small, family run business," said Amelia.

"You know it?"

"I may have passed by to take a brief look. Will you send in the police?" asked Amelia.

"Not while we are unsure of their dependability. We have a lead; the last thing we want to do is alert our enemies to that fact. The police can be of no use to us at this stage. In the meantime, we shall do some discreet digging of our own."

"Where to next, Prime Minister?" asked Amelia, rubbing her hands.

"For now, I need you to return to Oxford and your students. We don't know whose attention your investigations may have attracted, and I would not put you in harm's way."

Amelia raised her hand in objection, but Felix swiftly cut her off.

"You can still be of service to me from the college. Keep looking into the symbols on the cards. It's key that we understand their significance. I shall follow up with Houlston and Sons and see what information can be gathered."

"What about your enemies in there?" asked Amelia, reminding Felix of the barrage he had just received inside the Commons.

"I'll have Humphrey set up a meeting with the unions. I want to know what Cavendish has offered them in return for their support."

"I could do a lot more from here," pressed Amelia.

Felix checked the time on his pocket watch.

"If I recall, the train to Oxford leaves at ten minutes past the hour. That gives you just over thirty minutes to get to Paddington Station."

Houlston and Sons of Fleet Street

It was with great surprise that Humphrey opened the door to Number 10 to find Felix returned from Parliament early. He was used to the Commons overrunning and ruining his many well-laid plans but was yet to hear of it adjourning prematurely for any reason.

"Is the building on fire?" he asked jovially.

"Not physically, but metaphorically perhaps," replied Felix.

"Don't tell me; someone got a member's constituency name wrong again?"

"Cold," replied Felix.

"Someone lost the key to the wine cellar?"

"They wouldn't dare. Still cold."

"Someone snuck a woman into the chamber?"

"Warm," replied Felix.

Humphrey stared at Felix, studying his expression. "Oh dear. It has something to do with Amelia, doesn't it?"

"Hot!"

"Amelia is the reason you're home early?"

"Positively scorching!"

"And what, pray tell, has she been up to this time?"

Felix took a moment to explain the furore he had faced in the Commons, the growing anger and resentment on all sides and Amelia's timely intervention, before retiring to his study to document the day's events in his journal. As was customary, Humphrey lit a large fire and fetched a tray of sandwiches and a pot of tea from the kitchens.

"Will you be needing anything more?" he asked.

Felix took a moment to think. He was determined to make the trip across London to Fleet Street to investigate the printers on the slip of paper the masons had given Amelia. "Do you have your spectacles with you?" he asked.

"My spectacles?" questioned Humphrey. "Do you have a problem with your eyes?"

"No, I just need something to mask them. If I recall correctly, yours were a little weathered and bent out of shape."

"They're not weathered and bent out of shape, thank you very much. They're just well used," replied Humphrey, reaching into his pocket, taking out a long rectangular case and reluctantly handing it to Felix.

Felix opened the case and removed the spectacles. They were old and misshapen, with a small crack on the bridge held together with string. He placed them on his face, manoeuvring them into position.

"Very fetching," said Humphrey. "Now, will you tell me what this is about, or will I have to follow you around like I did when you were a mischievous child?"

"I have a lead in the case: nothing concrete, but a line of investigation. I need to disguise my appearance to carry out some…research."

"That is a job for the police, not the prime minister, surely?"

"I'm not entirely sure we can rely on the police in this matter," said Felix, repositioning the spectacles.

"What on earth do you mean?"

Felix turned to face his steward. He could sense the concern in his voice. "Amelia has been to see the masons. Someone has been leaking information to them."

"Surely you don't suspect—"

"I don't know," said Felix, cutting Humphrey short, "and therein lies the problem. The police, like the rest of the establishment, are well known to have ties to these secret societies, which makes them hard to rely on."

"But, Felix, think if you were to be discovered."

"I will take every care. Now, I must get back to work. Inform the staff that I do not wish to be disturbed and tell Mrs. Hughes I'll take a late supper this evening."

"Very well," said Humphrey, taking his leave.

Felix waited for Humphrey's footsteps to fade, then made his way over to the fireplace and carefully doused the fire. He turned the corbel ninety degrees and watched as the back panel began to retreat, unveiling the secret passage. Felix stepped into the tunnel and followed its ornate curved walls away from his study towards Old Pye Street.

Inside the secret office, Felix approached the giant model replica of London to plot his journey to Houlston and Sons. The most obvious path from Old Pye Street was along Whitehall, through Charing Cross and onto the Strand, leading directly onto Fleet Street. But it was risky. The chances of being seen increased dramatically on London's main roads and, as Humphrey had warned, Felix could not afford to be discovered under any circumstances. Instead, he studied the dark backroads and alleyways along the river Thames, mapping out an alternative route.

There was also the small matter of his appearance. Felix had already secured Humphrey's spectacles, but they alone would not be enough to hide his identity. He would need a story, a believable justification for questioning the printer on his business affairs.

Felix pulled one of the encyclopaedias off the dusty shelf, *The Complete Guide to Occupational Exploration*. He flicked through the long list of alphabetically arranged jobs, looking for one that might offer a plausible backstory. He scanned the A's, reading the descriptions for an actor, aircraft engineer and architect, before moving on to the B's and the specifics for a barrister, beekeeper and biologist. Having only progressed to the C's and a description of a carpenter, after a full hour, he finally decided to turn his attention to the collection of uniforms hanging from the clothes rail instead. He sifted through each disguise, considering every conceivable tradesman's uniform, but none gave off the impression of a man with a legitimate reason to study a company's accounts.

Exasperated by his lack of progress, Felix finally turned his attention to the messy pile of documents on the desk, a chaotic collection of scribbles, bills and letters previous prime ministers had mulled over while hidden away in Old Pye Street. Among them, Felix found a letter addressed to the Downing Street tax clerk with the royal crest sitting prominently at the head of the paper. He quickly gathered up Humphrey's spectacles, a top hat and a cane, and set out towards the front door and the narrow, cobbled streets beyond.

Felix emerged from Old Pye Street to the sound of silence. The rains had cleared the streets of people, leaving only the poor and destitute huddled together in small dry nooks around the city. It was a sight he had become accustomed to and promised himself he would rectify once in government. However, every time he'd tried to address the issue of London's needy in Parliament, it had been pushed aside in favour of a more politically agreeable cause, like increasing the navy's wage or providing better equipment for His Majesty's army. No politician in his right mind would agree to spend money on the homeless, not when it could be spent on the military. The dispossessed were of no use to anyone, whereas the Empire could always use more ships.

Felix made his way towards the Embankment, keeping to the back streets along the Thames before cutting up through Temple and finally onto Fleet Street. He could hear the roar of the printing presses all around him and taste the sewage rising off the Fleet, the largest of London's subterranean rivers. As a lawyer, Felix had spent many evenings in the area dining with colleagues at the Temple Inns. He had always known the printing houses to be small, overcrowded spaces bustling with energy and enterprise. However, over the past decade, Fleet Street had blossomed into the nerve centre of the world's news and information, and new buildings were being raised every year, each taller and more spectacular than the last.

Houlston and Sons, by contrast, was a small family holding set back from the main road, overshadowed by the expanding Fleet Street skyline. Felix noted how withered and unwelcoming the building looked. Its once vibrant green-and-gold family sign had faded and was barely legible, and the slatted wooden facade was weathered and bent out of shape. There was something eerie, almost improper, about its continued presence on Fleet Street. How had this old relic stayed afloat for so long, entombed in the shadows of this sprawling metropolis? It was like a mosquito lodged in the neck of a lion.

Felix approached the dilapidated building. The smell of dry ink and grease stung his nostrils as he pushed the door open and stepped into a large open room full of old, rickety printing presses working at full tilt, spitting out smoke and oil. It was a far cry from the new, state-of-the-art printing houses, almost like stepping back in time.

Felix walked across the factory floor towards a small desk at the far end of the room, surrounded by newspapers packed in bundles and ready to be delivered. He noted the array of foreign-language titles printed on various coloured and textured papers. It was clear that Houlston and Sons had come to specialise in rare overseas publications as a way of competing. He lifted one of the newspapers to study the paper it was printed on when a boy, no older than fifteen, with a pockmarked face and dark ink stains on his hands, approached.

"Can I help, sir?" he asked.

"What is your name and position here, boy?" asked Felix.

"I'm Alfred, Mr. Houlston's apprentice."

"Then run along and fetch your master for me," said Felix, flashing the document with the royal crest on it. "Tell him I have come from His Majesty's Tax Office and would like to discuss his accounts."

"Yes, sir," stuttered the young apprentice, scurrying off to the back of the shop to fetch Mr. Houlston.

Within moments an older man, far beyond retirement age with grey hair and thick glasses, slowly emerged, aided by the young apprentice.

"That's the man, Mr. Houlston, sir," said Alfred, pointing in Felix's direction.

"Thank you, Alfred," said Mr. Houlston, carefully pulling up a stool. "Fetch our guest a seat, will you?"

Alfred pulled up another stool and Mr. Houlston motioned for Felix to join him.

"You must excuse me. I am old, and it takes me an eternity to do most things, even walk across my own shop floor. What I wouldn't give for a pair of younger legs."

"That's quite alright," said Felix, taking a seat and placing his cane to one side.

"How can I be of assistance?" asked Mr. Houlston.

"We are carrying out routine checks on all the printing houses on Fleet Street, to ensure your accounts are up to date and to see if we can assist in any way."

"We had our accounts audited less than two months ago," said Mr. Houlston. "I doubt our rich neighbours are scrutinised half as often as we are."

Felix felt a sudden pang of guilt. "I can assure you, we show no favour to any business, large or small. We'll be moving on to the others as soon as we're finished here."

"You know, we've been on Fleet Street for over eighty years," continued Mr. Houlston. "We may be small, but our roots here are deep."

"If you could just have your books brought up, I'll be out of your hair in no time," pressed Felix.

"I know what they're trying to do," said Mr. Houlston, eyeing Felix with suspicion. "They want me out, but I refuse to go. I will not be intimidated by them or their chums at Westminster. I served my country, you know."

Becoming worked up, Mr. Houlston paused to steady himself. Felix watched as the older man took several deep breaths, eyeing him defiantly.

"What department did you say you were from again?" he spluttered.

Felix felt a wave of anxiety wash over him. He looked down at the document in his hand. His entire cover story depended on the small royal crest at the top of the page. It would not stand up to any scrutiny from the stubborn printer. All Mr. Houlston had to do was ask to see his appointment letter, and Felix would be entirely exposed.

"I'm not in cahoots with your competitors, if that's your concern," he said, leaning forward. "In fact, I think it takes great character to fight them off the way you have."

"You do," replied a shocked Mr. Houlston.

"It's not fair these big corporations squeezing the city's smaller family-run businesses. I applaud you for standing your ground. I'd be tempted to go a step further and invest in a new shopfront and refurbish the old family sign."

"A show of defiance? Perhaps I'll invite them to a grand opening party and play them at their own game. It would be worth the cost just to see the looks on their faces."

Felix nodded in agreement. He could hear the cogs turning in Mr. Houlston's mind and see the plans forming in his old calculating eyes.

"But to do that," continued Felix, "we need to ensure that your books are all above board for His Majesty's Clerk."

Mr. Houlston's eyes flickered from Felix to his printing presses and back as he weighed up his options and his guest's sincerity.

"Very well," he conceded. "Alfred, fetch my accounts."

"Yes, sir," replied Alfred, darting off into another room.

"There is nothing in there of any significance," said Mr. Houlston, slowly rising from his stool. "Let His Majesty's Clerk feast his eyes on our dwindling profits; perhaps it will disturb his sleep much as it has mine. Although, I doubt he has such a conscience."

It took Alfred only a short time to return with the company accounts, large, dusty old journals dating back more than eighty years, as Mr. Houlston had said. Felix organised each book by date, searching the most recent first and working his way back. It was more complicated than he had anticipated, with orders from all over the world and an array of exotic client names: Wong, Singh, Goldberg, DuPont, Garcia, Nakamura and Sequeira. They covered thousands of miles from the Americas to the Indian subcontinent and all the countries in between.

Alongside each order were the names of the products Houlston and Sons had sold over the years: linen, cotton and pulp. But there was no reference in the books to the bleached hemp the senior mason had recognised during Amelia's visit to the Freemasons' Tavern.

Felix continued to study the pages, increasingly aware of the passing of time. The longer he lingered, the more suspicious it looked, and soon the old printer would start to question his motives again. He turned from one page to another, quickly scanning the product names, when it dawned on him that perhaps he was looking for the wrong thing, or the wrong word, at least. Like most tradespeople, printers liked to give their products memorable titles rather than market them solely on their material components. Felix hurriedly skimmed back through the pages, examining the orders again. This time he noticed a series of catchy names alongside some of the entries.

"That's strange," he announced loudly enough for Alfred to hear.

Since bringing the accounts up, the young apprentice had turned his attention to an old printing press that had begun grinding its gears and spitting out smoke.

"What's that, sir?" he asked, looking up from the faulty machine.

"There seem to be several oddly named products listed here and there," said Felix. "What exactly do they refer to?"

Alfred shot Felix a worried look. He was about to turn and hurry off to fetch Mr. Houlston when Felix rose from his stool and stopped him in his tracks. He preferred to question the young apprentice rather than his wilier master, who would doubtless query Felix on his sudden interest in their products.

"Here, see for yourself," said Felix.

Alfred used the rag from his belt to wipe the grease off his hands, then buried his head in the book. After a short silence, he emerged, looking utterly confused.

"Well?" asked Felix.

"Sorry. I don't read," replied Alfred, his cheeks burning with embarrassment.

Felix thought for a moment. It was a delicate situation. He didn't want to disturb Mr. Houlston but having come so far, he was reluctant to leave without making a meaningful breakthrough.

"What if I were to read the orders out to you?" he asked. "Do you think you could explain what they are?"

"Most of them," nodded Alfred. "But I've only been Mr. Houlston's apprentice for eight months."

"Let's give it a try."

Felix took the book in his hand, ran his finger down the list and began reading out the names. "Classic Brown," he started.

"That's our wood pulp paper. Most of our customers use that one. It's our bestseller."

"Elegant White?"

"The White is our premium paper. It's made from cotton fibres and lasts longer than our other products. It keeps the inks well too."

"Rare Green?"

"Rare Green?" repeated Alfred. "That doesn't ring any bells."

"The Green is a hemp paper from India," said Mr. Houlston, appearing from the back of the shop. "We used to bleach it to remove the colour, many years ago now, when it was still in production."

"But there is a recent sale here," said Felix, pointing at the entry in the accounts.

The old printer approached the service desk, clutching its frame for balance. "Alfred, go out and fetch us a bottle of scotch will you, there's a good lad.' he said, shooting his apprentice an apprehensive glance.

Felix watched as Alfred turned and scuttled out of the shop.

"He does worry about my well-being," said Mr. Houlston, following Felix's gaze. "It's hard to find such honest folk these days, particularly in light of our recent struggles."

Felix turned to face Mr. Houlston. He couldn't understand the old printer's sudden hospitality. Mr. Houlston extended his hand, holding out a slip of paper.

"What is it?" asked Felix.

"It's a bill of sale for a pair of three-by-two-inch cards printed on aged Indian bleached hemp, as per the order in the book. You will see that the customer also purchased the press, the plates and all the inks associated with the job."

Felix took the bill of sale, lifting Humphrey's glasses away from his eyes to get a better look. He could barely believe what he was reading. At the top of the bill was a name.

"Tom Fellows?" he read lightly.

"A rather intimidating lump covered head to toe in tattoos and constantly reeking of alcohol, like every other crook from the Docklands. We contemplated sending him away, but his business was too valuable for us to turn down. Sometimes in life, we do what we must rather than what we would like."

Mr. Houlston stopped to take another deep breath. Felix noticed him subtly remove an object from the desk drawer and quickly place it in his pocket. Was it a gun or a knife, perhaps? Suddenly Felix realised why Mr. Houlston had become so agreeable, offering up fine scotch and free information. The crafty old printer was stalling, keeping him occupied just long enough to recover his weapon and hold Felix there until Alfred returned with the cavalry. Probably the same villainous group of people who had ordered the cards and abducted the two peers. Felix cursed himself for being so naive. Did he really think he could just walk into this man's family business and demand to see its most valuable secrets without arousing suspicion? How could he be so foolish? Now, with his cover likely blown and his life in danger, all he could think of were Humphrey's disapproving words and the potentially crushing newspaper headlines if he were to be exposed.

"Please, take a seat," said Mr. Houlston, directing Felix back towards one of the stools. "Alfred won't be long."

Felix hesitated, looking around the room for the nearest exit, but the only way in or out of the factory was the main door located all the way across the factory floor. He contemplated running, but it was too far, and he was unwilling to take the risk without knowing what the old printer had removed from the drawer and placed in his pocket. Instead, he reluctantly lowered himself onto the stool.

"Was it active service?" he asked, hitting on a strategy.

"Excuse me?"

"Earlier, you referred to your time in the armed forces. I was just wondering if you were engaged in active service."

"Of course," replied Mr. Houlston, puffing his chest out. "Ten years in the Fusiliers, including tours of India, South Africa and Burma."

"And now you're in another battle, to keep your business afloat?"

"This business has been in my family for generations. I won't be remembered as the failure that closed its doors. Not if there's even the slightest chance of saving it."

"But at what cost?"

"At any cost! We just need a few more clients, and then we can start to build up a head of steam."

Felix looked out over the factory floor and the old printing presses, including the rickety one Alfred had been attempting to fix.

"And what about your presses? How are you going to replace them?"

"They would've been on the scrap heap years ago if it weren't for young Alfred. The boy's a miracle worker."

"He won't be able to keep them running forever."

"Perhaps not," conceded Mr. Houlston, "but at least we'll still be in operation while I'm alive."

"So, you're holding out for death?" asked Felix.

"Something like that."

"Then what does it matter if you lose the business now or after you're gone? Either way, it's the same result: the doors will eventually shut."

"I promised my father on his deathbed that I would fight off these corporations, these vipers trying to put us out of business. They were the same reptiles who drove him to an early grave, and I will continue to fight them until the day I…"

Mr. Houlston spluttered, struggling to finish his sentence, the emotional exertion leaving him gasping for air.

Still plagued with doubts, Felix saw his chance to escape. With the old printer momentarily incapacitated, he sprang up from his stool to make his getaway. As he passed the faulty printing press, he pulled as hard as he could on the lever. The machine began to turn over, grinding its gears together and coughing up fountains of ink and thick plumes of smoke, slowly engulfing the shop. Amidst the chaos and confusion, Felix darted across the factory floor and made his exit.

Outside, the streets were busy with rush-hour traffic and the workers of Fleet Street were turning in their pens and inks for the evening. Felix welcomed the crowd, slipping into the herd's safety and out of sight. He could feel his heart racing. But as he walked away, another thought materialised. Should he stay and wait for Alfred to return so that he might get a look at these men Mr. Houlston had sent for?

He scanned the street, looking for a spot with a clear view of Houlston and Sons, when he noticed several members of the public stealing glances at him. He patted himself down, concerned he may have covered himself in ink or grease fleeing across the factory floor, but his face and clothes were clean. Suddenly it dawned on Felix that the crowd he was using as camouflage was made up of the people who wrote and distributed the news globally. Unlike most civilians, they would undoubtedly know what the prime minister looked like, even in his elaborate disguise. Remaining in Fleet Street was too risky, even with the opportunity of identifying potential suspects on offer. Besides, Felix had the bill of sale and, with it, a name. It was the breakthrough he had hoped for and the first shred of meaningful evidence they'd received since finding the cards at the scenes of both abductions.

With little option but to leave, Felix lowered his head and disappeared into London's dark backstreets and out of sight.

Sailortown

The clatter of breakfast trays roused Felix from a deep sleep the following morning.

Having navigated his way along the River Thames to Old Pye Street from Houlston and Sons the previous evening, he'd followed the secret tunnel to his study in Downing Street and made his way straight to his bedroom, collapsing on the bed with exhaustion. With everything that had happened, he was desperate for rest and passed out the second his head touched the soft sheets.

Felix looked up from his bed to see the curtains drawn and Humphrey standing over the bedside table, diligently preparing breakfast.

"Should I address you by another name this morning or are you resuming the role of Felix Grey today?" asked Humphrey.

"Felix will do just fine," replied Felix, sitting up.

"Well, seeing as you're back to playing prime minister, I suppose I must inform you that the Home Secretary is here to see you."

"What time is it?"

"Almost nine o'clock."

"Why didn't you wake me?"

"A man who falls asleep fully clothed is probably in need of additional rest."

Felix looked down, embarrassed to see that he was still wearing his suit from the previous evening.

"Now, will you want butter on your toast or strawberry jam?" asked Humphrey. "Mrs. Hughes has made a fresh batch."

"I can take it from here, thank you, Humphrey," replied Felix, stepping out of bed. "Inform the Home Secretary I'll be along in a few minutes."

"Very well," replied Humphrey, taking his leave.

Felix took little time washing his face, brushing his hair and changing into a clean suit before making his way to the study. He entered to find Thomas Percy drinking tea and eating scones.

"Apologies, Prime Minister," he said, brushing the crumbs off his chin. "Mrs. Hughes insisted and, well, I hear her scones are somewhat of a speciality."

"Is there news?" asked Felix.

"I'm afraid not. However, there has been another incident. This time at a printing house on Fleet Street."

Felix felt a wave of anxiety wash over him.

"A fire at one of the smaller family-run businesses," continued Percy. "A firm called Houlston and Sons."

"A fire?" questioned Felix, stunned.

"The flames ripped through the old wooden building in minutes, destroying everything in their path. A blazing inferno. As you can imagine, the unions are up in arms. They've put it down to more faulty machinery and blame us for doing little to help the ailing printers modernise. I have sent word to the unions expressing our regret and willingness to cooperate."

Percy paused.

"What is it, Thomas?" asked Felix.

"They found the body of the old owner, in the ashes."

Felix felt his legs go weak.

"He had his arms wrapped tightly around one of his old printing presses," continued Percy. "The firemen said it was almost like he was hugging it. Like he had chosen to burn with his beloved family shop. He'd worked there ever since he was a boy, you know."

"How awful," replied Felix.

"The consequences of these events will likely be significant and drawn out. The unions and the opposition will use it as a further stick with which to beat us, regardless of the horror."

It took Felix a few moments to absorb Percy's words. He could not fathom the terrible nature of Mr. Houlston's death. How had this happened? It had been less than twenty-four hours since he had spoken with the old printer and escaped from his shop. Had turning on the faulty press started the fire? It was spitting out lots of oil and smoke by the time he fled. Perhaps Mr. Houlston didn't have the strength to work the lever with Alfred gone. It was made of heavy cast iron, after all. Suddenly it dawned on Felix. Mr. Houlston wasn't hugging the old printing press out of some misplaced sense of loyalty or nostalgia; he was trying to turn it off.

"Are you alright, Felix?" asked Percy, noticing a change in him.

"I'm fine, thank you, Thomas. Just not sleeping very well, what with all that's happened. Is that everything?"

"Almost," replied Percy. "I've been in touch with Commissioner Thompson. His officers have questioned everyone at the East India Club for a second time but have made no further progress. They have also investigated Lord Monteagle's affairs, and it appears his Indian businesses were bringing in a steady income, far above his expenditure."

Felix looked back at Percy blankly. He had barely heard a word of the Home Secretary's update, his mind still swimming with the news of the fire and Mr. Houlston's death.

"Thank you," he said, turning to leave. "Humphrey will see you out."

"We will catch them, Prime Minister," said Percy, sensing Felix's melancholy. "We will right this wrong."

The walk back to his private chambers was a lonely one. Never had Felix felt so utterly discouraged. Not only had he failed in his attempts to solve the case, but his impetuousness had directly resulted in the death of an older man and the destruction of his family business.

The correct course of action would be to hand himself to the police and face trial for his part in the fire and Mr. Houlston's death. But there was something holding him back. A voice within telling him that he could still be of service to the missing lords, still make a valuable contribution to this case. With the police making little headway and the masons distancing themselves from the cards, Felix's covert work was the only line of enquiry bearing any fruit. He would have to continue or hand his evidence over to Thompson and his officers, but having heard Amelia's warning, he could no longer trust anyone connected with the establishment, not even the police commissioner.

Felix's mind was spinning as he tried to balance the correct moral path forward with the most rational one. Mr. Houlston was dead, but it made no logical sense to allow his tragic demise to impact the lives of the missing lords. They were still in danger, and Felix was obliged to help them if he could. He would not simply give up the search and condemn them to whatever fate their captors had in mind because of his own failings. Whilst there was still a chance to save them, he would push on with the case, resolved to hand himself over to the authorities once the peers were found and their abductors put behind bars. That, at least, would go some way to paying back the debt he now owed concerning the old printer's death, or so he hoped. In the meantime, he would set about finding Tom Fellows.

It was late when Felix eventually set off for London's notorious Docklands. He had spent the entire afternoon concocting a plausible story to use to approach his target, should he find him. He thought about taking the guise of a priest out to save the drunk and condemned souls of the Docklands' sin-strewn bars and brothels, but if Tom Fellows had played any part in the abductions, he would likely have little fear in the perceived wrath of God. He also considered playing the role of a police officer investigating a mistaken identity case, a lawyer looking to discuss a secret inheritance, or a property agent needing information to resolve a long-standing family land dispute. However, each character posed more problems than it solved.

After hours spent pacing around Old Pye Street, Felix finally decided on the identity least likely to scare off Tom Fellows, that of an illegal trafficker attempting to move illicit goods in and out of the docks and offering enormous rewards for any assistance. Fortunately, there were several pages of information on *London's Docklands* and *Britain's Untameable River Trade* in the giant encyclopaedias at Old Pye Street. Felix gathered as much knowledge as possible, reading about the type of boats the traders used, the cargo they were permitted to carry and the licences required. He removed a flat cap, a merchant's jacket and rubber boots from the Old Pye Street store and used the full-scale model of London to plot his course.

The journey to the Docklands was uneventful. Felix flagged down one of the new Herald petrol cabs, guiding its driver through a warren of quays and wharves along the Thames to what the old seafarers had affectionately nicknamed Sailortown. A ramshackle area centred around Wapping, Shadwell and Ratcliffe, Sailortown boasted a dingy array of pubs, opium dens and brothels. Many men had lost their fortunes and their minds in Sailortown, but it hadn't stopped the nightly stream of visitors arriving to indulge in the district's dark pleasures.

Felix stepped out of the Herald and onto the grimy Docklands pavement. He paid the driver double to linger for a few minutes, hoping to get noticed and create the illusion of wealth. If there was one thing that attracted the eyes of sailors and merchants alike, it was the prospect of making easy money. Felix noted the number of drunk and destitute figures already sleeping rough as he made his way towards the Prospect of Whitby, a lively-looking pub bursting at the seams with customers and chaos. He bustled his way through the crowded entrance, secured himself a table by the bar and ordered a large bottle of rum. It didn't take long for his presence to attract the interest of two thirsty sailors who pulled up chairs alongside him.

"You know, it can be awful lonely drinking a bottle of rum on your own," said the elder of the two sailors.

"It can even be considered rude in some cultures," continued his younger mate.

Felix took a moment to consider his strategy. He needed to show a level of hospitality but also make it clear that his company and, importantly, his rum did not come free.

"I suppose it is enjoyed better when shared with others," he agreed, signalling for the maid to bring two more glasses.

"Best social lubricant there is," said the older sailor, licking his lips greedily.

"However, I find a drink tastes better when it has been earned rather than given. Wouldn't you agree?" asked Felix.

"What are you after?" asked the older sailor.

"Information," replied Felix.

"We don't have any information," spat the younger sailor, rising from his seat.

"Not so fast," growled the older sailor, pulling his companion back to his seat. "That's just his inexperience speaking," he said, turning to reassure Felix. "What do you want to know?"

"I'm looking for someone to help me smuggle in a large shipment of goods," said Felix.

"That should be easy; the Docklands are full of men."

"Yes, but I'm looking for one in particular," continued Felix, pouring the men a drink. "He has come recommended."

The younger sailor looked around the bar nervously, cradling his rum. "What's this shipment then?" he asked.

"The contents of the shipment are of no concern to you," replied Felix, raising the bottle of rum temptingly.

"I suppose they're not," agreed the older sailor, knocking back his drink and lifting his glass for another measure. "What's this man's name then?" he asked.

"Tom Fellows," replied Felix.

There was a moment's silence. Felix could sense the name had struck a chord, particularly with the younger sailor, who quickly gulped down his drink, hopeful of leaving.

The older sailor, however, hesitated.

"Do you know him?" asked Felix.

"We know him alright," he replied. "The man you want is landlord at the George Inn."

The older sailor leant forward to claim his prize, only for Felix to snatch the bottle of rum off the table. There was more he wanted to know before giving up his best bargaining chip: how long had they known Tom Fellows? Had they ever met the missing lords? Were they ever seen in the Prospect of Whitby or the George Inn? But it wasn't that simple. The mere mention of lords or any men of title in the Docklands could have severe repercussions. Where there was wealth and privilege, there was also the law, and the law was not welcome in Sailortown.

"Which George Inn?" asked Felix, aware that many of the pubs in London had the same or a similar name.

The old sailor looked Felix up and down.

"Limehouse," he said, leaning over the table and gripping the top of the rum bottle. "Though, I'd stay away from it if I were you."

Felix released his hold on the bottle, and the sailors whisked it away to a dark corner of the pub, determined to enjoy the remaining rum and lose themselves for the night.

Outside, Felix hailed another Herald. He gave the driver his destination, and they set off through Sailortown towards Limehouse and the George Inn. Felix used the time to question the driver on his knowledge of the pub and its clientele. The driver explained how the George Inn was once a prominent destination for Royal Navy officers and wealthy merchants before falling into disrepair as the punters and their money began to move along the docks to the more buoyant areas around Wapping. In the last few years, there had been a sizeable drop in customers requesting to be taken to the pub; unless it was late in the evening and, heavily drunk, they desperately needed somewhere cheap to rest their heads.

True to the driver's words, the area around the George Inn was eerily quiet and run-down. Even though the journey had taken barely a few minutes, the contrast between Limehouse and Wapping was stark. It felt as though they were in a completely different city, one suffering the fallout of a long war or a crippling epidemic. Limehouse had previously been one of the most important ports along the Thames. Its thriving trade and bustling nightlife had attracted commerce from all over the continent. But several outbreaks of cholera, and the newly constructed ports further west along the Thames, had led to it becoming increasingly unpopular. In the last few years, a few Chinese communities had moved in, further decreasing its value, and filling the area with tea and eating houses and opium dens.

At the centre of Limehouse, on Salmon Lane, standing as a symbol of its past wealth and sudden decline, was the George Inn. Felix stared in disbelief at the pub's vast frame and high structure. It was a towering building compared to the pubs around Downing Street and the Square Mile and, although in need of repair, it retained a decadent elegance that stirred in Felix a desire to see it restored to its former glory. Perhaps if the George Inn rose like a phoenix from out of the Limehouse ashes, it would generate some interest in the area and bring back some much-needed trade and investment.

Felix stepped out of the cab and approached the faded pub door. He could see through the window that the lights were off, and the pub was no longer in use. He knocked gently and waited. Realising that anyone upstairs would have little chance of hearing him, he banged harder, sending a loud, echoing rumble into the silent Limehouse night. But there was still no answer.

Suddenly, Felix felt the glare of someone's eyes on his back and a presence move in the shadows behind him. He spun around, trying to catch a glimpse of whatever he had sensed in his peripheral vision, but there was still nothing there, only darkness. He scanned the area meticulously, but with no signs of life inside the pub or out in the street, and with the hour increasingly late, he finally returned to the cab, resolved to continue his search for Tom Fellows the following day.

The George Inn

Tom Fellows struck a match and lifted the flame towards his old lamp, casting a dim glow over the room he kept above the George Inn. It was late, and he had only just returned from running errands.

He threw off his wet coat and sat down, happy for a moment's rest. He took hold of the satchel by his feet, carefully untying the knot. There wasn't much inside, a hunk of bread and half a bottle of whiskey to keep the cold and hunger at bay. It had been months since he'd eaten a proper meal, and he longed for something hot to warm his bones. He tore into the bread, washing each piece down with a large gulp of whiskey, then leant back and closed his eyes, willing on sleep, when a loud bang on the cellar door disturbed his peace.

"What now?" he muttered, agitated by the intrusion.

Tom forced his weary body up from the chair, his bones creaking with every movement, picked up his lamp and made his way down the crooked staircase towards the pub.

The old bar-room was faded and run-down, and the smell of stale beer hung in the air, hovering between the few tables and chairs that still rested on the inn's broken and uneven floorboards. The elegantly tiled walls and long wooden beams hinted at a time when the inn had been popular and bustling with life. But Tom's drinking and gambling had hit the inn's profits hard, and he'd struggled to maintain the George, allowing it to slip into disrepair. It had since become a halfway house for sailors and merchants looking for a cheap place to sleep before going out to sea. They would often turn up drunk, looking for a warm bed or shelter from the rain, much to Tom's annoyance. But with little custom and growing debts, any business was good business.

Tom carried on towards the cellar. It was a damp room with a low ceiling and scores of beer barrels lining the walls and stone floor. Each barrel had a strategic part to play in the event of a raid on the George or an unwelcome guest showing up. The barrels by the door were to block an intruder's entrance, whereas those stacked by the stairs were to cover Tom's escape, should he need to be away on his heels.

Three more loud thuds shook the cellar door. Tom hesitated for a moment. Something about them seemed awry. They weren't as erratic as usual. They didn't follow the chaotic pattern of a drunk banging on the door, hoping for some respite from the cold. They were too considered, too equal in tone, and spread out to give him enough time to hear them. Tom felt a wave of anxiety wash over him. Something about this visitor made him nervous. He hoped it was just another down and out in need of some shelter, but it was earlier than usual and, deep down, he knew his hopes were vain.

Over the past twelve months, Tom had struggled to pay his bills and had turned to the Docklands underworld to make ends meet. It had been easy work in the main, picking up and dropping off packages to other links in the chain, but recently things had become more dangerous, and the last few jobs had involved some muscle work, a practice that made Tom feel very uncomfortable.

His father had always warned him about the dangers of dishonest work. He would say, *Don't go upsetting people because, one day, someone might just remember your face and catch you unawares*. It was a piece of advice Tom had taken to heart, probably the only advice his father had ever given him that resonated. The Docklands were large, and there was a constant stream of people coming and going, but it was still easy to bump into familiar faces, and the last few jobs had left Tom feeling vulnerable.

"Who's that then?" he called out.

"Ezra!" came the reply.

The name sent a shiver down Tom's spine. He quickly placed his lamp on one of the barrels and reached for his keys, unbolting the door.

Ezra Fox was a large man, tall with a barrel chest and bulging arms. His long, grey-streaked hair covered most of the scar that stretched along his cheek to the top of his forehead. But the red patch that covered his left eye was harder to conceal, and Ezra paraded it proudly as a badge of honour. He had lost his eye in a street fight with a drunken merchant when he was only sixteen. The encounter had brought him widespread fame and notoriety which he'd used over the years to significant effect, governing the Docklands and building his criminal network. He stepped forward, his large frame barely able to squeeze through the narrow cellar door. Tom took a few steps back. He had never seen Ezra in person; he usually received orders from one of his lackeys but not the great man himself. Ezra's presence meant one of two things; either Tom was in grave danger, or he was about to be in over his head.

"Are you alone?" asked Ezra, his good eye boring into Tom, probing him for any hesitation or signs of deceit.

"Yes," replied Tom nervously.

"Good. I have a special delivery for you."

Ezra raised his gnarled fingers to his lips and whistled loudly into the night. Two beams of light cut through the darkness, growing brighter as a motorised van approached, stopping outside the cellar. The driver opened his door and stepped out, followed by a crew of men dressed in overalls.

"Where do you want them?" the driver asked.

"Put them in the corner, out of the way," replied Ezra.

The driver signalled to his men, and they began unloading the van's cargo, several large wooden barrels.

"What's all this?" asked Tom, trying to hide his anxiety.

"I need you to store some ale for me," replied Ezra. "It's not for drinking, mind. I want it well hidden and out of the way. Understood?"

"Of course."

Ezra turned his attention to the cellar as the men rolled the barrels in and began to stack them. He took a moment to inspect the cargo, checking each barrel for the correct markings, occasionally rocking them to listen to the sound the contents made. Tom quietly sank into the shadows, hoping not to draw any more attention to himself, but Ezra didn't take long to set his gaze back on the errant landlord. Like most predators, Ezra could smell fear, and Tom's was everywhere. Ezra stepped forward, reaching into his pocket and removing a leather wallet.

"For your trouble," he said, placing a handful of banknotes on one of the barrels. "And be thankful for that. If I had my way, you'd be doing this out of the goodness of your black heart. But my employer insisted you be paid, to keep you honest."

It was the first time Tom had heard mention of anyone above Ezra. He had assumed that the pyramid of crime in the Docklands ended with Ezra at its apex. He wondered who this employer was and how formidable his character must be to have such a notorious figure under his control.

Tom took the money and placed it under his shirt. He knew that any hesitation or reluctance would be seen as a sign of weakness or distrust and could have grave consequences. Ezra's ruthless streak was legendary. Tom had heard countless tales in the pubs and inns around Sailortown of people disappearing or, even worse, their bodies showing up on the banks of the Thames. He did not want to become the next pub story, or the next body, bloated and swollen, floating down the river. Instead, he rolled up his sleeves and set to work, helping the men move the remaining barrels. It was tiring work, and he struggled to push the large wooden containers across the uneven stone floor. But with Ezra looking on, he summoned whatever strength he had and drove the barrels forward, stacking them with the rest of the cargo.

With the last barrel in place and Ezra satisfied, Tom finally sat down to catch his breath. His nose filled with a heavy and unfamiliar scent as he inhaled the dank cellar air. He looked around but couldn't sense where it was coming from. It didn't smell like beer or ale, nor did it smell of the cellar. It was musky and burnt his nostrils and throat the more he breathed it in. He subtly eyed the markings on the barrels. The lettering was foreign; German, he thought, but he was reluctant to press Ezra on the matter. It was clear that whatever was being stored in the barrels wasn't ale. But the more he knew about his mysterious delivery, the greater the risk. It was far safer to be kept in the dark.

Tom covered the barrels with a large sheet.

"They'll be safe here. You have my word," he said.

"Your word!?" mocked Ezra. "What good is the word of a drunken wretch? I prefer to have your fear."

Ezra stepped forward, raising himself to his full intimidating height, forcing Tom to stumble backwards, nearly losing his balance.

"If anyone asks," he growled menacingly, "we were never here."

"You were never here," replied Tom, shaken to his core. "None of you were!"

Ezra waited for the last of his men to leave. He reached for the lamp and curled his fingers around the flame, pinching the wick and extinguishing the light.

In the black silence, Tom heard the cellar door close and the motorised van pull away, leaving him alone in the dark, drenched in fear and the smell of burning air.

Confidence Vote

The sun had barely risen the following day when Felix set off from Downing Street for the short walk to Westminster. Having called an impromptu cabinet meeting to discuss the mounting pressure on his government, he'd decided to work from one of the offices within Parliament for the day rather than Number 10, hoping a change of scenery might lift his spirits.

Naturally, Humphrey had protested, aggrieved that Felix should leave so early without a warm breakfast in his belly or time to read the day's newspapers. But Felix liked to walk when he had things to mull over. It allowed him to work through his problems with a clear head. He'd covered many miles over the years and, in that time, solved many challenges.

However, today, Felix had more on his mind than usual. Having traced Tom Fellows' whereabouts to the dilapidated George Inn, he had missed the landlord and the opportunity to question him about the printers and the card. Unwilling to give up the chase, Felix had paid the cab driver extra to stake out the pub the following day and inform him the moment Fellows returned. A deal the driver was all too eager to accept and one that Felix could only hope he would honour.

Felix arrived at Westminster to the sound of silence. He made his way through St. Stephen's Hall on the western front of Parliament towards the Central Lobby, a lofty octagonal stone room with an intricately tiled floor and mosaic-covered vault; the crossroads at which the Lords, Commons and Westminster Hall met. He had planned to continue through the Commons Corridor moving east towards the Parliamentary Offices when he came upon Thomas Percy.

"Thomas?" he said, a little startled. "You're at it early this morning."

"Unfortunately so," said Percy, the strain of recent events beginning to show. "I, erm…"

"Can't sleep, either?"

"It's been almost a week since the lords' disappearance, and our leads are drying up. I'm at a loss as to what to do next."

Felix placed a consoling hand on Percy's broad back. He could sympathise with his colleague's despair; it was a feeling he had become used to of late.

"We will catch them, Thomas," he said, echoing the Home Secretary's consoling words the previous day. "We will right this wrong."

Percy nodded his thanks.

"Better dash, I've a meeting with the Speaker, probably another hour discussing the correlation between lunchtime drinking and falling standards in the house. Wish me luck!" the Home Secretary chimed, trying to muster some of his usual zest, before turning and disappearing back through the Central Lobby towards the Speaker's House.

Felix continued in the opposite direction towards the Parliamentary Offices. He'd decided the previous evening to address the complaints and criticisms he'd faced in the House of Commons the day before. Having settled into one of the small rooms, he began to write a detailed response to the question of the British military and its constant need for money in light of the emerging American and German forces. He also wrote about the British Empire as a beacon for democracy and social welfare. Naturally, this led to addressing the conditions in the mines and factories and the continued plight of the working class, a topic that resonated now more than ever, given the tragic deaths of Arthur Jenkins and Mr. Houlston.

The more Felix wrote, the more heartfelt his words became, and his document began to take the form of a personal statement rather than a manifesto. It felt liberating. With everything that had happened over the past few days and with little left to lose, he was suddenly free of the constraints of his position. It was unheard of for a prime minister to take a moral stance on such matters. To speak directly from the heart was seen as a weakness, a political suicide of sorts, but to Felix, it was progress and something that had been simmering in him long before the abductions.

Filled with a renewed sense of purpose, Felix waited anxiously for his colleagues in the cabinet to arrive. He watched the clock, counting down the minutes. The promise of decisive action made him feel like a child again, eagerly waiting for his parents to return home to tell them about the day's adventures and share his stories. Fortunately, he did not have long to wait before the door swung open and James Henry, the Chancellor of Exchequer popped his head in.

"Ah, there you are," he said, before turning to alert the others outside. "Found him. The prime minister is in this one."

Led by James Henry, the cabinet members started to filter into the room. Among those entering were senior cabinet ministers, Charles Joyce, the Lord Privy Seal, and the Secretary of State for Foreign Affairs, Francis Wood, followed by their undersecretaries and assistants.

Felix watched as they began to take their seats, noting their gloomy faces and lack of eye contact. He would take great pleasure in turning their negativity on its head.

With barely half the table filled, the steady stream of members entering finally stopped. Felix looked around, confused. His eyes questioned those present on why half his cabinet had chosen to snub his request for a meeting, but none of his colleagues would meet his gaze. He waited a few more minutes in the vain hope that perhaps they were running late, but it was evident from the mood inside the room that they were simply not coming. Felix's ambition burst like a parachute, yanking him out of his lofty hopes and bringing him back to earth with a thud. What good was a prime minister if he couldn't even form a cabinet?

The uneasy tension was broken by Percy's sudden arrival.

"Sorry I'm late," he said, slightly out of breath. "My meeting took a bit of an unexpected turn."

"At least you're here, Thomas," said Felix soberly. "As you can see, most of our colleagues didn't even manage that."

"Yes. Unfortunately, that comes as no surprise," said Percy, the promise of more bad news written on his face. "It appears the members have tabled a motion of no confidence in your leadership."

"They mean to vote me out," replied Felix, taken aback.

"Supported by some among our party, and cabinet."

The news hit Felix like a sledgehammer to the temple. Never in British political history had a governing party and its cabinet turned on its leader in such a manner. It was beyond damning. Felix looked around the room at the handful of cabinet members present. How many of them had been tempted to join the conspiracy? How many of them could he really trust?

"We have just under a week before the vote, to build our case with the House and win back favour," continued Percy. "It's not long, but it's something. We still have a fighting chance."

"A chance?" questioned Felix. "There is only one sensible course of action available now."

"Think of the odds, Thomas," said James Henry.

"Clearly, the odds are stacked against us. But opinions change quickly in the House," said Percy.

Once again, Felix had left it to the Home Secretary to encourage and reassure everyone. How many times had his loyal friend propped up his ailing premiership over the years? He deserved so much more, thought Felix; a knighthood, no, a sainthood—not the daily stream of problems that continued to land on his desk.

"Here," said Felix, sliding his work across the table.

"What is it?" asked Percy.

"An honest account of where we are as a country and plans for the future, for what they're worth. Do what you will with them. Show them to our supporters and even our enemies. They may make a difference, although I doubt it very much."

Felix turned to leave.

"Where are you going?" asked Percy.

"I have something pressing to attend to."

"More pressing than this?"

"Speak to our members, Thomas. Make a list of who we can rely on and who we have lost. We'll review it tomorrow."

Back at his study in Number 10 that evening, Felix grabbed a bottle of scotch and a tumbler and disappeared through the secret walkway towards Old Pye Street. When he reached the secret room he sat at the desk, opened the bottle and poured himself a large glass. As he lifted it to his mouth, ready to drown his sorrows and lament his failures, he stopped to study the stern, determined faces of the former prime ministers depicted on the walls. How had he followed in the footsteps of these great men? How had he walked the same halls, worked at the same desk, and occupied the same great seat of power? The more he thought about it, the more absurd it felt.

Felix's soul-searching was suddenly disturbed by a sound at the Old Pye Street door. He stood up quietly and crept into the narrow hallway towards the front of the rickety old building. Through the small stained-glass window, he could see the silhouette of a man snooping around outside. Although anxious, Felix remained completely still, eager not to draw attention to his presence. The figure approached the door and lent down, slipping a folded note underneath. Felix waited for him to leave, then grabbed the paper and unfolded it, reading the message:

The landlord has returned to the George Inn.

Felix stared at the words in shock. He'd been so overcome with the no-confidence motion and his self-doubt that he'd forgotten entirely about his deal with the cab driver. Suddenly presented with a lifeline, Felix quickly changed, replacing his formal clothes with a pair of workman's trousers, a merchant's coat and rubber boots. He stuffed the note in his pocket, gave the prime ministers one final look and stepped out onto Old Pye Street with a renewed sense of purpose.

Having flagged down a cab on Victoria Street and instructed the driver to take him to the Docklands, Felix used the journey to reacquaint himself with his cover story, determined to master the details and avoid another tragedy like the one he'd created at Houlston and Sons.

Arriving at Limehouse under cover of night, Felix stepped out of the cab and approached the run-down pub. He knocked loudly on the faded door, sending a series of thuds echoing into the surrounding streets. He stepped back and waited anxiously. Concerned that he'd arrived too late to catch the landlord at home again, Felix at last heard the faint sound of footsteps coming from inside.

"Who is it?" called a voice from behind the door.

"I'm here to see Tom Fellows," replied Felix.

"I asked who you were," repeated the agitated voice.

"My name is John Bishop. I'm an importer of foreign goods. I was hoping to conduct a little business with Mr. Fellows."

"What kind of goods?"

"The kind I'm not comfortable speaking about on an east London street full of listening ears."

Felix waited, worried he might have scared the landlord off, when he heard metal bolts being drawn, and the door finally swung open to reveal Tom Fellows.

"Quickly then," said Fellows, ushering Felix inside.

Felix was surprised by the landlord's meek appearance and nervous disposition. He had been expecting a hardened sailor with a weathered face and battle scars. Instead, Fellows was a small, frail-looking man with blotchy skin and a red nose. His eyes looked like he should have been in his middle years, but his body told a different story, one of alcohol consumption and opium abuse.

"You can never be too careful," said Fellows, leading Felix through the forlorn inn towards a narrow staircase. "Especially around here. There are crooks and villains everywhere."

Fellows lit a bright lamp and led the way down the stairs to the inn's dark cellar. Felix followed, covering his eyes from the glare of the flame. He opened them at the bottom of the staircase to find himself in a dank room surrounded by barrels.

"Now, what's this business you wanted to discuss?" asked Fellows.

"I have a shipment of goods coming into the Docklands. I need a crew I can trust and someone who knows how to get them past the authorities undetected," replied Felix.

"Why me?"

"Because you have a reputation for smuggling," said Felix, looking around the cellar, "and needing the money."

"How much are you offering, exactly?" called a rasping voice from the darkness.

Felix spun around to see a tall figure standing in the shadows. "Who's asking?"

Ezra stepped forward, revealing his menacing frame and prominent red eye patch. He crossed the room and unbolted the cellar door, allowing a group of rugged-looking men to pour into the cellar. Felix's heart skipped a beat. He recognised the two sailors he had questioned at the Prospect of Whitby the previous evening amongst the rabble.

"Is this him?" asked Ezra, addressing the sailors.

"That's the man," said the younger of the two.

Ezra turned and approached Felix, his intimidating size casting a shadow over the cellar walls.

"So, tell me about this shipment of yours."

"It's arriving in a fortnight from Iberia," said Felix, trying to maintain an air of confidence, "full to the rafters with sherry and port. Enough to flood the London market and push out the competition."

"I haven't heard about any shipments," said Ezra, "and I make it my business to hear about everything coming in and out of these docks, especially if there's a tax due."

"It's been kept secret. You never know who you can trust these days," replied Felix, shooting Fellows a stern look.

"A fine story, I'll give you that," said Ezra, signalling to his men.

They rushed forward and took hold of Felix, forcing him to the ground.

"What is the meaning of this?" protested Felix.

He tried to fight them off, but he was vastly outnumbered and the men didn't take long to subdue him, wrapping a heavy sailor's rope around Felix's chest and arms and tying him to one of the barrels.

"You're making a big mistake," he called out. "There's enough money in this deal to make us all rich."

"Now, why would I want to be rich?" chortled Ezra. "Where's the fun in that?"

"If it's not money you're after, then what is it?" asked Felix.

"I want to know why you're here. I've got informants all over these docks, and none has ever heard of you or any shipment."

Felix tried to think of a convincing answer, but his mind was blank. The more he tried to concentrate, the more his thoughts scattered.

"Well?" pressed Ezra, beginning to lose his patience.

Felix took a few deep breaths, trying to regulate his racing heart. It was a method he'd been taught by the family doctor, who'd learnt the technique on a visit to India tending to an ailing Himalayan prince. Fortunately, the breathing was enough to calm Felix down and restore clarity to his thoughts. It was pointless trying to carry on with his current pretence. His merchant story had been transparent from the start. The only thing it had accomplished was to lead him here, to this point, strapped to a barrel and fighting for his life. He had to think quickly and devise another character that might resonate enough to get him out of his precarious situation.

"I'm a detective at Scotland Yard," he blurted out.

Felix felt the mood in the cellar change immediately. These men were criminals, law-breakers to the core, but none of them wanted the abduction of a high-profile police officer hanging over their heads.

"The commissioner has assigned me to gather information on a case," he continued. "I just want to ask a few questions."

The men anxiously turned to Ezra, hoping he might see sense and untie their prisoner. But instead, he spun around to face Tom Fellows.

"If you have anything of value upstairs, now is the time to fetch it," he warned the landlord.

"What do you mean?" asked Fellows.

Ezra approached one of the barrels. He removed a cudgel from inside his long coat and struck the wooden frame until a crack appeared, and a stream of fine black powder began to pour out.

Fellows looked at Ezra in disbelief.

"This pub is all I have left," he pleaded.

"All YOU have left?" scoffed Ezra. "The last I checked, the pub was under new ownership."

"Yes, for now. But I was going to raise the money and buy it back—"

"Enough!" bellowed Ezra. "The George has been compromised. God knows how many more blue boys will show up. It's time to go."

Ezra grabbed the barrel in his large hands and spun it around, dragging it across the cellar floor, creating a gunpowder trail back to the other barrels.

"What about the copper?" asked the young sailor.

"One less nark to worry about."

Felix felt his heart sink. They meant to kill him. To blow him up, along with the downtrodden inn. "Let me go!" he shouted in desperation. "You can't do this!"

Ezra's men turned to leave.

"Let me go! Please! You can't. I'm the…"

Felix's words were drowned out by the cellar door closing. Within moments the men had cleared out, covering the room in darkness. He continued shouting his pleas into the void, but it was no good; they weren't coming back.

Felix sat back against the barrel. He could hear their muffled voices outside, followed by the sound of car engines and then vehicles driving away. After a few moments, all that remained was silence. He suddenly felt a wave of hope wash over him. Maybe they'd forgotten about him or had decided to spare the pub after all. But just as he was breathing a sigh of relief, he heard the faint sound of a match striking and the crackling noise of the gunpowder catching alight. He watched the cellar door as a tiny spark appeared, entering beneath its warped wooden frame. It moved across the floor at speed, gathering pace as it ate through the meandering black line, drawing closer to him and the surrounding pile of barrels.

Felix tried to stretch out his leg, hoping to reach the gunpowder and break the line, but it was agonisingly just out of reach. Ezra was far too wise to make a mistake like that. He'd laid the gunpowder close enough to give Felix hope but far enough away to make it unreachable.

Felix watched as the spark darted past his outstretched leg towards its destination. He had often read about the emotions people were supposed to feel when faced with their own death, but he did not feel anything besides regret. He closed his eyes, concentrating on the depth and rhythm of his breath, hoping the end would somehow be easier to bear by remaining calm. He began a countdown in his head, another trick to take his mind off the spark and the barrels, when he heard a noise outside the cellar door. Someone was pulling at the lock, trying to get in.

"Help! Help! I'm in here!" he shouted.

The door finally burst open, and to Felix's surprise, Mr. Houlston's young apprentice Alfred rushed in. He froze for a second, taking in the scene.

"Quickly!" shouted Felix, motioning towards the spark hurrying along the line of gunpowder.

Alfred rushed over and stamped on it before sweeping the line of gunpowder away with his foot and breaking its connection to the barrels.

Felix opened his mouth to thank the young man, then turned to his side and vomited.

"Sorry, it's the shock,"

Alfred nodded, unsure where to look. He leant down and untied Felix.

"What were you doing outside?" asked Felix, wiping his mouth.

"I've been here since the fire and…"

Alfred stopped, unable to finish his sentence. Felix looked at the struggling young man.

"I was sorry to hear about your master."

"He was a good man." replied Alfred, looking away to hide his tearful eyes.

Felix pushed himself up off the floor.

"Thank you for saving me" he said warmly.

"I couldn't just stand aside and watch them do it again, not to another innocent."

Felix felt a wave of guilt wash over him.

"Alfred, I'm not a tax clerk."

"I know, I was listening at the door."

"What were you doing out there?"

Alfred hesitated. "It sounds foolish now that I think about it."

"Try me."

Alfred took a breath. "I was waiting for the right moment to grab Fellows and take him to the police. He's usually drunk by this time of night. But there's been so many comings and goings that the opportunity never quite presented itself."

"That's admirable, but not a job for a boy your age. These people are dangerous."

"I know," agreed Alfred. "But after what they did to the shop and Mr. Houlston…It's just not right!"

"What do you mean?" asked Felix.

"It's all my fault," replied Alfred, welling up. "If I hadn't told them you'd been in the shop asking questions. Me and my big mouth!"

"I can help you, Alfred," said Felix, comforting the young man. "But I need to know what happened once you left the shop."

Alfred nodded, taking a few more breaths to hold back the tears.

"After Mr. Houlston sent me out, I jumped in a carriage and came straight here. The landlord's business had kept us afloat the past year. In return, all he asked was to be told if any strangers turned up asking questions about our work or his order. So, when you appeared asking to look at our books, I thought I should tell him. I felt obliged. Only, he got all nervous when I mentioned it, said he needed to leave. He even gave me a bottle of scotch for free. When I returned, you'd gone, and Mr. Houlston was closing everything down."

"He was alright?' asked Felix, shocked.

"Well, he wasn't quite himself. He was annoyed about something, probably the press that was playing up. But I fixed that before turning in for the night. I knew those presses inside out, you see. They were like family to me. I lived with them. I didn't have a home of my own, so Mr. Houlston let me sleep in the back. It'd been a long day, and I fell straight off. I woke up to a commotion coming from the shop floor. I came out to see the walls all covered in flames and Mr. Houlston… tied to the printing press. I tried to free him, but I couldn't cut through the rope in time. I tried my best, I swear!"

"It's not your fault, Alfred."

"The smoke got so thick, so quickly, I just couldn't see him. But I could hear him. He begged me to leave, to save myself. I didn't know what to do, so I just ran. I knew the shop floor like the back of my hand and found my way out. When I got outside, that's when I saw him, the landlord, just standing there, watching. Making sure it all burnt to the ground. He didn't see me though. His eyes were fixed on the flames."

Alfred stopped to take a breath.

"I came to the inn the following night to find him. That's when I saw you standing outside, knocking on the door."

"That was you?"

Alfred nodded. "I was waiting for him."

Felix took a moment to absorb the information. Alfred's revelations had left a bittersweet taste in his mouth. He was relieved not to have been directly responsible for the fire and the old printer's death, but his presence at the shop had indeed set a series of disastrous events in motion. Suddenly, it all began to make sense. By sending for scotch, Mr. Houlston had hoped to charm Felix into turning a blind eye to the illegal work he'd conducted for Tom Fellows. He'd known that the card job was crooked, but he needed the money to keep the shop afloat. Felix remembered the old printer's fatal words, *at any cost*.

Felix turned his attention back to the young apprentice. He looked tired and dirty. Having had a home and a trade with a considerate mentor, he was now jobless and destitute, the victim of a political game far above his station or comprehension.

Felix considered giving him some money to find a room for the night. But how long would it be until he was out on the streets again, another lost soul sleeping rough? If Felix was going to make any meaningful change to the lives of the poor and needy, it would have to start now.

"Do you have anywhere to go?" he asked.

Alfred shook his head, embarrassed.

"Well, I may know of a place," said Felix, leading the young apprentice out of the cellar and back onto London's cobbled streets.

The early morning light was beginning to appear by the time Felix and Alfred arrived at Old Pye Street. Felix watched his young companion examine his surroundings with growing curiosity. Alfred had likely assumed that travelling with a gentleman like Felix would mean heading for an upmarket part of town, rather than one of London's run-down and forgotten back streets.

They approached the narrow terraced house, and Felix opened the door, ushering Alfred inside. They made their way along the tight hallway towards the sizeable oval office. Felix turned on the generator, casting a dim light over the secret room and bringing it to life. Alfred looked around in awe. He had never seen anything like it: the large oak desk, the telephone switchboard, the hanging portraits, the full-scale model of London. It was like stepping into an adventure story, not real life.

Felix observed the young man struggling to make sense of it all. He had thought long and hard in the cab about how best to explain it to Alfred, but nothing he could say would prepare the young apprentice for such a moment. He simply had to see Old Pye Street for himself.

"You're probably wondering what this is all about."

"You could say that," mumbled Alfred.

"The truth is, I'm not a tax clerk, a police officer, or even a detective," said Felix. "I'm the prime minister."

"Give over," laughed Alfred. "You can't be the prime minister."

"I realise it's a lot to take in, and there'll be plenty of time for explanations tomorrow. But, for now, we could probably both use some rest. You'll be safe here for the night. I'll be back in the morning with some food and clean clothes."

Alfred looked up at Felix, the slightest hint of doubt suddenly forming in his glazed eyes.

"Sleep well, Alfred," smiled Felix before turning towards the hallway and the tunnel back to Number 10.

The Gambler

The kitchen was alive with activity when Felix entered the following morning. The staff were busy preparing the household breakfast while Mrs. Hughes tended to a large basket, packed to the brim with some of her favourite homemade delights. Felix had informed Humphrey that he would be travelling for the day and needed a sizeable basket of food prepared for the journey. As usual, the wily old steward had questioned him on the nature of his mysterious trip and, unsure how to explain the past few days' events to his faithful friend, Felix was forced to concoct an elaborate cover story.

"There's freshly baked bread, scones and biscuits in there, along with some smoked meat, apples from the garden, and my famous homemade jam," explained Mrs. Hughes, proudly folding a towel over the basket.

"What's in the homemade jam?" asked Felix.

"I'll agree to share my secrets when you agree to a month's paid leave."

"A month!?" chortled Felix.

A ripple of laughter spread among the listening kitchen staff.

"You don't get owt for nowt in this world, Prime Minister," said Mrs. Hughes, handing Felix the basket. "We learn that lesson quickly up north."

Felix thanked the head cook and returned to his office with the basket. Waiting on his desk was a pile of freshly cleaned uniforms he'd requested from the laundry room, alongside some basic grooming apparatus. He took the supplies and returned through the fireplace towards Old Pye Street.

To his amazement, the secret office had come to life. The previously dull bulbs shone brightly, and the lifeless telephone switchboard had miraculously awakened, with small lights flicking on and off as calls were being made or hung up on the exchange.

Felix looked around the room in disbelief, finally locating Alfred sitting by the buzzing generator covered in wires and old machine parts.

"I thought you might like to see it all up and running," said Alfred, trying to twist himself out of the mess. "Would be a shame to waste a machine like this."

"But how did you manage it?" asked Felix.

"I don't know. Just good at fixing things, I s'ppose. D'you wanna give it a try?"

Alfred held out the telephone mouthpiece and receiver. Felix took them in his hands and sat down at the switchboard. He considered who to call and connected one of the cords to a socket.

"Professor Amelia Woodruff. Corpus Christi. Oxford," he announced into the mouthpiece, waiting to be connected. He looked around the newly lit room, suddenly vibrant and ready for service, and smiled warmly at the young apprentice.

"Thank you."

"For what, exactly?" came a voice through the receiver. "My unrelenting charm and intellect?"

"Amelia, it's me," said Felix, lifting the mouthpiece.

"Yes, I know. I could tell from the heartfelt tone and, frankly, saccharine sincerity. You made it out of the printer's alive, then?"

"You haven't heard the news?" asked Felix, surprised.

"News?" repeated Amelia, enthused by the promise of misadventure.

Felix explained the past few days' events, starting with his visit to Houlston and Sons before moving on to the motion of no confidence and Alfred's timely intervention at the George Inn. Unsurprisingly, Amelia was sour to have missed out on the fun but was pleased to hear that Felix had escaped unscathed. To Felix, however, the past few days had been anything but fun, and he certainly didn't feel unscathed. Over the past twenty-four hours, his position in government had become untenable, and he'd managed to put his life in danger, only surviving by the smallest of coincidences.

There was, however, one saving grace. Having repeatedly played out his ordeal at the George, Felix had hit upon something he thought might be helpful to the case. While tied to the barrel, he had witnessed a brief exchange between Tom Fellows and the one-eyed man, suggesting that ownership of the pub had recently changed hands. There were many ways to control a person, but as the old printer had proven, chief among them was money. Whoever's name was on those deeds would almost certainly have a connection to the case.

"I need you to do some digging, Amelia," said Felix. "Can you find out whose name is on the title deeds for the George Inn at Limehouse?"

"I can have one of my students look into it. She's like a dog with a bone once she gets going."

Felix thanked Amelia before putting the receiver down. He stood up to face Alfred, who was looking around the room anxiously, pretending not to have listened to his conversation.

"There you have it," said Felix. "Now that you know the whole truth, I would understand if you wished to leave. We can find you an apprenticeship somewhere, with food and board, and good prospects."

"No. I would like to stay," said Alfred.

"It will be dangerous. I don't want you to feel obliged."

"Mr. Houlston was good to me. He took me in, even when he knew I didn't have a proper education. I want to help. I need to."

Felix considered Alfred for a moment. There was a burning intensity in his young eyes. After what happened, how could he deny the young man the chance to see things put right?

"Things will undoubtedly get worse before they get better," he said, giving Alfred one last chance to change his mind.

"I'd still like to stay."

"Understood. But you must promise to keep our work here a secret. No one must ever know about my involvement in the case or the location of this office. Not while I'm in government. However long that may be."

"Cross my heart and hope to die," promised Alfred.

"And, when this is all over, you will take up my offer of an apprenticeship and never look back. Not for a moment."

Alfred nodded his acceptance of the terms.

Feeling reassured, Felix lifted the basket onto the oak desk and removed the towel, revealing the delicious array of food Mrs. Hughes had prepared. Alfred had never seen such a magnificent spread. He waited patiently for Felix to take the first piece before launching himself head-first into the basket. As Alfred gorged himself on scones and jam, Felix took the opportunity to enquire about his family and background, mindful not to push the young man too much.

Between bites, Alfred explained that his mother had been a seamstress for a wealthy family and had been given temporary lodgings in their basement. The family had paid her to stay with them three nights a week to be on hand for the lady of the house and her two daughters. After some years, the damp walls began to take their toll on her breathing, ending her life prematurely. His father was a tradesman. He took great pride in the quality of his work and in passing down his knowledge to Alfred, his only son. But the loss of his wife was crushing, and after her death he descended into a depression, turning to alcohol and opium for comfort. Unable to cope with his father's addictions and determined to carve out his own path, Alfred left home at thirteen only to find himself on the streets, where Mr. Houlston eventually discovered him. He'd been sleeping rough outside a union building when Mr. Houlston arrived to enquire about an apprentice to help maintain his printing presses. Fortunately for Alfred, the union had one apprentice left and was reluctant to let him go. Having overheard the conversation and witnessed Mr. Houlston's disappointment, Alfred approached the old printer and offered his services. Naturally, Mr. Houlston was reluctant to begin with, but when Alfred explained his situation, the old printer agreed to give him a trial, which Alfred passed with flying colours.

Alfred's story reminded Felix of just how unforgiving society could be. One stroke of misfortune could turn a person's life upside down. Fortunately for Alfred, he'd met a good man willing to offer him a second chance. Countless others hadn't been so lucky. It was the type of issue that had attracted Felix to politics in the first place; the desire to help those less well-off or in desperate need of benevolence. Unfortunately, he'd allowed himself to be distracted from the country's growing social issues by the constant political point-scoring in the Commons. However, having seen the plight of so many over the past few days, it had become abundantly clear just how out of touch Felix was with the lives of ordinary people. He would need to speak to the union man who confronted him at Downing Street and listen openly to his grievances if he genuinely wanted to make the changes that had stirred him into becoming a politician in the first place.

"Is everything alright?" spluttered Alfred, chomping on some cheese. He had noticed a sudden change in Felix's mood and a far-off look in his eyes.

"Yes. I was just thinking you'll need some sheets and a pillow if you're to be comfortable here."

Felix rose from his chair and set off for the corridor back towards Downing Street. Once in his study, he checked his drawers, searching for the petition the union man had handed him on the evening of his parliamentary dinner. He found the scroll hidden beneath some heavy books alongside Thompson's note informing him of Lord Cecil's abduction.

Felix took a moment to study the long petition. There were thousands of signatures, some with accompanying comments; workers venting their anger and frustration at their working conditions and the government's lack of action. Each name Felix read reminded him of Arthur Jenkins, the unfortunate young man who had died at Silverwood. How many more Arthur Jenkins were on this list? he thought to himself. How many more lives at risk?

Felix reached for some paper and began to compose a letter. He responded to the union's concerns about working conditions and the lack of investment in new machinery, then followed that up with a passionate response to the workers' comments, empathising with their worries and fears and promising to make far-reaching changes if he retained the power to do so. He finished by inviting the union leaders to meet him at their chosen time and place before folding his letter in half and placing it inside an envelope. He found the name of the union man and his organisation at the top of the petition document. It read:

To be presented to the prime minister by the hand of William Foster on behalf of the Industrial Workers Union.

Felix had barely finished sealing the envelope when there was a knock at the door, and Humphrey entered.

"Will you need me to light the fire?" he asked. "Or will you be off on another of your escapades this evening?"

"The fire can wait. I need you to send a letter for me. And have the staff bring up some fresh sheets and a pillow."

"Are you intending to sleep in your study now?"

"They are for someone else. A rough sleeper in need of some comfort."

"Then they should use the staff's old sheets."

"Nonsense," said Felix, brushing Humphrey's protestations aside. "Some of mine will do fine."

Humphrey didn't take long to return with the sheets and pillow. He reluctantly handed them to Felix before taking the letter. Felix waited for his steward to leave the study before turning the marble corbel on the fireplace and activating the secret passage. He had hoped to tell Humphrey all about Old Pye Street and Alfred, but there had been little time to explain, and he was sure his steward would disapprove. There had barely been a secret between them since he was a boy, but Felix knew he could only reveal the truth once he could prove their benefit to the case.

Felix found Alfred back at work on the other side of the tunnel. Having devoured Mrs. Hughes's feast, the young man had turned his attention to fixing the holes in the walls, hoping to block out the draught that occasionally engulfed Old Pye Street.

"Do you ever rest?" asked Felix.

"I like to keep busy. Stops me thinking about…things too much."

"I can understand that," said Felix, laying out the sheets to make Alfred's bed. "This must be my first time preparing a bed. I've always had someone else do it for me. Pathetic, when you think about it."

"It's not your fault. You didn't choose the life you was born into."

"Neither did you," replied Felix, finishing the bed, and turning to help Alfred.

It was close to ten o'clock when they finally finished working. In that time, they covered all the draughts, fixed the doors firmly onto their hinges, straightened out the bowed wooden shelves and organised the library of encyclopaedias into neatly aligned rows, indexed in alphabetical order.

Felix looked at the clock, unsure where the day had gone. He was about to retire for the evening when a light began to blink on the telephone switchboard. Curious, he reached for the receiver, switched the cord jack, and spoke into the mouthpiece.

"Hello…?"

"It's me…" came the muffled sound of Amelia's voice.

"Amelia? Can you speak up?" said Felix, barely able to hear.

"I have…come to…quick as you can," she replied, her voice cutting in and out.

"Amelia? I can't hear you. Speak up."

"Meet…the lobby."

"Where are you, Amelia? I missed the location."

"…Club."

Felix caught the last word before the phone cut out.

"She's gone," he said, turning to face Alfred. "She said something about a club, but I didn't catch which one."

Alfred approached the switchboard. He looked down at the connecting cords. "The call came from an exchange in London. Area code 470."

Felix quickly scanned the area codes on a list pinned to the side of the machine. "Blast it! I told her to stay in Oxford and not to do anything rash!"

He quickly placed the receiver back on the switchboard and grabbed his jacket.

"Do you know where she is?" asked Alfred.

"The call came from St. James's Square. She's at the East India Club."

"Can I come with you?"

"I don't think that's a good idea."

"I can keep an eye out. Watch the doors in case anyone tries to slip in or out."

Felix considered the young man for a moment. He was adept at hiding in the shadows, as he had proven while staking out the George Inn, and with the events of the past few days, it couldn't hurt to have an extra pair of eyes keeping watch.

"On one condition," he replied. "If you see even the slightest hint of trouble, I want you to return and send word to the police. I don't want you putting yourself in harm's way regardless of what happens to Amelia or me. Understood?"

Alfred nodded in agreement. He followed Felix to the full-scale model of London in the centre of the room, where they plotted his journey from Old Pye Street through the backroads and cobblestones to St. James's Square. Felix did not want Alfred to be seen arriving with him, potentially putting him at risk, so he sent the young man out on foot, then waited thirty minutes before leaving to give him a head start.

On arrival in St. James's Square, Felix checked the shadows for any signs of Alfred before approaching the steps to the East India Club. To his relief, the young man was nowhere to be seen, meaning he had listened and stayed out of sight. Felix stepped into the club lobby, where he was met by the elegant hostess, Seema Sharma.

"This way, Prime Minister," she said, leading Felix through reception towards a long corridor with doors on both sides. "Your American colleague has taken some private rooms and is anxious to see you."

They approached a thin door with a small carving of the Hindu monkey god, Hanuman. Seema Sharma pushed the door open and led Felix into a small cluster of rooms beautifully decorated in authentic Indian designs. Felix noted the rich array of ivory and terracotta ornaments and the vibrant silk curtains hanging from the ceiling to the floor. He stepped through the main suite into a small tearoom covered in green and gold cushions where Amelia sat, drinking sweet tea from an emerald teacup and looking very pleased with herself.

"I see you made it then," she said, sipping from her cup. "You really must try this tea. It's simply delicious."

"Christ, Amelia," sighed Felix. "I rushed here as fast as I could. I thought you were in danger."

"In danger? Whatever gave you that idea?"

"Your message..."

"What about my message?"

"It was all garbled and fuzzy before it dramatically cut out. You sounded like you were in distress."

"Me, in distress? How strange," chortled Amelia.

"Apologies," interjected Seema Sharma, "we are having some difficulties with our new telephone line."

"You see," said Amelia, jumping up from her seat. "They're having some difficulties with their new telephone line."

"Then why did you ask me to come? I've got"—Felix stopped, suddenly aware of Seema Sharma's presence—"things that require my immediate attention."

Amelia looked over at the watching hostess. "Would you mind?" she said apologetically. "Sensitive information about to be disclosed, I fear."

"Of course," whispered Seema Sharma, departing and closing the door behind her.

Amelia listened to the hostess's footsteps fading before turning to face Felix. "My student followed up on your lead, and it appears your instincts were correct. The George Inn has recently changed hands to a Mr. G. Pulleyn. Have you heard of him?"

Felix shook his head.

"Nor I, or any of my associates, which I find odd, seeing as they make it their business to know anyone of note in London. So, having taken up the challenge of uncovering more information about this Mr. G. Pulleyn, I decided to dig into his affairs, only to reach more dead ends. It appears someone has gone to great lengths to keep his business dealings out of the public eye."

"He must have friends in high places?"

"Possibly. The few financial records there were led to Philcher & Co, a small legal firm in York. Naturally, they were reluctant to speak about their client in any way."

"Naturally."

"And they decided to cut off communication entirely when we pushed them on the matter. But just as we were about to give up on our search, one of my more tenacious students uncovered a fascinating piece of information."

"You're recruiting your students?" asked Felix, stunned.

"Only the most trustworthy, with the minds for such a task."

"And what exactly was so fascinating about this piece of information?"

"Well, it so happens, that the same week Mr. G. Pulleyn took ownership of the George Inn, his name also appeared on another set of property deeds. This time for a far more significant holding: the Burbage estates in India and London."

"Burbage?" questioned Felix. He knew the name but couldn't quite recall how or why.

"Jonathan Burbage," replied Amelia, motioning around the room. "Think about where we are."

"Monteagle's associate from the poker night!" remembered Felix.

"Correct! Burbage was here on the night of the abduction. He invited Monteagle to the club to play poker with a group of his business associates. Now we know why."

"Do we?" asked Felix, still not completely sure.

Amelia rolled her eyes.

"He was clearly struggling to meet his financial obligations and was prepared to cut a deal to save his estate. That deal included laying the ground for Monteagle's abduction. He has motive."

"Astonishing," said Felix. "Then why are we not out looking for Burbage?"

"It's all in hand, Prime Minister," replied Amelia casually.

"What do you mean, it's all in hand?" asked Felix, suddenly concerned.

"Burbage is currently upstairs at one of the club's poker tables. He's been there for some hours now and is a little drunk and heavily in debt."

"Amelia…"

"His opponent is a gentleman named Phillip Masters, a noted academic and mathematician and a close colleague of mine at the university. He is well known in Oxford circles for his love of games and strategies and, importantly for us, his ability to count cards."

"I asked you to do some digging, not to put yourself and your colleagues in danger," said Felix, a little vexed at not having been consulted on the plan.

"What's life without a little risk?"

Felix opened his mouth to respond when they were disturbed by a knock at the main door. Amelia finished the last of her tea and straightened out her clothes. "It's probably best if you stay in here. We wouldn't want to spook them now, would we?"

Felix reluctantly sat on one of the tearoom stools, out of sight but close enough to hear, while Amelia entered the main room and opened the door. Phillip Masters, a tall, bookish man, entered accompanied by a drunk and crestfallen Jonathan Burbage.

"Please, take a seat," said Amelia, motioning towards the sofa. "Sweet tea?"

"Just get on with it," replied Burbage coldly.

"Very well," said Amelia, turning towards Masters. "What is the level of Mr. Burbage's debt to you?"

"Fifty pounds," replied Masters.

"Fifty pounds," repeated Amelia theatrically. "That's quite a sum. And can you pay it?" she asked, facing Burbage.

"You know I can't."

"What a pity. My father always said that the safest way to double your money was to fold it over and put it back in your pocket. But I suppose it's a little late for old Texan sayings; the damage has already been done. However, fortunately for you, there may still be a way to avoid this embarrassment and save your reputation."

Burbage looked up at Amelia, confused but hopeful.

"I would like to buy Mr. Burbage's debt, if you'll agree to sell it?" said Amelia, offering her hand to Masters. "I doubt you'll see a penny otherwise."

Masters hesitated, pretending to consider the offer to avoid Burbage realising he'd been lured into a trap. Having deliberated for just the right amount of time, he finally stepped forward and shook Amelia's hand, securing the deal. With the debt passed over, Masters wished them a good night and turned, leaving the office and Amelia to question Burbage.

"How about that tea?" said Amelia, pouring two cups from an ornate amber teapot.

"What do you want from me?" asked Burbage.

"I just want to ask a few simple questions," she replied, handing Burbage a cup. "And, depending on the sincerity of your answers, I may see fit to wipe your debt. What do you think about that?"

Burbage took a moment to consider Amelia's offer. He was torn between the need to manage the situation and the risk of disclosing sensitive information. But with the substantial debt hanging over his head and his reputation in the balance, he had no choice but to agree to Amelia's terms.

"How long have you known Lord Monteagle?" asked Amelia, sitting down opposite the stricken man.

"Over twenty years. We set up our businesses in India together."

"Are you friendly?"

"As friendly as one can be with a lord; they're not known for their congeniality."

"Yet you invited him to your club to play cards?"

"It's common for gentlemen to discuss business over a poker game."

"Is it also common for them to be drugged and abducted from one of your games?"

"I had nothing to do with that horrid business!"

Amelia gave her guest a moment to settle down. She had learnt over her years of lecturing students that a well-timed silence could be just as effective as any flurry of words.

"I know about the financial issues you've had with your estates," she said, breaking the silence. "I also know about your involvement with a Mr. G. Pulleyn."

Burbage looked up, his eyes full of worry. It was clear that Amelia had struck a chord.

"Tell me," she continued, "was it this Pulleyn's idea to arrange your poker game and invite Lord Monteagle?"

Burbage hesitated. "He was having trouble expanding his interests in India. He was new money, you see. And the old families, well, they refused to deal with him. Typical establishment. When he found out I'd worked with Monteagle in India, he demanded I set up the meeting and introduce the lord to some of his associates. A game of poker seemed like the ideal opportunity."

"What do you mean by associates?" asked Amelia.

"The plantation brothers and the insurer," replied Burbage.

"You mean to tell me you didn't know them beforehand?"

"It was the first time I'd met any of them. He...Mr. Pulleyn, was adamant that I pretended to be in business with them. He said it would keep Monteagle attentive and make the meeting seem more legitimate."

"And you agreed to all of this?"

Burbage's eyes filled with shame. "I realise it seems ill-considered to you, but he offered me a way out. A healthy commission, if I could just facilitate the meeting. I had no idea that they were going to take him. I swear it!"

Amelia took a moment to absorb this new information. She'd been sure of Burbage's involvement from the moment her student found the amendments to the Burbage deeds, but she hadn't counted on Burbage having been hoodwinked.

"Where is Pulleyn now?" she asked.

"I have no idea. I've never met the man."

"What?" replied Amelia, shocked.

"He did all his communicating via a runner. A drunk publican from the Docklands."

"You handed over half of your assets to a man you've never met?"

"He offered me a way to save my family estate. I had no choice."

"There is always a choice," said Amelia. "And now, you are faced with another. I will clear your gambling debt and preserve your reputation and in return you will tell no one of this meeting, not a soul. And should this Mr. G. Pulleyn try to contact you again, you will feed that information directly to me. Is that understood?"

Burbage nodded.

"Then you are free to go," said Amelia, dismissing him.

She waited for Burbage to leave before turning to face Felix, who, having heard the shamed gambler depart, had entered from the tearoom.

"Well, there you have it. Is there anything you British won't do to protect your precious reputations?"

"Did you believe him?" asked Felix.

"People often do the unthinkable when they are desperate. He seemed sincere enough."

"See what else your students can dig up about Mr. G. Pulleyn."

"What will you do?" asked Amelia.

"Speak to these associates of his. Now that we know they were hand-picked for the poker game, they won't be able to hide behind their false statements or Burbage's protection any longer. If they haven't already gone to ground, that is."

Armed with nothing more than an obscure name, Felix thanked Amelia and slipped out of the East India Club into a waiting car. He directed the driver through the backroads from St. James's Square to Westminster, keeping an eye out for Alfred along the way. Back at Number 10, he hurried to his study and made his way through the secret passage towards Old Pye Street, where he waited for over an hour, checking his watch anxiously before Alfred finally returned.

Relieved to see his young ward back safely, Felix explained the night's revelations and Jonathan Burbage's involvement with the mysterious Mr. G. Pulleyn. His words, however, lacked their usual pluck. He could not hide his disappointment with how the evening had played out. Having exposed Burbage's role in Monteagle's abduction, Felix had been hopeful of finally solving the case, only to have left the club no closer to finding the missing lords or their abductors.

It was a recurring pattern. Every time they'd unearthed a meaningful lead, it either evaporated into thin air or ended in tragedy. Maybe it was finally time to speak to Commissioner Thompson, thought Felix. He had already devoted too much energy to the case when he should have been focusing on his role as the British prime minister and protecting his position in government. His enemies were circling, and the impending vote was an opportunity to put the final nail in his coffin. He needed to strike back and prove to his cabinet and the parliamentary members that he still had enough fight to do the job.

If there was one thing that Burbage's situation had proven, it was that a person needed to maintain a strong position in life to avoid compromising themselves or their principles.

Game of Trust

Despite having gone late to bed, Felix rose with a sense of purpose the following day. He set straight to work writing a detailed account of the recent events and revelations in his journal, ready to hand it over to Commissioner Thompson and relieve himself of the burden. He documented his exploits at Houlston and Sons and the George Inn before writing a comprehensive account of Amelia's meeting with Jonathan Burbage and his links to the mysterious Mr. G. Pulleyn.

It wasn't until later that morning when Humphrey entered with a tray of tea and the day's newspapers that Felix finally looked up from his work.

"Is the bed on fire?" asked Humphrey.

"Not quite," replied Felix, clearing space for the tray. "There is lots to be done if we still hope to turn our fortunes around."

"Oh, you're back to being Prime Minister today. Do excuse me; it is rather hard to keep up."

"Enjoy the moment, old man," said Felix, ignoring Humphrey's priggish grin. "I do admit your advice may have been a touch merited."

"Just a touch?"

"No one likes a know-it-all. Besides, from now on, we shall be concentrating our efforts on governing and governing alone. Send word to Percy. It's time to start planning our campaign strategy."

"It would be my pleasure," replied Humphrey, bounding off to conduct affairs.

With the written account for Thompson finally completed and his steward departed, Felix turned his attention to the day's newspapers. He unfolded one of the large broadsheets, peeling the pages away to reveal a startling headline: *The Worst Industrial Disaster since the Albion Colliery.*

Felix scanned the article, shocked to discover that there had been a series of explosions at factories on the outskirts of London. In the early morning hours *inferno-like fires* had engulfed factory buildings in Morden and Worcester Park, ripping through them in minutes, whilst a massive explosion at a mill in Surbiton had torn the front of the old brick building clean off. Many workers had been reported missing, feared dead.

There was little known about the cause of the tragedies, but what was evident from the article was its unforgiving tone. Aside from the strongly worded attacks on the factory owners and the government, whom the newspaper blamed for this current spate of catastrophes, there were also several accusatory questions: *Why were the factories still running in the early morning hours? Why were staff being made to work such unrelenting shifts? Why were exhausted workers operating faulty machinery?*

For each question, the answer was soberingly obvious: the pursuit of profit. And who was reaping the rewards of these profits? The factory owners and the government.

Felix thought about the poor souls caught up in the fires and their families receiving the news of their loss. He thought too about Arthur Jenkins and Mr. Houlston and, to his shame, about the impact this news would have on the impending confidence vote. With his position in government looking ever more precarious, these factory disasters couldn't have come at a worse time. He hated himself for considering it, but was it possible that the unfortunate timing of these terrible events was more than just a coincidence? Were his opponents ruthless enough to coordinate such destruction and loss of life simply to oust him from government and wrestle power for themselves?

Felix was finally distracted from his thoughts by Humphrey returning with news that Commissioner Thompson had arrived at Downing Street seeking an audience. Having dressed and taken hold of his journal, Felix entered the study to find Thompson standing in the same spot he had occupied on his previous visit, clearly a creature of habit, a hangover from his time in the army.

However, to Felix's surprise, the commissioner looked unusually dishevelled, with a few locks of his pristine grey and black peppered hair out of place, and his trousers, although still perfectly creased, now stained and scuffed like his usually polished shoes.

"Do excuse my appearance, Prime Minister," began Thompson. "I am yet to return home. I've been all over the city visiting the factory sites, you see."

It was the first time Felix had witnessed the commissioner looking anything but immaculate. It made him seem more human and reassured Felix of Thompson's honesty and dedication to the job.

"Please, don't apologise. I have just been catching up with the news myself."

"A terrible, terrible business, sir."

"Do we have an estimate on the casualties?"

"Unfortunately not. The factories in Morden and Worcester Park are still on fire, and our heroic firefighters are struggling to control them, despite their best efforts. There's been no opportunity to enter the buildings and assess the full extent of the destruction, but I'm sure the human cost will be…extensive."

"Do we have any idea who might be responsible?"

"We'll know more once the fires are out and we can start our investigations. Assuming there was any foul play, of course."

"Surely you don't believe this is simply a coincidence: three factories at once?"

"It's not about what I believe. It's about the evidence. I'll wait for some more meaningful information before jumping to conclusions."

Felix nodded his acceptance of the point. "Is there anything we can do to help?"

"We'll need men and machinery to help clear the debris."

"I'll speak to the Home Secretary."

"And I would consider deploying the army."

"The army?" said Felix, a little taken aback. "Why would we need the military?"

"Rioting has already begun, Prime Minister. They started this morning in London and have already reached as far as Yorkshire. God only knows how bad things will get by this afternoon."

Felix considered the commissioner's words. He could sense Thompson's anxiety at containing widespread riots, having already asked so much of his officers. However, deploying the army was not something any prime minister wanted on their record, particularly not a liberally minded one like Felix. No matter how he manoeuvred, Felix knew that his colleagues in the Commons would view his actions as a failure. If he engaged the army, he would be called a tyrant; if he chose not to, it would be seen as yet another sign of weakness by his enemies.

"I have a better idea," said Felix, thinking aloud. "I will speak with the trade unions. Let's see if they can't appease their workers before we take any drastic measures."

"The unions!" scoffed Thompson. "They probably started these riots in the first place. Opportunists, the lot of them."

"Perhaps," agreed Felix, eyeing the commissioner's fire-stained clothes, "but they have good reason in light of recent events."

"Perhaps…in light of recent events," conceded Thompson.

"That's settled then," said Felix, closing the meeting. "In the meantime, I'll ensure you have every available resource."

The commissioner nodded his thanks and turned for the door.

"Sorry, one last thing, Commissioner," remembered Felix, stopping Thompson mid-stride.

He looked down at the journal in his hand, containing the case details. He stepped towards Thompson, ready to hand it over when he suddenly found himself reluctant. Perhaps it was inappropriate, he thought, given the circumstances and the need to concentrate on the factory fires, or maybe he'd just become too close to the case. Whatever the reason, something in Felix's gut was holding him back, preventing him from cutting ties.

Rather than hand over the journal, Felix gave Thompson a brief account of Burbage's debts and his financial arrangement with Mr. G. Pulleyn.

"And how did you come about this information?" asked Thompson, amazed by Felix's revelations.

"You know what these gentlemen's clubs are like, Commissioner. No one's financial affairs are their own. I simply heard a rumour that Burbage's estates were in trouble and had someone investigate the deeds for me. I'm surprised you hadn't heard about it yourself."

"As am I," replied Thompson, embarrassed to receive this information from the prime minister and not one of his investigating officers.

Having agreed to investigate the identity of Mr. G. Pulleyn and to bring the other poker players in for further questioning, the commissioner departed. Felix took a moment to reflect on their meeting. He scolded himself for holding back. He may have doubted the police, but it was not for a prime minister to deceive or mislead those trying to assist him. It was just another reason as to why he doubted his suitability for the role. The Iron Duke would never have acted in such a way, scrambling to concoct a false story and telling half-truths to cover his tracks.

Fortunately for Felix, he only had a little time to analyse his growing list of failures before Percy arrived. The Home Secretary had been hard on the campaign trail over the past twenty-four hours, petitioning members and giving rousing speeches to galvanise the party's support. Unfortunately, the factory disasters had gone a long way to undoing his excellent work, and he looked like a spent force by the time he limped into Felix's study.

"I take it you've seen the news?" he said, slumping into one of the study chairs.

"Unfortunately," replied Felix.

"It may very well have put an end to our chances, old boy," lamented Percy, reaching for the plate of biscuits on Felix's desk. "And just when I was getting some traction with the members."

"Maybe it's a sign, Thomas?"

"Well, if it is, it's a particularly brutal one," replied Percy, munching on a shortbread.

"Or, perhaps, its shows that we're concentrating our efforts in the wrong places," said Felix, thinking aloud.

"What on earth do you mean?"

Felix took a moment to organise his thoughts. "We have been so focused on trying to convince the members of our suitability to lead that we've stopped leading."

He moved around the desk to face Percy, a hint of optimism shining in his eyes. "Rather than being judged by our words, let them judge us by our actions. We'll show them what effective leadership looks like by responding to these disasters with everything we've got. We can start by sending all the resources we can muster to help our public servants do their jobs. I want the police force, the fire service and our wonderful medics given every possible assistance. I want to put them at the centre of everything we do from this point on. And I want the people, the newspapers and our members to see us doing it."

"Sounds dangerously like socialism to me, Felix."

"Call it what you will, Thomas. But I want our great British workers to emerge as the heroes of these disasters. Their support will hold the key to our success."

With lunch concluded and Percy departed, Felix set off for Old Pye Street to relay the day's revelations to Alfred. He wasn't sure how Alfred, having witnessed the fire at the printer's and the death of Mr. Houlston first-hand, would react to the news. He wanted to be the one to tell him and be on hand to help the young man through any unhappy recollections.

He arrived at the office to find Alfred sitting at the telephone switchboard, engrossed in a flurry of flashing lights.

"What going on?" he asked, alerting Alfred to his presence.

"The network's gone crazy," replied Alfred, pointing at the brightly lit panel. "Something big's happened."

"Yes, unfortunately so," said Felix, approaching the young man. "I've just had the police commissioner and the Home Secretary pay me a visit. There have been some incidents at several factories around London. Large fires."

Alfred stepped away from the switchboard.

"Is everyone okay?" he asked.

"We're still waiting for information."

Alfred nodded, his eyes slowly filling with tears.

"Why don't I fetch us some tea?" suggested Felix.

"I've stayed too long," murmured Alfred, casting a glance around Old Pye, suddenly ashamed.

Having found solace in his new home, and purpose, he'd forgotten entirely about bringing Mr Houlston's killer to justice.

"I should be out there, looking for Fellows."

Felix stepped forward and placed a warm hand on the young man's shoulder.

"He's gone, Alfred. No good will come of carrying this guilt or roaming the cold streets looking for dangerous criminals."

"I need to make it right." whispered Alfred.

"The best course of action is to wait and allow the police do their job."

"I can't wait." replied Alfred. "I need to do something now."

"You can't just leave," insisted Felix. "We had an agreement. You gave your word."

"I haven't forgotten my promise," replied Alfred, hastily grabbing a handful of leftovers from Mrs. Hughes' food basket. "I'll return, as soon as I've found Tom Fellows."

With the food stuffed into his pockets, Alfred made a quick dash for the door.

Trades Union Congress

Although he had only known Alfred a short time, Felix couldn't help but feel responsible for the young man and anxious about his sudden departure. With the boy's chances of learning a trade with a caring master having gone up in flames at Houlston and Sons, he was now back on the streets, where Mr. Houlston had found him. It seemed selfish and improper that Felix hadn't taken the opportunity to correct the trajectory of his short life by insisting he take up an apprenticeship rather than keep him at Old Pye Street to assist with the case. Now, all Felix could do was wait and hope for Alfred's safe return and a chance to put things right. In the meantime, he would set his mind to doing whatever he could to stop the riots sweeping across the country.

Having arranged a meeting with the head of the Trades Union Congress, Humphrey prepared the state car, a new Daimler 12 h.p., for Felix's journey along the Thames to Farringdon Street. While it had been of the utmost importance to remain anonymous when investigating the case, visiting the TUC required a very different approach. The tenacious spirit of the union representatives was legendary, and Felix was determined to show the full might of his prime ministerial authority and influence before negotiating with them.

It was late afternoon by the time Felix's car pulled to a halt outside the Congregational Memorial Hall. He exited the vehicle and approached the imposing building, taking in its large steeple and Gothic architecture. It had been erected on the old Fleet Prison site and had become home to many left-wing groups and trade union bodies. They had gathered there four years earlier to create the Labour Party, a political arm to represent them and their workers in Parliament. A dogged group of MPs well known in the Commons for their brash manners and hardened politics.

Felix took a deep breath and stepped into the building's reception hall. It was surprisingly grand for a socialist headquarters, with high ceilings and a vast lobby filled with light pouring in through its enormous windows. He watched in awe at the buzz of workers ferrying documents and tea trays around, barely avoiding knocking into one another.

"I have an appointment with Mr. Ernest Booth," he said, approaching the lobby desk.

"He'll be ready shortly," replied the receptionist casually, without looking up from her book.

Surprised by her dismissive tone, Felix stepped closer to her desk. "Do you not require my name or the nature of my business?" he asked.

"That won't be necessary, Prime Minister," she replied, turning the page.

Felix was about to respond when it suddenly dawned on him that the receptionist's disregard for his presence was likely a ploy to unsettle him before his meeting. The unions were well known for engaging in such psychological tactics. Unperturbed, Felix smiled at the receptionist and took a seat. After some time observing the organised chaos, he was finally greeted by a thin, older man in an oversized suit.

"I'm to take you up," he said, extending his hand. "Tim's my name."

Felix observed Tim's black-stained palm before shaking it.

"A life spent down the pits," said Tim, following Felix's eyes. "I've tried everything—soap, alcohol, sand—but it won't come out. S'ppose you can't hide what you are, no matter how many fancy suits they put you in, eh?"

There was an unfortunate truth to the man's words that resonated with Felix, yet his tone felt forced, almost rehearsed. Having negotiated the dismissive receptionist, Felix realised that he was now faced with the second character in the union's pre-meeting pantomime: the veteran miner.

"No more digging for me now, though," continued Tim, "not since the union found me this job, on account of my age and troublesome back."

"That's very decent of them," agreed Felix, playing along.

"I'd say so. God knows where I'd be now, probably six feet under. I'm just thankful to still be in work."

"Well, let's hope we can stop this rioting and get more people back to work," replied Felix.

"Right you are." The old miner nodded, leading Felix through the melee towards an old service lift. He opened the gates and invited Felix to step inside.

"Fourth floor, please, Errol," he said, instructing the equally decrepit lift operator.

Errol shut the gates and pulled the lever, bringing the rickety lift to life. As it stuttered upwards, Felix watched Tim disappear beneath him, wondering what other surprises the TUC had in store for him.

"Errol, is it?" he asked, facing the lift operator. "Let me guess: you've been here for under a year, probably transferred from one of the collieries because of your age and physical condition, and you couldn't be more thankful for the opportunity?"

"Spot on," exclaimed Errol, "but how'd you—?"

"Call it intuition," answered Felix before Errol could finish his question.

The fourth floor was less chaotic than the bustling reception hall, with portraits of influential union men lining the corridor walls on both sides. Felix stepped out of the lift to find William Foster, the union man he'd encountered at his parliamentary dinner, waiting eagerly for him.

"We meet again, Prime Minister," said Foster in his thick Yorkshire accent. "Only this time, you're in my house."

"It would appear so," replied Felix.

"I did warn you, didn't I? I did say we'd strike all over the country, but you'd not listen, would yeh? Not to the likes of me, anyway."

"You were intruding."

"Yeah, I was, and with good reason. You needed to understand the severity of the situation."

"There's never a good reason to break into another man's home."

"That's where we differ, us lowly folk and you privileged lot. We don't care two hoots for your gentlemanly dos and don'ts. All we care about is survival, and we go about that any way we can."

Felix took a moment to consider Foster's words. He understood the cause more than most in Parliament, but disagreed with the union's tactics. Regardless, there was little point in arguing with the miner, not when he'd come to ask the TUC for help. Instead, Felix nodded his way through Foster's justifications with reticence before finally being led down the corridor towards the meeting room.

"Don't think they'll be impressed by you in there," said Foster, stopping outside the door. "There are no prime ministers here, or kings or queens. Only men and women."

Foster pushed the door open, and Felix entered. His eyes were immediately hit by a bright light. He lifted his hands to block out the glare, suddenly realising that he was facing two huge windows looking out onto St. Bartholomew's Hospital to the east and Fleet Street to the west.

"The two contrasting sides of this great city, eh?" called out another broad Yorkshire accent.

Felix swung around to see two figures sitting at an oval table. Nearest was the voice's owner, Ernest Booth, a lump of a man dressed in a simple suit and union tie. Alongside him was Agnes Lock, a much older lady dressed in a faded frock with her hair hidden under a scraggy boater hat.

"On the one side, you've got Barts," continued Ernest, "a haven for the poor and destitute in our society, and on t'other side, the epicentre of the civilised world. And slap-bang in the middle of it all is us, fighting to bridge the gap between the rich and the poor. The question is, Prime Minister, who are you here representing?"

"Everyone," replied Felix, taking a seat. "That's the nature of the job."

"Sounds like a thankless task to me."

"It can be," nodded Felix. "That's why I need your help. I want to bring this rioting to an end."

"Is that right?" chuckled Ernest, amused. "You want us to help you? I'm not sure that would be very popular with our members. You see, you've got blood on your hands, Prime Minister."

"No more than you."

"What are you talking about?"

"I wonder how your members would react if they knew you were making deals with the likes of Milton Cavendish?"

"Divide and conquer, the establishment's oldest and most effective weapon," muttered Agnes.

"Fortunately, no amount of propaganda would have our members believe anything of the sort," added Ernest.

"So, you deny it then?" asked Felix.

"Wholeheartedly," replied Ernest. "Although, we've heard about your little popularity vote int' Commons. Perhaps it might suit us to back the winning horse for a change."

"If I lose that vote, we all lose, including the unions."

"That's a touch dramatic, isn't it, Prime Minister?"

"Think about it for a moment," said Felix. "These riots are opening the door to the opposition, most of whom have vested interests in these businesses you are striking against. How do you think they'll respond once they're in power?"

"You're all part of the same club. It matters little to us which of you is in power."

"You couldn't be more wrong," said Felix. "And believe it or not, after everything your workers have been through, you, their union representatives, are currently the biggest threat to their cause."

"He's scaremongering," observed Agnes quietly.

"Now, now, Prime Minister, play fair," said Ernest, wagging his finger at Felix.

"There's no time for games, sir. I'm one of the few politicians in the Commons with both the influence and the desire to see things radically changed. But with the workers rioting and the country in chaos, there is little chance of me winning this vote and staying in office. Should I lose, Parliament will be dissolved, and there will be a snap general election. Unfortunately for you, that will mean losing your current momentum and returning fairly quickly to the status quo."

"You don't know that for sure."

"No, I don't," replied Felix, rising from his seat. "But what I do know is that it takes weeks, even months, to form a new government, which could leave your members out of work. And then what? Even if by some miracle the workers don't turn on you, what do you think will happen once the opposition is in power? Do you really think Cavendish will simply cave to your demands? Isn't it more likely he'll take as hard a line as possible with you to show the voters that his is a strong and steady administration? Like I said, if I lose, we all lose."

"What are you offering?" asked Agnes.

"The chance to make a real difference."

"That's hardly a tangible offer, Prime Minister. We're going to need something more than emotional rhetoric."

Felix considered Agnes for a moment, then stood up tall and determined. "If you call off your strike and help me put a stop to these riots, I will take your demands to the Commons and fight for them with everything I have. And if my efforts should fall on deaf ears, I will resign from my post and stand aside. You have my word on it."

Shocked, Ernest looked from Felix to Agnes and back again.

"We'll need time to think it through," he said.

Felix nodded his acceptance. He was stepping away from the table to leave when a thought suddenly struck him.

"One last thing," he said, facing his hosts. "If not by Cavendish, how did your man break into Number 10?"

"Oh no, sir," replied Ernest, the bounce returning to his voice. "We can't possibly divulge that kind of information. Not unless you have something more to offer in return. You don't get owt for nowt in this world, Prime Minister."

Felix took a moment to consider Ernest's words. There was something oddly familiar about his last comment. He was sure he'd heard it somewhere before. He racked his brains, trying to recall where and when he may have come across the saying when suddenly it hit him. It was a phrase Mrs. Hughes used on occasion. Another of her strange Yorkshire proverbs. A thought began to form in Felix's mind: William Foster, Ernest Booth and even Mr. G. Pulleyn's lawyers, Philcher & Co, were all from Yorkshire, just like Mrs. Hughes. Even the young miner, Arthur Jenkins, who died so needlessly at the Silverwood Colliery, was from the county. This series of unfortunate events began with his accidental death at the Rotherham coal site. Could it be more than just a geographical coincidence?

The journey back to Downing Street was bittersweet. Although satisfied with the outcome of the meeting, Felix could not help thinking about William Foster and his sudden appearance at the parliamentary dinner. How had he managed it? Surely Mrs. Hughes hadn't helped the union man break into Number 10. She'd been with the Grey family almost as long as Humphrey and had always been a trusted and dependable figure in his life. Felix tried to think back on all her years of loyal service. She'd always seemed happy enough, content in her role. It had become customary in the Grey household to reward their staff every Easter and Christmas, and Mrs. Hughes had often commented on the family's excessive generosity. Why, then, would she engage in such treacherous behaviour? It simply wasn't possible.

Death's Own Carriage

Having banished all thoughts of his cook and the union man from his mind, Felix returned to Number 10 determined to prepare for the vote. He marched through the house, towards his study, when he was intercepted by Humphrey.

"Prime Minister, the staff are engaged in a minor hysteria over a scotch stain on the study floor. Did you happen to drop—?"

"Not now, Humphrey," barked Felix without stopping.

"Is everything alright?" asked Humphrey, following after him.

"Everything is fine. Do you not have chores or some errand to see to?"

"Nothing that can't wait," replied Humphrey, struggling to keep up.

"In that case, allow yourself some personal time."

"No, I'd prefer to stay with you, actually."

"And why is that?" asked Felix.

"Because I've seen that face on more than a few occasions over the years. You look troubled, Felix."

Felix stopped and looked back at his faithful steward. How well Humphrey knew him. He felt a surge of gratitude rush through his body, accompanied by one of guilt at his recent dishonesties.

"Now, will you tell me what has got the prime minister marching through his own house like a man possessed?" asked Humphrey.

Felix hesitated, unsure how much to divulge. Although unconvinced of any connection between Mrs. Hughes, the miner and the TUC, there was still a slight nagging in his mind, the curious lawyer inside him that need to be sure, to know for certain.

"Would you mind following me to the kitchens?" he asked.

"Is that what this is about, your stomach?" sighed Humphrey. "If so, I can have something brought up to your study. Like I do most evenings."

"It's not my stomach. I just need to scratch and itch, that's all."

Inside the kitchens, the staff were busy preparing the evening meal. Several pots and pans were bubbling on the stoves, and the kitchen hands were busy chopping their way through a mountain of vegetables. Felix scanned the large room, looking for Mrs. Hughes. Shocked by his unusually stern demeanour, the staff stopped what they were doing and stood to attention.

"Mrs. Hughes?" asked Felix firmly.

After a short silence, one of the kitchen maids nervously pointed towards a door at the far end of the room. "She's in her office, sir."

Felix crossed the kitchen, watched by the curious staff.

"As you were," said Humphrey, beckoning them back to work.

Felix stopped outside Mrs. Hughes' office. He took hold of the door handle, then paused, having second thoughts.

"Are you going to tell me what all this is about?" asked Humphrey, concerned by Felix's behaviour.

"Do you remember the union man who decided to attend our parliamentary dinner, uninvited?"

"How could I forget? He ruined a perfectly executed evening."

"Do you think he might of had an accomplice?" asked Felix nervously.

Humphrey looked at the door. "Mrs. Hughes? Don't be ridiculous! No. I can't believe that, not for one second."

"I sincerely hope you're right," said Felix, finally turning the handle and opening the door.

The head cook's office was a small, uneven room with a low ceiling and crooked walls. It had once been the house larder before a newer and more modern kitchen was installed, freeing up space for the head cook to occupy and conduct her affairs. Mrs. Hughes was sitting at her lopsided desk, finishing her monthly supplies list, when the men suddenly entered unannounced.

"Prime Minister?" she squeaked, surprised to see Felix. "Is everything alright?"

"Do you have a moment?" he asked, eyeing the paperwork on her desk.

"Now, if it's about your food, I can assure you that everything is bought from as nearby as we can manage, just like you requested."

"I've not come to discuss the food. Unfortunately, I am here about another matter."

"Really? Whatever is the problem?" asked Mrs. Hughes.

"I've just returned from a meeting with the Trade Union Congress. During our conversation something was said that got me thinking back to the evening of the parliamentary dinner and the appearance of our unexpected union guest."

"Something that was said?" repeated Mrs. Hughes.

"An old Yorkshire saying, actually. The kind you like to use on occasion."

"Those sayings are very popular with folk these days," said Mrs. Hughes.

"I'm sure, only, something interesting occurred to me after hearing that old saying. The union man who broke into this house, the TUC leaders, even the poor miner who died at Silverwood, Arthur Jenkins, they're all from Yorkshire.

"Yorkshire's a big place, prime minister." said Mrs. Hughes.

"Yes, of course it is," replied Felix, suddenly realising the absurdity of the situation and the tenuous nature of his connection. "Never mind. I'm sorry to have disturbed you, Mrs. Hughes."

Embarrassed, Felix turned for door when he was stopped by the sound of Mrs. Hughes whimpering.

"Whatever is the matter, Eleanor?" asked Humphrey, stepping forward to offer her a handkerchief.

Felix spun around to see the head cook wiping tears from her eyes. There was a momentary silence as she struggled to gather herself and speak.

"If you don't mind," she stuttered, "I should like to leave my post quietly and without any fuss."

"I don't understand," said Humphrey, shocked.

Felix felt the guilt rising in his throat.

"I'm sorry if my questions implied any blame on your part, Mrs. Hughes." he began "It was foolish of me to entertain such thoughts. Please allow me to explain."

"I had no choice," Mrs. Hughes muttered through her tears, cutting Felix off. "They were going to take our family home."

"Who were? The TUC?" asked Felix, confused.

"No, the banks," replied Mrs. Hughes, taking a breath. "My brother lost his job, you see. He couldn't keep up with his payments. The banks threatened to take the house unless I covered the shortfall. The house my father built with his own hands."

"Who gave you the money?" asked Felix.

"I wouldn't, not for any sum of money," replied Mrs. Hughes, hurt by the implication.

"Then why?" asked Humphrey.

"The union helped my brother find a job and gave him an advance to cover his debt? He worked hard to repay their kindness. Lots of long hours and late nights. Then one day, they pulled him into the office to meet some well-to-do politician. He said that working conditions in the plants had never been so awful and that the government was ignoring the workers' pleas. That somebody could die. He implored my brother to help for the sake of his colleagues and their families. They wanted to get their message to the government, and someone had heard about my role here. They said that if I could get a man into the house to present their petition directly, it would make a huge difference. My brother didn't feel like he could say no, what with how they'd helped him, well us. They told him he'd be a hero among the workers."

"Do you know the name of the politician?" asked Felix.

"He didn't give a name, and my brother was too respectful to ask."

"What about the company your brother works for?"

"They're called the Blossom Street Carriage Works. They're a local York firm."

Felix turned to Humphrey. "Contact Amelia. Explain what has happened here and ask her to have her students look into the board of directors at the Blossom Street Carriage Works and their political affiliations."

"The vote is only a matter of days away—…"

"More reason to act quickly," replied Felix, cutting across Humphrey's concerns. Humphrey nodded his consent and reluctantly departed to carry out his orders.

"I should like to pack my belongings, if I may?" asked Mrs. Hughes.

"That won't be necessary," said Felix. "You won't be leaving our services today, Mrs. Hughes."

"I won't?"

"You've been the victim of a rather sinister plot against me, for which I can only apologise. However, you should've come to me the moment they approached you."

"If I could go back to that day, that is precisely what I would do."

Felix took a moment to observe his long-serving cook. Although hard to watch, her heartbreak had reassured him of her sincerity.

"Let us leave this in the past," he said. "If you wish to help me now, carry on with your duties as usual. I don't want our enemies to think anything has changed or that we are on to them."

Mrs. Hughes smiled warmly through her teary eyes. "Thank you, Felix."

Felix's head was swimming by the time he returned to his study. He poured himself a glass of scotch and watched the sun setting outside his window.

Even though disappointed, he could not blame Mrs. Hughes for her actions. She, like Alfred, was a victim of circumstance. A target for those looking to undermine Felix and the British government. It was a valuable lesson for Felix, who had naively believed his staff's loyalty was unfaltering. Unfortunately, everybody was vulnerable in some way, and on this occasion,

Felix's enemies had managed to uncover a chink in his head cook's armour and use it to their advantage. Had the same thing happened in the cases of Monteagle and Cecil? Had these dark forces infiltrated their homes and inner circles, clearing the way for their swift and professional abductions?

Having resolved things with Mrs. Hughes, Felix focused his mind back on the vote and the job of governing. He set about writing a letter for publication in the national newspapers, addressing the families of those presumed missing in the factory disasters, praying for their safe return, and promising all the help and support the government could muster. Over the past few weeks, he'd become all too familiar with writing these types of letters. It had both deepened his resolve and made him feel deeply inadequate as a leader. He poured himself a second scotch, preparing to settle in for the evening, when the study telephone rang. He picked up the receiver and pulled it to his ear, only to hear the metronome-like voice of Commissioner Thompson on the other end.

"Hello. Prime Minister," began Thompson as though dictating a telegram, clearly unused to the workings of a telephone. "Body found. Shad Thames. En route now. Meet at the scene."

Having delivered his message, the commissioner hung up immediately. Felix's heart began to race. Could it be one of the abducted lords? They'd been missing for some time, long enough for the gases to build in a dead body and help it rise to the water's surface if not weighed down properly. Then another thought occurred to Felix and he felt his stomach lurch. What if it was Alfred? He'd feared for the boy's safety the moment he'd left Old Pye Street to pursue Tom Fellows. What if he'd been captured by the crooked innkeeper and his cronies? Or worse, the man with the red eye patch? Felix had witnessed his disregard for human life first-hand. He wouldn't have thought twice about murdering Alfred and throwing his body into the Thames.

Felix reached for his coat and hurried out of the study. He ran down the stairs, whizzing past his shocked staff, and departed

Number 10, stepping onto Downing Street. He continued down the cobbled walkway, weaving through groups of onlookers, agog to see the prime minister suddenly emerge from the famous address and hail down a cab like an ordinary member of the public. But public perception was the last thing on Felix's mind. All he could think about was the dead body and Alfred.

Felix directed his driver to Shad Thames, guiding him through several small roads and backstreets that even he, a professional driver, had never heard of; such was the level of knowledge Felix had acquired about London's roads from the full-scale model at Old Pye Street. Having crossed the river at Westminster Bridge, they proceeded through Lambeth and Southwark before finally joining the main road at Tooley Street and turning onto Shad Thames, where a police blockade greeted them. Felix paid the driver and exited the cab, stepping through the police barriers towards the crime scene.

"Prime Minister," called Thompson from a small gathering of officers.

Felix approached the men, only to find them huddled around two figures splayed out on the riverbank.

"We've just fished a second one out," said Thompson.

Felix could barely bring himself to look. To his great relief, neither of the bodies belonged to Alfred or the missing lords. However, it didn't take long for Felix to recognise the men. They were the sailors he had encountered in Sailortown and then again at the George Inn.

"Sailors?" he asked, pointing at the tattoos on their arms and necks.

"Probably got into a skirmish and copped it," said one of the officers. "You know what these sea dogs are like; they don't half love to drink and fight."

"That will be all chaps," said Thompson. "Have their bodies taken to the mortuary for identification."

The officers placed the bodies on wooden stretchers before transferring them to a waiting carriage. Felix watched as the dead men were loaded into the tall gothic vehicle and pulled into the night by huge, black horses. It was the type of otherworldly scene one would expect to read about in a penny dreadful, not witness on the banks of the Thames; death's own carriage delivering two more black dark souls to his dark gates. But why had the sailors been murdered and dumped? Had they seen too much? Surely the man with the red eye patch would have heard about Felix's escape from the George Inn by now. If he believed Felix's cover story, he would undoubtedly assume that the entire police force was searching for him. It would then stand to reason that, if on the run, he might feel the need to dispose of anyone who might be a liability or, even worse, lead the police to his whereabouts. Like the officer said, sailors liked to drink, and when they drank, they often got into trouble. But why had Thompson summoned him here, when he knew nothing of Felix's connection to the sailors?

"Prime Minister," said Thompson, as if on cue. "Walk with me for a moment, if you will."

Thompson led Felix away from the crime scene to a quiet spot along the river, out of the way of any listening ears.

"I know the identity of one of the corpses," he said, looking over his shoulder to ensure they weren't being listened to. "His name is John Williams. He was one of my officers working secretly in the Docklands area. Well, before he turned, that is."

"You mean he switched sides?" asked Felix.

"He stopped communicating with us over three months ago. We don't know why. Generally, it's either down to money or fear. Or, perhaps, he just preferred the life of a criminal. Either way, he became a huge problem for Scotland Yard."

"Are you implying that someone inside the police might be responsible for these murders?"

"It's a possibility. They may have got wind of his identity and decided to profit from the information. I'm loath to admit it, but there are still officers among our ranks who are easily corrupted."

"And the alternative?" asked Felix.

"The alternative is that perhaps he got too close to the organisation's secrets and paid the price. These criminals like to reduce their numbers from time to time. Trimming the fat helps to weed out any informants in their ranks. Particularly if they felt we were getting close to them. It tends to happen before they go to ground."

"And then what?" asked Felix.

"London is like a great warren of rat holes," replied Thompson. "Perfect for society's vermin to disappear into. If they have decided to lie low, then there's little chance of us flushing them out anytime soon."

"Then why did you ask me to meet you here, Commissioner?" asked Felix, suddenly confused.

Thompson took a moment to consider Felix's words. "Because, Prime Minister, I need you to see and understand what we're up against. And, I need to know if there's anything more you may have heard in your gentlemen's clubs that you're not telling me."

Felix observed Thompson, a little taken aback by the boldness of his words. "Are you implying that I'm keeping secrets from the police?" he asked.

"Not secrets," replied Thompson. "Information, perhaps."

"And why would I do that?"

"I asked around the East India Club, as you suggested, and it appears that Burbage's financial woes are far from common knowledge. In fact, there was no knowledge of them at all. Which made me think: how did the prime minister come across such valuable information?"

"It's not what you know, Commissioner; it is who."

"And who do you know with such access to a person's private financial affairs?"

Felix hesitated. He couldn't name Amelia or explain her students' efforts without divulging the ploy to trap Burbage at the poker table and giving away the rest of his work on the case.

"I'm the prime minister, Commissioner. I know many people in high places."

"And there's nothing more these *people* have expressed to you that I, as the head of the police, should know?"

"If there were anything more to be said, you would have heard it," replied Felix, turning abruptly and departing.

Lost to his thoughts, Felix barely registered the journey back from Shad Thames. It was almost as if he'd stepped into the cab, passed through the vehicle and out the other side already at Downing Street. He returned to his study to document the day's revelations. He wrote a detailed account of everything he'd witnessed at Shad Thames and the content of his private conversation with Thompson. Usually, committing his thoughts to paper calmed Felix, but on this occasion, it simply magnified his anxiety. Surprisingly, it wasn't the sight of the two dead bodies on the riverbank playing on Felix's mind, but the sudden sense that the case was slipping through his fingers and, with it, any chance of ever finding the missing lords. It had been a week since their disappearance and, without Tom Fellows or the one-eyed man, there was little else to go on.

Felix examined his notes, trying to piece together all that had happened over the past few days, but the case was still as vague and disjointed as it had been since the news of Monteagle's disappearance. The only line of enquiry appeared to revolve around Mr. G. Pulleyn and his connection to the gamblers at Burbage's poker table. But whoever Burbage's mysterious benefactor was, he had gone to great lengths to protect his identity. There was also the tenuous link to Yorkshire. Could it be merely a coincidence that Mr. G. Pulleyn's lawyers, William Foster, and the politician who callously plotted his entry into Number 10 were all from the county? Either way, Felix would have to wait for news from Amelia about the Blossom Street Carriage Works and the commissioner's investigation into the poker players before he could even hope to start piecing it all together.

Carlton Club

Felix awoke the following day to a tray of messages. Humphrey had left him to catch up on some much-needed sleep, placing a light breakfast of smoked fish and bread on his desk beside the neatly folded newspapers and a small pile of envelopes.

The first message Felix opened was from Amelia. Her students had discovered some interesting information on the Blossom Street Carriage Works and, sick of being cooped up at the university, she had purchased a ticket on the afternoon train to London to present her findings to Felix in person. It would be good to have the professor's energy around the place, thought Felix. Having spent another night tossing and turning, he desperately needed an injection of optimism, and Amelia administered those in abundance.

The second note was from Commissioner Thompson. It was characteristically blunt and to the point, informing Felix that the factory fires had finally been put out and the smoke cleared, paving the way for the police to enter and carry out their investigation.

The third note, however, took Felix entirely by surprise. It had come from the Leader of the Opposition, Milton Cavendish.

Prime Minister,

With the confidence vote looming, the investigation into the lords bearing no fruits, and the country in the grip of widespread rioting, I feel it only fitting that we, the leaders of the two major parties, meet to discuss a meaningful solution to mending our broken country. Therefore, I invite you to meet me at the Carlton Club this afternoon to discuss these most extraordinary times and make the necessary arrangements before the State Opening.

Milton Cavendish

Felix placed the note to one side, unsure how to feel about his opponent's invitation. It was unlike Cavendish to offer an olive branch when there was an opportunity to use the stick. But these were *extraordinary times*, as Cavendish had noted, and perhaps he was prepared to put his duty for his country above his ambitions for the time being. Curious to uncover the truth, Felix prepared himself for the journey to Pall Mall and an audience with his great nemesis.

The Carlton Club, where Conservatives met, was an elegant-looking building that stood imperiously on the corner of Pall Mall and Carlton Gardens, curiously close to the Reform Club, the famous Liberal Party equivalent. It was another great oddity of the British political establishment that, not fully satisfied with crossing each other's paths in the great halls of Westminster, these political foes had chosen to set up their members' clubs a mere stone's throw away from each other.

"Prime Minister?" called a crisp voice, garnering Felix's attention as he entered the lobby.

Felix turned to see the club's host approaching. He was an older man, immaculately dressed in a tailored suit with a member's pin on the collar of his double-breasted jacket next to his regimental Dragoon Guards badge. He limped slightly as he walked and used a stick with a silver horse's head in recognition of his time in the British Cavalry.

"Mr. Cavendish is awaiting your presence," he said formally. "If you could follow me."

Felix followed the host through the hall and up the ornate staircase. The older man's laboured pace gave the watching members time to study Felix as he passed, much to his annoyance.

He had hoped to make a quiet entrance into the Conservative stronghold rather than have his presence trumpeted around the club within moments of entering. If it had been planned this way, it was a masterstroke from Cavendish, another point in their game of cat and mouse. Alerting the political establishment to Felix's arrival at the club would only add more buzz to the speculation surrounding his future, creating further uncertainty for Felix's few remaining supporters.

At the top of the stairs, the host finally came to a stop by a stained oak door. He knocked twice, then opened it, ushering Felix inside.

The room was surprisingly dark, with heavy brocade curtains covering the tall windows. In the dull light, Felix could make out sets of Chesterfields, separated by elegant mahogany tables, and portraits of prominent Conservative leaders lining the walls between rows of bookshelves and ornately framed mirrors. His eyes were suddenly drawn to a cloud of smoke drifting above a trolley laden with scotch and crystal glasses.

"I wouldn't usually indulge at this time of the day," said Cavendish, stepping into the light, puffing on a cigar, "however, with no one here to entertain me, I found myself getting rather bored. Does that ever happen to you, Felix? Does your mind require something to fill the silence?"

"I rarely receive the gift of silence," replied Felix. "There is always so much to think about in this job."

"Then consider yourself fortunate. My father used to say, a busy man is a content man."

"Or a dog-tired one."

"Scotch?" proposed Cavendish. "Parliament is in recess after all."

"Not for me, thank you," replied Felix.

"Suit yourself," said Cavendish, pouring himself a small measure. "My father also liked to say that, at times, a man can take on more than he can endure. Whatever his intentions, he will end up causing more harm than good."

"And by *a man*, am I to assume you're referring to me?" deduced Felix.

"Well, naturally," replied Cavendish, raising his glass with a smile.

"You invited me, and I'm here," said Felix, trying to hide his irritation. "So, how would you have us save this great country of ours?"

"I would've thought that was obvious," replied Cavendish scornfully. "Oh, come now, Felix, surely you never really expected to stay the full term? The tide of popularism that sailed you into power was always likely to drag you back out, kicking and screaming. That, unfortunately, is how tides work."

"I'm aware of the mechanics of tides."

"You see, old boy, trivial fancies may last a few years, but true leaders," declared Cavendish waving his cigar at the figures on the walls, "well, they last for generations."

Felix took a moment to look around the elegant room. He studied the large portraits, the towering bookshelves and the beautifully crafted furniture. It oozed wealth and privilege from every corner and, undeniably, success. He turned back to Cavendish, supping on scotch and smoking his cigar, when it suddenly dawned on him that this wasn't a meeting at all but a victory parade. A chance for his adversary to lord it over him before delivering the decisive blow in the Commons. Cavendish was not merely content with winning; he wanted to savour the moment in front of the great Conservatives of the past.

"Perhaps I will have that scotch after all," said Felix.

"That's the spirit, old boy," clapped Cavendish, pouring Felix a glass.

"What with the riots and the missing lords, not to mention the tenuous support in my own cabinet, what would be the point in continuing?"

"I couldn't agree more." said Cavendish. "I suggest we inform His Majesty of your desire to step down immediately and spare your reputation the unnecessary embarrassment of a vote."

"Although, this rather irritating voice in the back of my mind keeps telling me that there is much more at stake here than just you or I."

"What could be more important than being the British prime minister?" scoffed Cavendish.

"Does it not seem odd to you that all of these events are happening simultaneously? The abductions, the factory disasters, the riots? You said it yourself in your message, *these most extraordinary times*."

"It never rains but it pours…"

"Until it stops entirely," replied Felix. "I don't suspect I'll be visiting His Majesty any time soon. Not while there's still a chance."

"A chance? There is no chance!" barked Cavendish. "You will lose this vote and, with it, your government and any last semblance of a reputation."

"Perhaps," replied Felix. "But not without a fight."

Cavendish opened his mouth to respond when he was halted by a commotion coming from outside in the hallway. Agitated, he marched across the room and swung the door open.

"What's all the racket about?" he bellowed. "I am trying to conduct a meeting in here!"

"The riots have stopped, Milton," came a voice from out in the hall. "All up and down the country, the TUC have called it off."

"What do you mean they've called it off?" exclaimed Cavendish, his anger rising.

Felix allowed himself a wry smile. He had managed to persuade the notoriously stubborn and suspicious unionists that his deal was their best option. He had succeeded in bringing a stop to the riots.

"And just like that, the sun pokes its head through the clouds," he said, placing his untouched drink on the table. "See you in the Commons, Milton."

Felix felt a surge of euphoria wash over him as he stepped out of the Carlton Club and onto Pall Mall. It had been a small victory in the grand scheme of things, but rather than sealing his fate, the meeting had laid the ground for a potential recovery. Instead of returning to Parliament defeated, he could now rejoin his cabinet with his head held high, having not only brought an end to the riots but also faced down the opposition leader in his own gentlemen's club. It was the kind of tabloid fodder that had made prime ministers, not broken them. However, his sense of relief ended abruptly when a convoy of police wagons galloped past him at full tilt before turning onto St. James's Square. Concerned, Felix followed, turning the corner a few moments later to find the carriages parked outside the East India Club.

Felix entered the members club to find the main hall cordoned off and the police preventing anyone from leaving. The primary focus of their investigation seemed to be a room at the far end of the hallway. Felix lifted the cordon and headed down the corridor, immediately recognising the door from its small carving of the Hindu monkey god, Hanuman, on the outside. It was the same room in which Amelia had questioned Jonathan Burbage a few days earlier. He stepped inside only to find the once gloriously decorated cluster of rooms ransacked and plundered. The beautifully crafted ivory and terracotta ornaments that had caught Felix's eye were now missing, and the bright silk curtains had been torn and ripped from their hooks.

"When was she last seen?" asked a familiar voice from the adjoining room.

Felix turned the corner to see Commissioner Thompson and a handful of officers deep in discussion.

"Commissioner?" he said, alerting Thompson to his presence.

"That will be all, chaps," said Thompson, quickly clearing the room. "How did you know we were here?" he asked, facing Felix.

"I stepped out of a meeting at the Carlton Club when I saw your carriages hurtling down Pall Mall."

"Rather convenient, wouldn't you say?" replied Thompson.

"If you don't believe me, have your men look into it. I'm sure half of Westminster could verify my whereabouts by now. I was in a meeting with the Leader of the Opposition."

"I see," mumbled Thompson. "Apologies, it's been a trying few days."

"No apologies required," said Felix, looking around the small emerald room with its ornate tea sets and handmade sculptures twisted and strewn everywhere. "Who do you suspect did this?"

"We know who did it. The question is, why?" said Thompson, closing the door to give the men some privacy. "We received a message from the club reporting a burglary. One of the staff had walked in on the Indian hostess looting the room of all its valuable antiquities. When he tried to stop her, he was struck with a club, leaving him unconscious."

"And where is the hostess now?" asked Felix.

"Gone," replied Thompson. "And I don't have much hope of finding her, either."

"That's rather pessimistic, even by your standards, Commissioner," said Felix.

"Everything you see here has been staged, Prime Minister," replied Thompson, motioning around the room. "The robbery, the vandalism, even the eyewitness. It's all been carefully crafted to make us believe that the hostess fled, having carried out a callous robbery."

"But why?"

"After our meeting at Downing Street, I had my officers bring in the poker players who'd shared the table with Lord Monteagle. It soon became apparent under questioning that neither James nor Henry Coleridge, or that slimy insurance man they associate with, Clement Morris, had ever heard or done any business with anyone named Mr. G. Pulleyn."

"And you believe they were telling the truth?"

"I do," replied Thompson. "They did, however, furnish us with some fascinating information. It wasn't Jonathan Burbage who invited them to the East India Club to play cards on the evening of Monteagle's abduction. Neither was it Mr. G. Pulleyn. Each of the guests received a hand-delivered invitation from…"

"The hostess," answered Felix.

"Precisely," said Thompson. "Once word got out that a connection had been made to Burbage's estate debts, she knew it was only a matter of time until we uncovered her involvement in Monteagle's abduction. The evidence would inevitably lead to her. Having realised the game was up, she planned to stage a robbery, hoping to throw us off the scent and buy herself some time. Unfortunately for her, she was caught in the act. So, she took the most valuable artefacts and made her escape."

"Going to ground," concluded Felix.

"I'm afraid so," replied Thompson gravely. "I have deployed some of my best men to find her, but I suspect she is very far from reach by now."

"But why still take the artefacts, if she'd been seen?" asked Felix.

"Who knows, perhaps for sentimental reasons or to bargain her way out of the country."

Felix took a moment to consider Thompson's explanation of events. He knew that Burbage hadn't been familiar with his guests before the night of the poker match but had assumed that by being hand-picked to attend, each man would have had a personal connection to Burbage's mysterious benefactor. The police would only have to question them to find the link. He hadn't considered that the hostess might have organised their attendance on Pulleyn's behalf, no matter how obvious it seemed now.

How quickly one's fortunes changed in this world, thought Felix. He'd barely stepped out of the Carlton Club, enthused for the first time in weeks, when his attention had turned to the East India Club and another loose end. There was also the continued absence of Alfred. Barely had a moment passed when he had not been in Felix's thoughts. With the vote looming and much to document, Felix made the journey back to Downing Street, determined to complete his work and begin his search for the young man, when he was greeted in the hallway by a disgruntled-looking Humphrey.

"Is everything alright?" he asked, surprised to see his steward so flustered.

"The Texan is in the Cabinet Room," bristled Humphrey, taking Felix's coat. "She's regaling the footmen with stories of her time lassoing cattle in the Wild West."

"I see," said Felix, trying to mask his amusement. "Leave it with me. I'll see to it that she stops distracting the staff."

"If you could, Prime Minister," replied Humphrey.

The Cabinet Room was long and rectangular, with high ceilings supported by Corinthian columns. Midway along the south-facing wall stood a colossal marble fireplace with a portrait of Sir Robert Walpole sitting imperiously above it, flanked on either side by two bookcases housing the prime minister's library. The cabinet table sat in the middle of the room as the central feature, and sitting in the prime minister's seat, holding court with a handful of Downing Street staff, was Amelia Woodruff.

Amelia was dressed in a curious outfit, a collision of American and British fashion, consisting of a cravat and braces alongside the type of full-length leather hide overcoat one would typically associate with a rancher.

"…and that's why I never accept a drink from anyone carrying a rope or spitting tobacco!" she concluded, accentuating her Texan accent, much to the amusement of the watching staff.

"Not the most orthodox cabinet meeting I've ever witnessed," said Felix, entering the room. "Nor is it the worst."

"Apologies, Prime Minister," one of the young footmen said with a bow, quickly hurrying out of the room, followed closely by his colleagues.

"Am I in trouble?" quipped Amelia, watching them depart.

"They'll be treading on eggshells around me for months now," replied Felix.

"Perhaps Humphrey can reassure them. It will help him develop his more sensitive side. Come to mention it, where is the great man? He was here one minute and gone the next. You don't think he dabbles in black magic, do you?"

"If he did, I'm sure you'd be the first target on his list. Now, have you come to cause havoc with my staff or assist me?" asked Felix. "You mentioned some information about the Blossom Street Carriage Works in your note?"

"To business then, if we must," replied Amelia, sitting up straighter. "Blossom Street Carriage Works is a large manufacturer of train engines and carriages, as the name so cunningly suggests. They've been established for nearly twenty years and employ many local men and women. As you can imagine, they wield great influence in the area and are connected to several local politicians, all looking to garner support for their campaigns. However!" exclaimed Amelia, pausing for effect. "There is a person of particular interest who sits on their board and recently helped them raise a large sum of money to extend their premises."

"Well?" pressed Felix after another of Amelia's exaggerated silences.

"None other than the Honourable Member for Wakefield, Mr. Barnaby Shaw."

"The Shadow Chancellor?"

"Precisely," replied Amelia, sitting back in Felix's chair.

"He would know how a factory works…" mused Felix.

"I should hope so," joked Amelia. "Or he'd be a pretty substandard choice to run one."

"That's not what I meant. To orchestrate the factory disasters, a person would need to know how an industrial plant operates."

"Agreed." Amelia nodded.

"They would also need the financial and political means to influence people and conceal their involvement."

"That too."

"Now consider the profile of Shaw. He is from a wealthy and influential Yorkshire family. He has a vested interest in toppling the government and, given his relationship with the Blossom Street Carriage Works, he also knows the workings of a factory. He could have planned these disasters and made them look like accidents to stir up unrest among the workers."

"The theory has merit."

"He would even have the luxury of watching the political fallout from each event in the Commons," continued Felix, on a roll, "simply instructing his cronies in the unions to strike as and when required."

"Yes, but why, then, would the TUC decide to call off the riots?" asked Amelia.

"Perhaps they were unaware of his plan and believed the factory disasters to be genuine accidents, as most others did."

"Or perhaps they decided to switch sides," suggested Amelia. "You know what you Brits are like; you'll do anything to back the winning horse."

"I'm hardly winning, as Cavendish was so quick to point out during our meeting. But you're right; the union connection doesn't make sense. There's still a missing link."

As Felix pondered the information, Humphrey entered to inform them that Percy had arrived. However, before the old steward could finish his announcement, the Home Secretary marched past him, looking red-faced and agitated.

"Now, Felix," he began without so much as a hello, "I realise it has been an extremely testing time and on the surface of it all, things may seem a tad hopeless," he blurted out without taking a breath, "but I must insist that you refrain from agreeing on any deals with that snake Cavendish and face this vote head-on. The riots have stopped, and our fortunes are turning!"

"It's fine, Thomas," said Felix, concerned by his colleague's pulsating chest. "There will be no deals," he continued, lowering Percy into one of the chairs to catch his breath.

"But I heard you were at the Carlton Club."

"Cavendish requested a meeting. He wanted to bask in my humiliation and persuade me to step down. But I refused."

"Thank God," puffed Percy, finally relaxing. "The arrogance of the man, to think we would step aside for him and his chums without a fight!"

"Yes, well, the fight is far from won, but with the riots ended, we may have just given ourselves an outside chance."

"Then there is no time to waste!" exclaimed Percy, springing back out of his chair. "We need to maximise our every advantage. I'll rally our members and have the whips whipping up a storm," he said, bounding out of the Cabinet Room with a renewed vigour, much to Felix's and Amelia's amazement.

Old Kent Road

Back in his study, Felix jotted down a record of his meeting with Cavendish, followed by the events at the East India Club and Amelia's findings on the Blossom Street Carriage Works. As he committed the details to paper, Felix's mind drifted back to his previous meetings with Thompson, the appearance of William Foster at Number 10, and even his time at Houlston and Sons, searching for a link that might complete the chain and unlock the entire mystery.

He flicked back through the journal, reading past accounts. Could the Shadow Chancellor connect the various elements of the case? Shaw had managed to keep his business affairs out of the public eye, much like Pulleyn had done. A thought suddenly struck Felix. What if Shaw was Pulleyn? He had unparalleled access to Parliament and the missing lords' schedules. He would only have had to follow them briefly to learn their routines and plan the ideal moment to strike. Once the abductions were committed, he could simply sit back and conduct his affairs from Westminster, keeping informed of the police's progress and manoeuvring his footmen as required. It all added up, except for the most important detail: why?

Felix could understand the need for the factory disasters. They provided the opportunity to cause large-scale unrest, weakening his position in government and leading to a vote of no confidence. But why the lords? Why would Shaw go to the trouble of abducting such highly regarded men? It was a gaping hole in his reasoning, alongside his uncertainty over any link to the TUC. In reality, Shaw's only crime was his connection to the Blossom Street Carriage Works, a local company in his constituency. Felix could name several parliamentarians with affiliations to local businesses in their voting area. It was common practice and certainly not evidence enough to convince Thompson of any wrongdoing. Felix would need something more concrete before daring to accuse a fellow member of Parliament of anything so heinous.

Felix closed his journal and reached for the crystal decanter housing his scotch. He had barely removed the stopper when he heard a scratching sound coming from the fireplace. He crossed the room, looking curiously at the marble mantelpiece, when a soft voice echoed from behind the coal-stained panel.

"Prime Minister," it called softly. "It's me."

Felix quickly turned the marble corbel, opening the secret passage, and Alfred stepped through the fireplace into the study. He looked scruffy, with wild hair and puffy eyes, as if he hadn't slept or washed in weeks.

"Welcome back," said Felix gently. "You have been missed."

Alfred's face turned red. He'd rarely received such warmth from his own father, let alone from the British prime minister.

"I've found him. Tom Fellows," he blurted out, bursting with nervous energy. "He's holed up on the Old Kent Road. If we go now, we'll be able to catch him before he—"

"Slow down," said Felix. "Tell me how you came to find him."

Alfred nodded, taking a few deep breaths. "When I left," he began, "I went straight to the Docklands to look for him. I checked every pub and inn on the waterfront, but there was no sign of him anywhere. I thought about coming back, seeing as how cold it was on the streets and all, but every time I thought about it, I could see Mr. Houlston's face tied to that old printing press staring back at me. So, I went back to the George Inn and waited there, hoping he'd show his face. And he did. Only for a moment, mind. He came back to pick something up and was in and out before you knew it. I didn't recognise him at first. He had a hooded coat on, covering his eyes, and he'd let his beard grow out, obviously trying to disguise himself."

"What was he picking up?"

"Money. I saw him counting it through the window before he left. There was a bit. Enough to keep him going for a while anyway."

"Then what?"

"I followed him to Old Kent Road. He walked all the way. It took forever. He kept stopping to look over his shoulder. Nervous he was being followed."

"Are you sure he didn't see you?"

"I'm sure," said Alfred. "Anyway, I don't think he was looking for the likes of me. He looked scared out of his wits."

"Where is he now?"

"He's taken a room in a pub."

Having listened to Alfred's account and desperate not to let another lead slip through his fingers, Felix decided to journey to Old Kent Road to confront the villainous innkeeper himself. He led the way back through the study fireplace and down the secret passage towards Old Pye Street, where he replaced his tailored suit jacket and Oxford shoes with a tradesman's coat, hat and boots from the collection.

"I'll flag us a cab," said Alfred eagerly.

"That won't be necessary," said Felix, stopping him in his tracks. "I want you to stay here."

"I don't understand," replied Alfred. "I found him. I waited all those hours in the cold for him to come back. I need to—"

"Rest," said Felix, cutting in. "You need to rest. You've done what you set out to do, Alfred. You found him. Now let me do what I must, while you regain your strength."

"But—"

"I insist," said Felix. "You can't do it alone, and nor should you have to. Not when you have friends in your corner."

Alfred reluctantly nodded, turning even redder than before. He gave Felix details of the pub where Tom Fellows was staying and a more detailed description of the landlord's disguise so that he would recognise him immediately, then collapsed on his makeshift bed to rest.

Outside, Felix could smell the moisture in the air. He hurried through Old Pye Street and onto Victoria Street, where he hailed a hansom cab before the heavens finally opened, covering London in another of its famous downpours. Felix instructed the driver and they set off eastwards towards Old Kent Road. He hadn't realised he'd fallen asleep until the driver banged on the carriage box to wake him.

"Here we go then!" he called out. "The Bricklayers Arms, Old Kent Road."

Felix quickly rose and stepped out of the carriage. He paid the driver, who, having pocketed the money, quickly pulled on the reins and ordered his horses away, reluctant to hover in the area any longer than necessary. Old Kent Road was one of London's most notorious thoroughfares. Part of an ancient trackway built by the Romans linking London to the coast, it had been repeatedly shortened over the years, housing groups of industrial workers and blossoming into a haven for organised crime.

Felix took a moment to study his surroundings. The area was a hub of commercial activity, with narrow streets of stall owners and barrow boys selling all manner of unusual and exotic trinkets. The carriage had barely departed when Felix was offered the first of his many *deals of a century* on goods ranging from Spanish ivory to elegant silks from India.

Having navigated the energetic merchants with his wallet still intact, Felix crossed the dirty cobbled street towards the Bricklayers Arms. The pub was a large building set over four floors at the end of a row of terraced cottages. Green and maroon tiles covered the outer walls, and a vast red-and-white sign advertising the pub's stout adorned the upper level. Felix took a deep breath and entered.

The pub was overflowing with industrial workers washing off the dust from a long day on the job. Felix slowly walked through the crowd, carefully observing each face as he passed, looking for Tom Fellows. He could see why the errant landlord had chosen Old Kent Road as his hiding place. With such a massive volume of people passing through every day, it was the perfect place for a person to disappear. Even the locals would struggle to bump into a familiar face from one day to the next.

Having walked the length of the pub with no sign of Fellows, Felix was about to circle back when a man in an ill-fitting suit and flat cap stepped in front of him, holding an expensive-looking leather suitcase with two brass locks and a briefcase of the same style.

"You look like a man of taste," he said, flashing the items in Felix's face. "How would you like to be the proud owner of one of these fine cases?"

"I'm not interested," said Felix, trying to step past the man.

"Hold your horses," protested the salesman, blocking Felix's path. "You haven't even looked at them yet." He held up the leather suitcase. "This one 'ere is what the gentlemen in Mayfair call, 'and luggage. You could go a long way being seen with one of these in your 'ands."

"I said I'm not interested," repeated Felix.

"On the other 'and, this one," continued the salesman, raising his other arm to showcase the briefcase, "is more your City of London style item. All the bankers carry these. Make you look like you're from proper stock. And you can't put a price on that now, can you?"

Irritated by the intrusion, Felix had stepped to the side to leave when he spotted a shadowy figure weaving through the crowds towards the exit. Out of the window, he saw a scruffy, bearded Tom Fellows depart the Bricklayers Arms and step into the hubbub outside. Felix looked back at the salesman, suddenly realising what was happening. Having spotted him enter the pub, Fellows had paid the salesman to keep Felix occupied long enough for him to escape. Felix quickly pushed past the decoy and fought his way back through the crowds, exiting the pub, only to find that Fellows had disappeared. Evaporated into the chaos of Old Kent Road.

Felix berated himself. How could he have failed so soon and so spectacularly? How could he have been so foolish? Clearly, the streetwise landlord would have been on high alert, looking closely for enemies trying to find him. He would always have eyes and ears on the pub door, just waiting for the moment to flee. Simply strolling in, his face undisguised, was always destined to fail.

He scanned the street in both directions, as far as his eyes could see, but with so much life around him, it was like looking for a black cat in a coal cellar. He was about to turn and leave when he heard a loud yelp from one of the adjoining streets. He turned and sprinted towards the alleyway, only to find Fellows knelt on the cobbled floor, cradling his arm in agony. Standing over the landlord, gripping a length of scrap piping, was Alfred.

"He was trying to get away," said the young man apologetically.

"You were supposed to stay back and rest, Alfred" replied Felix.

"I tried to but I couldn't sleep. I was too worried about what might happen when you…"

Alfred stopped, realising that Fellows was watching.

"I was just going to keep an eye out, in case you needed me. Honest. Until I saw him run like the rat he is."

Alfred pointed the pipe at Fellows.

"Don't hit me," cried Fellows, curling his thin frame into a ball on the floor.

Felix took a moment to study Fellows. He suddenly looked pathetic, a far cry from the man he'd met just a few days ago at the George Inn.

"We aren't going to hurt you," said Felix.

"You're not?" said Fellows, cautiously looking up.

"No, we're going to take you back inside that pub, and you're going to tell us everything you know. Or, I'll have you arrested right now and put behind bars. Understood?"

"Understood," replied Fellows.

Felix secured a table in a quiet corner of the pub and ordered a jug of stout to help settle Fellows' nerves before commencing with his questions.

"Where are the missing lords?" he asked in a low voice, mindful of any listening ears.

"What are you talking about?" sneered Fellows. "I don't know anything about any missing lords."

Felix studied Fellows. He seemed genuinely perplexed by the mention of the lords. Was it possible that he didn't know what the cards he printed were for?

"You expect us to believe you?" bristled Alfred, finding it hard to contain his anger sat opposite his master's killer.

Fellows took a long swig of stout, wiping the foam off his beard with his sleeve.

"Believe what you want, young'un," he said. "It doesn't matter to me either way."

"Maybe this will matter to you," replied Felix. "Two lords have been abducted. One from his home and the other snatched from his members' club. Those cards you had printed at Houlston and Sons were found at each of the crime scenes, left behind by their abductors."

"You can't pin that on me. I didn't know what they were using those cards for. I swear! I'm just one of their lackeys. They tell me what to pick up and drop off, and I do it. I don't ask any questions. That's how you end up dead."

"Like Mr. Houlston?" asked Alfred.

"I had nothing to do with that!"

"What about your two sailor friends?" added Felix. "We fished them out of Shad Thames last night."

Fellows' eyes dropped to the table.

"I had nothing to do with that either," he said, taking another gulp of his drink. "I may be many things: a crook, a thief, an alcoholic. But I'm not a murderer."

"That seems hard to believe, given the circumstances," said Felix.

"It's the truth!" barked Fellows.

"Then tell us what happened," pressed Felix. "We might be able to help."

"I'm beyond helping," replied Fellows, holding his head in his hands. "I didn't know what he was planning. I can still hear them now, clawing at the door to get out," he continued, gulping down the rest of his drink. "More stout!" he shouted across the bar.

"Who can you hear?" asked Felix, shocked.

"Them poor workers in those factories," replied Fellows, looking up sorrowfully. "It was just like at the printer's. We were only supposed to damage the building. You know, make it look like an accident. The old printer even stood to make a pretty penny on the insurance. But that wasn't enough for him. No, he needed to destroy it all, even the old man. He tied him to that machine and just stood there, watching him burn. It was the same at the factories. He had us bolt the doors, trapping everyone inside. We couldn't do anything about it. No one would dare question him."

"Who?" asked Alfred, shocked.

"The one-eyed man," replied Felix, putting it all together.

"Ezra Fox is his name," whispered Fellows, looking over his shoulder nervously. "He's the devil."

"Where is he now?" asked Felix.

"I don't know. I fled as soon as I got the chance. After what happened to the others, I guessed I was next on his list."

"What's Fox's connection to those factories?"

"No idea, but if he's taking orders from someone else, they must be very high-up and powerful. Let's just say Ezra's usually the one calling the shots."

"Did he ever mention anyone?"

"Not to me."

"Come on you must've heard something?" pressed Felix.

"I told you! I'm just a nobody. Someone he kicked around and used, like a stray dog."

"Listen to me," said Felix, trying to pull Fellows out of the melancholy rapidly consuming him, along with the stout. "If everything you say is true, then you still have a chance. But you need to help us find him before he causes any more destruction. Is there anything else you can remember, anything at all? It could make all the difference. It could save lives."

Fellows looked up at Felix, struggling to hold back his tears. It was clear that the past few days' events had weighed heavily on his shoulders and that he believed any hope of redemption had turned to ash, along with the factories.

"I did overhear them speaking about something," he said, trying to recall the conversation. "One last job, somewhere in east London. *A place with a unique collection of workers* is what Ezra said. *The kind of job no one would ever forget.*"

"Do you have any idea where?" asked Felix.

"That's all I heard."

"Think!" pressed Felix. "Is there anything else that might help us to find it?"

"He did say something about the flames," replied Fellows.

"What flames?" asked Felix.

"I can't remember fully!" said Fellows. "Something about the wood and chemicals, and the flames…"

"Wood and chemicals?" repeated Felix, frustrated. "That could be any factory in the country! What else?"

"I don't know!" bellowed Fellows, starting to shake. "I can't think. I just kept my head down and obeyed orders," he mumbled, tears streaming down his face. "I was scared. I was so scared."

Alfred stood up, unsure where to look. It was hard to witness Fellows breaking down in front of him. He'd been so sure this man was responsible for Mr. Houlston's death that he suddenly felt a tug of remorse hearing his explanation and seeing his grief.

Having noticed Alfred's discomfort, Felix rose from his seat. "It's okay," he said, placing a hand on the young man's shoulder. "We're finished here."

"You're going?" asked Fellows. "What am I supposed to do now?" he asked, the panic returning to his voice.

"Leave and go straight to Scotland Yard," said Felix. "When you get there, ask for Commissioner Thompson and tell him everything you have just told me."

"Hand myself in?" replied Fellows with a wry laugh.

"You could stay here and take your chances," said Felix. "Although, if we managed to find you, I'm sure it won't be long until your enemies do the same. The police are your only hope."

"Hope?" scoffed Fellows. "All my hope died with them poor folk in those factories."

Fellows gulped down the remainder of his stout and pulled the large jug towards him, ready to lose himself for the night.

With little left to say, Felix turned and led the way back through the rowdy punters and out of the Bricklayers Arms, followed closely by Alfred.

Bryant & May Matchmakers

Dismayed by the news of another impending disaster, Felix and Alfred returned to Old Pye Street, determined to uncover the location of the new factory target before Ezra Fox and his men could cause any more death or destruction. Based on the account Fellows had given of a conversation he'd overheard while in Ezra's employment, they were looking for a site in east London with a *unique collection of workers*. It would have to be a large manufacturer with a sizeable staff if the plan was to match or exceed the significance of the previous factory disasters, and truly become a *job no one would ever forget*. But large enterprises were hardly few and far between. Over the past few years, east London's population had boomed, and large commercial sites had popped up all over the East End. Felix had even patronised two earlier in the year, the new Hartley's jam factory in Bermondsey, and the Truman Brewery, which showed no signs of slowing down its expansion in Brick Lane.

However, there was one distinguishing detail from the case that could help narrow the search. Each of the previous attacks had occurred at a long-established factory with seemingly old or malfunctioning machinery. Ezra Fox and his cronies had capitalised on the workers' anxiety around their outdated equipment to plan the disasters and conceal their involvement, making each tragedy appear the consequence of political failings rather than foul play. If they were to locate the target, Felix and Alfred would have to find a site of both the appropriate size and age.

Before turning his attention to the Old Pye Street encyclopaedias, Felix drafted a letter to the Chief Record Keeper at the Public Record Office asking for lists of all the large-scale factories operating in the east London area over the past twenty years. Alfred watched the telephone switchboard, hoping to spot any call patterns that might prove relevant to the case. Neither looked up from their work for hours until a ray of light broke through the crooked window frame, bouncing off Felix's desk. Felix checked his pocket watch; it was almost six in the morning. He stepped away from his desk and approached the telephone switchboard.

"Alfred, the sun is rising; we've worked through the night," he said, placing a hand on the young man's shoulder.

To his amazement, exhausted, Alfred had fallen fast asleep upright in his chair. Felix carefully lowered him onto the makeshift bed he'd set up on the floor and covered him with a sheet before quietly gathering his papers and leaving.

Having passed through the secret passage back to his study at Downing Street, Felix placed his papers on the desk with a note requesting that Humphrey deliver his letter to the Public Record Office, then went to his bedroom to change clothes and prepare for the day.

Felix entered the dining room to find Amelia sitting at the long table with her head buried in a letter. She was dressed in a green and red tartan jacket with a matching shirt and wore a Texan rancher's hat with its brim edges rolled up, exposing her face. It had been a while since Felix had seen Amelia so quiet or the environment around her so tranquil. It was a troubling feeling that gave the immediate impression that something terrible had happened.

"What is it, Amelia?" he asked, approaching the professor.

"A message from my students. They've been looking into the name Pulleyn, hoping to shed some light on its etymology."

"And?"

"And it appears that the name was quite active, until the early seventeenth century when it suddenly died out. Well, until now, of course," Amelia said with a sly grin.

"Then why are you smiling?"

"Because it means, Prime Minister, that this Mr. G. Pulleyn isn't real. It's a spurious name."

"You mean we've been searching for someone who doesn't exist?"

"Yes! Wonderful, isn't it?" beamed Amelia.

"No, it's not wonderful, Amelia," said Felix. "I don't see how chasing after a shadow this whole time can be a good thing. Not when people are being murdered."

"Whomever Pulleyn really is," said Amelia, placing the note on the table, "he would've known about the name and its obsolescence; otherwise, it seems hugely coincidental that he would've opted to use it and not simply concoct some meaningless entity instead. You see, there must be some connection to the name, some method to it. A reason for him to want to retain it."

"What kind of connection?"

"I'm not sure, but if we can uncover why it disappeared as it did, it may give us a clue as to who has resurrected it and for what reason."

"How do we find out why the name disappeared?" asked Felix.

Amelia toyed with the brim of her hat, considering the question. "Why does a name die out?" she asked.

"By natural process?" suggested Felix. "Perhaps the last remaining Pulleyns were incapable of conceiving any children?"

"It's possible, as is the prospect of financial ruin, social exclusion or disease. My knowledge of historical epidemics is a little hazy, but I believe there were several outbreaks of the plague during the mid-seventeenth century. That would have done away with whole towns of people and generations of family names."

Felix had barely had the chance to consider Amelia's words when Humphrey entered, looking a little flustered.

"Commissioner Thompson is here to see you," he said, glancing from Felix to Amelia and then back again.

"Is that your not-so-subtle way of asking me to leave?" questioned Amelia.

"You really are picking up on our customs marvellously," replied Humphrey.

"You know something, Humphrey," said Amelia, standing up and straightening her clothes, "if it doesn't work out for you here, you could always start a career in hospitality. I could see you as the host at some well-to-do gentlemen's club or even as a pub landlord, with that delicate touch of yours."

"Pubs are for commoners and blow-hards," replied Humphrey. "Perhaps you might find one while the prime minister conducts his business with the commissioner?"

Amelia smiled and stepped away from the table.

"It's taken some time, but you're finally starting to warm to me!" she declared.

"Like cattle to a lasso," replied Humphrey.

"I knew it! I knew you couldn't resist listening to my little narrations."

"I may have overheard a word or two. It's my job to be the eyes and ears of this house. Likewise, if I were looking for a name that had mysteriously died out but had since been resurrected by a criminal, I would first investigate any historical references to its criminal past. Criminality breeds criminality, you see."

"Of course!" said Amelia. "Had the name passed into infamy, then there would have been an execution or a long imprisonment, which would have been documented."

"And which may have left a lingering sense of injustice and the need for retribution," added Humphrey.

Excited, Amelia reached for her overcoat.

"Where are you going?" asked Felix.

"To visit an old friend," replied Amelia, hurrying for the door.

With the calm restored, Humphrey led Commissioner Thompson into the dining room.

"Tea?" offered Felix, pouring himself a cup from a freshly brewed pot.

"Not for me, thank you," replied Thompson. "I don't intend to take up too much of your time. I've come to disclose some recent information."

Felix looked up from the tea tray, intrigued.

"This morning, a rather peculiar incident occurred at the station. A shabby and destitute-looking man named Tom Fellows walked into Scotland Yard and asked for me directly. He said he was involved in the disasters at Silverwood, Morden, Worcester Park and Surbiton, all of which had been planned and executed by a group of criminals from the London Docklands led by a local ruffian by the name of Ezra Fox. He also said that he had been persuaded by one of my investigating officers to hand himself in. Yet, having questioned my men, it appears that none of them has ever heard of this Tom Fellows, let alone advised him to come forward."

"That does sound peculiar," agreed Felix, trying to look surprised.

"He did, however, describe this investigating officer," Thompson continued, reaching into his pocket, and taking out a folded piece of paper. "I had my best man sketch a rough version of his face."

Thompson unfolded the paper and handed it to Felix.

Felix studied the drawing. The likeness was unquestionable. It was as though he was looking at himself in a mirror. He felt his stomach lurch. He knew how damaging this could be to the case and the impending vote should news of his involvement get out. It was almost unthinkable for the prime minister to engage in such low behaviour. Felix turned his attention back to Thompson. Over the past week, he had begun to respect the commissioner's diligent work ethic and commitment to the job, but there was still a question mark in his mind over which side he was working for. If recent events had taught Felix anything, it was that nobody was ever quite what they seemed.

"This is absurd," he said, returning the paper to Thompson. "He has clearly given a description of me to deflect from your investigation."

"But why would he," asked Thompson, "when he has handed himself in and willingly given over valuable information?"

"Perhaps he wanted to derive some merriment at your expense?"

"So, you've never met with this Tom Fellows?" asked Thompson.

"And where exactly was I supposed to have encountered this criminal? Here? In the Commons? At Buckingham Palace?"

"The Old Kent Road…" said Thompson, suddenly aware of how absurd his accusation sounded when spoken out loud.

"Let me see if I understand what you're suggesting, Commissioner," said Felix. "You believe that the prime minister, already busy with a spate of industrial disasters, national riots and with a vote of confidence in a mere two days, has had the time—let alone the inclination—to have been conducting meetings with criminals on the Old Kent Road?"

"Well, when you say it like that—"

"Interesting theory," continued Felix, cutting across Thompson. "Let's try some alternative theories, shall we? You said that this man, this Fellows, had been prompted to hand himself in by one of your investigating officers. Is that correct?"

"Yes," replied Thompson.

"You also said that none of your men had come forward to claim their involvement in his sudden appearance at Scotland Yard?"

"That's correct."

"Had it not occurred to you, then, that perhaps this investigating officer of yours, keen to protect his identity, given that one of your other officers was recently fished out of the Thames, had sworn Fellows to secrecy? Or perhaps, this Fellows chap, having realised the game was up and decided to hand himself in, has concocted this story to help his cause?"

"There is merit in both possibilities."

"Either way," continued Felix, on a roll, "when asked to describe the investigating officer, and keen not to disappoint, he probably recalled a familiar face from a newspaper or pamphlet. It could just as easily have been the King's face or Captain Scott's. I suppose I should be flattered. It's not often I get preferential treatment from the public."

"Yes, well, I think I've taken up quite enough of your time, Prime Minister," said Thompson sheepishly. "I should probably be making my way back to the Yard. We have reason to believe that these criminals may be planning another attack somewhere in London."

"Do you have any promising information or leads?" asked Felix, pretending to be surprised.

"Nothing of any substance. We believe the target to be closer to the east of London than the previous attacks and larger in scale. We have men scouring the area, assessing as many sites as possible, but we simply don't have the manpower to watch them all."

"Of course not," sympathised Felix. "Let me know if I can help in any way," he added, ending the meeting cordially.

"Thank you, Prime Minister," said Thompson, taking his leave.

Although the meeting had been trying, news that the police were also looking for the next factory target filled Felix with the hope that they may still find Ezra Fox and his men before it was too late. By informing the police of the impending disaster, Tom Fellows had taken the first step on a long road to redemption and, in the process, ensured that hundreds of bobbies would be out on the streets, monitoring industrial sites all over east London. If Felix and Alfred could find a way to uncover the target, they would have every resource needed to apprehend these criminals.

Felix returned to Old Pye Street to continue his search. He entered the oval-shaped office to find Alfred back at the telephone switchboard, hard at work. He watched the young man for a few seconds, impressed by his perseverance. If only half the politicians in Westminster had the same sense of purpose or enviable moral compass.

"Morning, Alfred," he said, alerting the young man to his presence.

Alfred turned to face Felix. "Sorry about last night. I, erm, must've nodded off," he stuttered.

"That's quite alright. You must have been exhausted. Anything of any note?" asked Felix, pointing at the telephone switchboard.

"Not yet," replied Alfred.

Felix approached the large, full-scale model of London in the centre of the room, scanning its flawless detail, looking for anything that might assist their search.

"Why east London?" he mused. "There are police on every street. Eyes everywhere."

"Maybe on every street, but not the river," said Alfred.

"There are no police on the river?" questioned Felix, surprised.

"Some," replied Alfred, stepping away from the telephone switchboard, "near Westminster and the city, where the rich folks are. But once you get a bit further down the river," he said, pointing at the area around London Bridge and leading out east, "there's not a bobby in sight. That's how we smuggled materials into the city from the docks."

Alfred stopped, suddenly realising what he was admitting and to whom. "We, erm...only did it to keep the business afloat."

"At times, we do what we must to survive," said Felix reassuringly before returning to the model. "So, they could use the river to avoid the police."

"That's their best bet," replied Alfred.

After hours spent scouring the encyclopaedias at Old Pye Street and learning everything there was to know about the quays and wharves of east London, Felix returned to Downing Street to fetch some food for himself and Alfred. He had barely stepped out of the secret passage and sealed the entrance when the study door opened, and Humphrey entered.

"Lunch will be served at one o'clock sharp," he said, stalking across the room to place a handful of letters on Felix's desk. "It will be roasted chicken with a black truffle sauce and vegetables."

"Could you have it sent up? I plan to continue working this afternoon. And have Mrs. Hughes fill the plate. I'm feeling surprisingly hungry today."

"One chicken or two?" mocked Humphrey.

"One will suffice," replied Felix, approaching his desk to check the newly delivered post.

At the top of the pile was a large envelope with an official government stamp emblazoned on it. Felix quickly opened it. As he had hoped, the letter was from the Chief Record Keeper at the Public Record Office, returning a list of all the major factories operating in the east London area over the last twenty years. The list was endless. Felix could feel his heart sinking further with every page he turned.

"Fire?" asked Humphrey.

"I'm not thirsty," replied Felix, focused on the letter.

"I said, fire," repeated Humphrey, rattling a box of matches to get Felix's attention.

Felix looked up. He stared at the large box of matches in Humphrey's hand. On the front, in bold letters, were the words *Bryant & May's Special Safety Match*. His mind immediately jumped back to his journey to Oxford, to present the card to Amelia, and the article mentioning the Bryant & May matchmaking factory in the East End with its impressive site and the large-scale employment of women and young girls. He thought back to his recent conversation with Tom Fellows in the Bricklayers Arms the day before, recalling the broken man's words, *something about the wood and chemicals, and the flames, a place with a unique collection of workers*.

Suddenly it all started to make sense. It wasn't merely the size of the factory that would make this disaster more significant in scale or meaningful in people's minds. It was the fact that the target was a famous factory which employed large numbers of women: mothers, sisters, daughters and wives. And a factory filled with highly flammable phosphorus and wood was sure to go up with a bang,

"I asked about the fire," repeated Humphrey, getting irritated.

"Not for now, thank you," said Felix, "just the food."

He waited patiently for Humphrey to leave, inwardly counting every second, then sprung from his seat and hurried to the fireplace, activating the secret passage. He sprinted through the long tunnel, arriving at Old Pye Street sweaty and out of breath.

"Put me through to Scotland Yard!" he called to Alfred, bursting into the room.

Alfred lifted the cord and placed it in the appropriate jack, making the connection. He handed the receiver to Felix.

"Commissioner Thompson," bellowed Felix down the mouthpiece. "I don't care if he's busy. You tell him it's the prime minister on the line."

Within moments Felix heard the regimented voice of Commissioner Thompson on the other end of the call.

"Prime Minister?"

"Commissioner. I have reason to believe the next attack will be at the Bryant & May matchmaking factory in Bow. They have nearly two thousand staff there, mainly women and young girls. I cannot disclose how I came about this information, but rest assured, it has come from a credible source. I need you to immediately divert your men to the site. Time is of the essence."

Felix placed the telephone receiver back on the switchboard and hurriedly exited the building via the Old Pye Street entrance, followed closely by Alfred. He hailed a cab and instructed the driver to follow the river east towards Bow and the Bryant & May matchmaking factory.

A calm silence welcomed Felix and Alfred as their cab approached the factory gates. Felix studied the industrial site, appraising the state of affairs before stepping out of the vehicle. He had learnt his lessons the hard way at Houlston and Sons and the George Inn, and was determined not to rush in and potentially plunge himself into another compromising situation.

The factory was made up of a cluster of huge red brick buildings with sprawling walls covering many acres of land and encasing two large courtyards. Each courtyard had an impressive tower that burst into the sky and could be seen for miles. Historically, the site had been used to manufacture candles, crinoline and rope before Bryant & May moved in and regenerated the dilapidated buildings to manufacture their matches. The high roadside walls and the director's cottage were set in front of the imposing site, and a second-floor bay window overlooked the tall factory gates, with the brand's emblem, an image of Noah's Ark and the word security emblazoned on them.

On the surface of things, nothing seemed to be out of the ordinary. There were groups of workers, predominantly women, moving in and out of the buildings and going about their daily routines. Some even had time to gather outside for a chat, a well-earned cigarette, and a cup of tea. It seemed like just another ordinary day at the factory.

Felix approached the open gates, confused. He felt a sudden anxiety building in his chest. What if he had got it wrong? What if he'd just diverted the police's attention away from the actual site to a fictitious threat at the matchmaking factory? After all, it was entirely possible that he may have read too deeply into Tom Fellows' words and the Bryant & May mention in the newspaper.

"What now?" asked Alfred, staring up at Felix.

"I'm not sure," he replied. "Maybe we should take a look around."

Felix led the way through the gates, across the grass bank and into the first courtyard, where he was greeted by one of the site foremen.

"Can I help?" he asked, looking Felix and Alfred up and down.

They were an odd pair, Felix in his tailored suit and Alfred in his simple apprentice clobber.

"We were hoping to look around your site," replied Felix casually.

"You'll have to get approval from the directors, I'm afraid," coughed the foreman, suffering from years of overexposure to the white phosphorous found in the matches.

"It's nothing formal. We're simply visiting out of whimsical curiosity. Surely, you can allow a few minutes for an interested party?" pressed Felix.

"It's not down to me," replied the foreman. "It's company policy. You never know who's trying to steal your ideas."

Felix was about to protest when he saw a group of men in workers' overalls hurrying across the courtyard towards the gates. He watched them curiously as they quickened their pace and finally broke into a sprint. One of them, a large, intimidating man had a patch over one eye.

Realising the worst, Felix grabbed Alfred, about to pull him away when a loud explosion shook the courtyard, lifting Felix, Alfred and the foreman off their feet and sending them hurtling onto the grass bank.

It took Felix a few breaths to regain his senses. He could hear a cacophony of shouting and screaming and saw a large plume of smoke reaching into the sky above one of the factory buildings.

Carefully, he rose to his feet, relieved to see Alfred and the foreman slowly peel themselves off the grass bank, shaken but thankfully uninjured. He hurriedly led them towards the burning building. Through the smoke and chaos, he could hear a group of women calling out for help as they strained to force open the large factory doors, with little success.

"It's locked from the inside!" shouted the foreman through a gap in the door. "You need to remove the wooden latch!"

But his voice was drowned out by the cries of fear and panic from those trapped inside. With the flames rising and their hopes fading, the foreman tried using brute force, charging at the doors with all his might. But the thick oak panels hardly moved under his weight. Suddenly another, smaller, explosion could be heard coming from inside the factory.

"There's a lot of chemicals in there," warned the foreman, "The whole thing's gonna go up any moment now."

"Stay here," Felix instructed Alfred.

He turned and sped away, tracing the perimeter of the factory wall, searching for another way into the building. To his dismay, the factory windows were all too high and out of reach. Strewn across the ground lay the broken pieces of a ladder, evidence of the intruders' entry and exit.

Undeterred, Felix persisted, eventually discovering a small, boarded-up shaft, a forgotten passage for passing buckets of waste in and out of the site.

He stepped back and using the heel of his shoe, broke straight through its wooden frame, revealing a small gap barely big enough to fit a person. Determined, Felix removed his jacket and emptied his pockets of anything that might catch before dropping to his knees and wriggling his body through the small opening.

Inside, black smoke had engulfed the large room, making it difficult for Felix to see. He reached out, touching the wall, and used it as a guide to feel his way back towards the factory entrance. As he got closer, Felix ran into a crowd of panic-stricken workers trying to get to the exit and escape. They were coughing heavily, screaming and crying. Felix used all his strength to force his way through the melee to the front. He could feel his energy draining with every exertion and the heavy smoke beginning to clog his lungs.

He finally reached the doors and felt around in the darkness until his hands landed on the large wooden plank trapping everyone inside. He tried to lift it, but the plank wouldn't budge; it was far too heavy for one person to move. He could hear the muffled voices of the women, Alfred, and the foreman on the other side of the door, shouting at the trapped workers to lift the wooden plank, but organising them from the courtyard was futile.

Felix began to cough, finding it difficult to breathe. There was no going back now. He needed to act quickly if he was going to save the lives of the people trapped inside, including his own.

Suddenly, another explosion sounded in the distance, shaking the ground beneath his feet. Panicked, Felix leaned forward using all his weight to try and shift the plank, but it still wouldn't move.

Desperate, he threw himself at the door again and again until he felt a woman calmly take hold of his hand. Shocked, Felix stopped and allowed her to guide it towards the bottom of the wooden plank. She tapped his hand on the heavy beam twice, trying to communicate an instruction. Realising what she meant, Felix quickly found the hand of the next woman along and did the same, guiding it towards the bottom of the plank and tapping it twice to relay the directions.

There was confusion at first amidst the panic, but slowly and surely, one by one, the women began to understand. Each woman did the same to the woman next to her and then the ones next to them until there was a line of women with their hands on the vast wooden plank.

Together, the women and Felix began to lift, exerting their remaining energy to finally shift the heavy latch and unlock the large factory doors. Within seconds, relieved workers burst out of the building, gasping for air. It was like a stampede as they bolted toward the light pouring over Felix and the exhausted line of women on the front row, who collapsed under their weight.

Those who witnessed the incident from outside hurried to help colleagues who had passed out or who were trapped under the feet of the rushing herd. Alfred's eyes caught sight of Felix sprawled out on the floor. He pushed through the crowd of workers and seized Felix by the arm, trying to pull him to safety, but struggled with the weight of his limp body.

In the background, he could hear the police arriving, along with the fire service. It was pandemonium, as people from all corners of the site rushed to put out the colossal fire and assist the stricken workers.

"Help!" shouted Alfred desperately over his tears. "I need help!"

But his words were lost in the chaos.

Distraught, Alfred wrapped his arms around Felix, unsure if he was still alive or if he was cradling the prime minister's dead body in his hands. He leant over, placing his ear close to Felix's mouth, anxiously listening for his breath. It was a trick he'd learnt as a young boy when his booze-stricken father wouldn't wake after a long night on the gin. But Alfred couldn't hear anything. There was no sign of life, just the stillness of Felix's chest.

Alfred slumped to the floor in despair when he felt Felix's hand softly touch his arm.

"Prime Minister?" he said leaning back down.

"Old…Pye…Street," murmured Felix.

"You're alive!" exclaimed Alfred, overcome with relief.

He felt a sudden surge of adrenaline rush through his body. He wrapped Felix's weak arms around his neck and spoke into his ear.

"We have to get you out of here. But I need your help, I can't lift you on my own. I need you to pull on my neck as hard as you can. Do you understand? Ready? Now…PULL!"

Alfred felt Felix tug on his neck. The young apprentice planted his heels into the hard ground and pushed with all his strength, slowly lifting Felix off the floor and onto his feet. He grabbed Felix around his waist to steady him, and together they slowly staggered out through the large gates of Bryant & May, away from another horrifying disaster.

Tower of London

The Thames was busy for the time of year, with tugboats carrying goods from the processing plants and warehouses in the East of London to the fashionable shops and department stores all across the capital. The few remaining passenger steamboats that still ferried people up and down were less frequent than in previous years as the industry continued to shrink under the growing expansion of the London Underground.

With little sign of a steamer approaching, Amelia hailed a longboat and paid the ageing waterman a few coins to carry her east down the river towards Tower Hill.

"Yankee, are you?" he asked, dipping his oars into the water.

"Do you know the United States?" asked Amelia.

"Can't say that I do. I could tell from that hat and your accent. We get a lot of your kind looking to visit the Tower."

"I'm not a tourist," protested Amelia, "I live here, and I'm conducting research at the Tower, not sightseeing."

"Research, you say. You're not looking into the ghosts, are you?" asked the waterman.

"A ghost of sorts."

"You know that Anne Boleyn still haunts the place? If you look up from the river at night, you can sometimes see her spectre on the ramparts of the Bloody Tower."

"Is that so?" asked Amelia. "Sounds a little far-fetched to me."

"That's 'cause you're an American, see," replied the waterman. "You ain't got enough history to have proper ghosts."

"Nonsense! There were natives in America for thousands of years before we landed. Next, you'll tell me that you can see Guy Fawkes' head floating around on a spike if you look closely enough."

"It wouldn't surprise me," replied the waterman.

"Well, have you seen any of these phantoms?" asked Amelia.

"No, not personally. But plenty of others working these waters have."

"And it didn't strike you as odd that they all told the same story?"

"It just proves that it's true," said the waterman. "Why?" he asked, suddenly curious.

"Because, my good man, repetition is how fiction, to the superstitious mind, morphs into fact."

The waterman opened his mouth to respond, then stopped, perplexed by Amelia's words. Unsure what she meant and too proud to ask, he turned his attention back to rowing, mumbling about ghosts under his breath, much to Amelia's amusement. He steered the boat alongside the Embankment and past Temple towards Blackfriars. Amelia took the opportunity to absorb the many incredible sights along the riverbank. As an enthusiastic anglophile, she loved being surrounded by the city's historical treasures, and Somerset House, the Inns of Court and St. Paul's Cathedral were among her favourites.

Having passed through Southwark, they soon reached London Bridge, the busiest crossing in the city with thousands of pedestrians and vehicles passing over it every hour. Two years earlier, the bridge had been widened to help with traffic flow when it was discovered that it had been sinking by an eighth of an inch every year.

The waterman guided the longboat under the bridge's dark arch, emerging on the other side. An accomplished rower, he had won the Doggett's Coat and Badge, the oldest continuous rowing race in the world, in his youth. He came from a long line of watermen, each generation having rowed in the race, and one or two even serving as Royal Watermen, responsible for ferrying Kings and Queens, along the waterways of London.

Amelia rose from her seat to take in the commanding sight of Tower Bridge and the Tower of London in the distance. The bridge, a feat of architectural and engineering mastery, had taken nearly a decade to build and had become a symbol of

London's greatness. One newspaper had even quoted William Wordsworth's immortal sentence, *Earth has not anything to show more fair,* to describe it. It was a sight that Amelia never tired of.

After a mundane journey for the waterman, who had navigated the route countless times, but a rare and majestic turn on the river for Amelia, the vessel finally arrived at the Tower of London, docking between the Byward Tower and Traitors' Gate. Amelia thanked the waterman in her usual theatrical manner, much to the old seadog's displeasure, and then disembarked.

The Tower of London was a mishmash of buildings, towers and grounds, all set within two concentric rings of defensive walls and a moat. It was best known for its use as a notorious medieval prison and torture chamber but also served as a grand palace, a royal residence, an armoury, a treasury, a menagerie, and the home of the Crown Jewels of England. But it was the Tower's historical use as a public record office that Amelia was interested in. Its records were rumoured to go back as far as William the Conqueror and held every state secret since the Norman Conquest.

Publicly, the last Keeper of the Records at the Tower had left his position in the mid-nineteenth century when the records were sent to the new Public Record Office in Chancery Lane. However, Amelia knew that this was not entirely accurate and that a particular collection of documents had secretly remained. Having been granted access to the site for a research project some years earlier, she had decided to explore the infamous and highly restricted lower chambers of the White Tower. Evading the yeoman warders, Amelia made her way to the basement, where she discovered a small room, unchanged since medieval times, with rows of battered shelves housing historical documents, ledgers and rolls. As she settled down to read one of the old manuscripts, she was disturbed by the Tower's senior curator. Aghast to find Amelia in the secret chamber, he reluctantly explained the room's history and significance, provided she agreed to leave and never come back.

The hidden archive was all that remained of the fabled Black Hall, the Tower's original record office, which had supposedly been consigned to history some centuries earlier. While many of the Tower's records had been relocated, they had been mostly copies or less controversial documents like land registry deeds and birth and marriage certificates. Unbeknown to the public, who associated the Tower with the missing Plantagenet princes and, more recently, the Crown Jewels, the original records remained, secretly housed in the remnants of the Black Hall, too valuable and murky to risk moving.

It was the same senior curator who had caught her in the act and explained the Black Hall's mysterious history that Amelia now sought out as she approached two yeoman warders at the Tower's Henry III Watergate.

"I'm here to see Mr. Francis Banks," she said, appearing from the riverside walkway.

"The tourist entrance is at the Byward Tower," replied one of the warders.

"I am not a tourist," Amelia bristled. "I am a professor."

"Course you are!" scoffed the other warder, certain that there was no such thing as a female professor, particularly one dressed so oddly and with a mild American accent.

Amelia reached into her pocket and took out her university identification, waving it in the air.

"I am Amelia Woodruff, a professor at Corpus Christi College, Oxford University. Ever heard of it? It's a little seat of learning just north-west of here. Now, if you would kindly inform Mr. Banks of my arrival, I am certain we can resolve this matter quicker than you can say, South Texan Longhorn."

"Of course, Professor," said one of the warders, quickly scampering off to enquire.

After a few moments, he returned with a smartly dressed, academic-looking man.

"I was under the impression we had an agreement, Professor Woodruff," said Francis Banks frostily. "I enlighten you about our little room, and you never return unless in line with the other tourists?"

"That was our agreement, and it was struck in good faith. However, something unforeseen has occurred, a matter of national security, which unfortunately necessitates that I further examine the contents of our little room."

"Remind me, what was your excuse for being down there last time?" asked Francis. "Ah, yes. You were in search of Turrim Vespertilio, the notorious—"

"Tower bat," interjected Amelia, glancing at the amused warders. "Yes, that was a touch fanciful, but you must believe me; this is of the utmost importance."

"Do you have the story of the boy who cried wolf in America, Professor?"

"Indeed, we do. If we could just go inside and talk, I would be happy to explain the situation, and if you are not entirely convinced, I promise I'll leave without a fuss. You have my word, and a Texan's word is stronger than oak."

Francis took a long, unconvinced look at Amelia, then turned and marched back towards the large wooden doors.

"Err, Mr. Banks?" called Amelia, confused.

"You've got five minutes," he replied, pushing the doors open. "Make them count."

Amelia quickly scampered after Francis as he marched into the castle's innermost ward, cutting a path through the tourists and across the large grass bank towards the White Tower. Amelia tried to keep in step but found herself constantly slowed by the incredible displays, including the magnificent tournament armour of Henry VIII.

"You do realise this is eating into your time?" warned Francis, turning to see her gazing in awe at the gilded armours of Charles I and James II.

"Yes, of course, apologies!" replied Amelia, hurrying after him.

Having passed through the Tower's main exhibition chamber, they entered a quiet staff room with a small table, chairs and a series of notes nailed to the beautiful Portland and Kentish ragstone walls.

"So," began Francis, facing Amelia, "I'm listening."

"Not even a cup of tea first?" quipped Amelia, trying to thaw the frost. "This is most un-British."

"Three minutes to go," replied Francis, checking his watch. "I really would get a move on, if I were you."

"Straight to it then," said Amelia, sitting on one of the chairs and crossing her legs as though about to read a bedtime story. "I'll tell you what I can, but there are certain details and persons that, for reasons of a sensitive nature, must remain a secret."

Francis nodded his agreement and Amelia began. First, she explained the abductions of the lords, the cards left at the crime scenes and their odd symbols. Then, with the curator engrossed, she quickly and theatrically moved on to the masons, Houlston and Sons, the poker match at the East India Club and her questioning of the gambler, Jonathan Burbage. Like any great detective, having laid out the setting, the crime and the mystery, Amelia then concluded by listing the suspects and the sequence of events that had led her to the Tower of London.

"How utterly fascinating," said Francis, pulling up a seat beside Amelia. "It certainly beats explaining the difference between tournament and battle armour to a gaggle of Neanderthal tourists. So, you think the last Pulleyn died here in the Tower?"

"I can't be sure, but if they'd been notorious criminals or had committed treason, that would certainly explain the name's sudden disappearance. Who would keep a name that is mired in shame and ignominy?"

"You do realise how many criminals have passed through these gates over the past nine hundred years? It would take an army of researchers to get through all those ledgers."

"It's the best chance we have," conceded Amelia.

"That's why I'm going to help you," declared Francis, suddenly alive with adventure. "I know these archives better than anyone. If the answer is down there, I will help you find it."

Having guided the way back out of the staff room, through numerous corridors and down several flights of stairs, Francis finally led Amelia into White Tower's basement and the forgotten Black Hall.

"Where do we start?" puffed Amelia, scanning the medieval room, out of breath.

"The old keeper had a unique archiving system," replied Francis, pulling over a small wooden ladder. "He used a combination of registers, indexes and other finding aids he'd created over the years to keep a tab on everything. Early seventeenth century, you said?"

"Yes, that's right," nodded Amelia.

Francis positioned the ladder under a dusty old shelf full of parchment scrolls. He climbed up and read the tags on each, passing a selection down to Amelia, who carefully placed them on a long table in the centre of the Black Hall. He continued along the shelves, removing other scrolls and faded leather-bound journals and passing each into Amelia's waiting hands.

"That should see us through the night," he said, looking down at a sizeable collection safely assembled on the table.

Amelia smiled at Francis in admiration. She'd never met a man who could match her enthusiasm for research before.

"Thank you," she said, uncharacteristically self-aware.

"What for?" asked Francis.

"For believing me and for helping."

"You can thank me once we've found our man," replied Francis, sitting at the table and handing Amelia a scroll. "Now, if you will, Professor."

Together, they unrolled their parchments and buried their heads in their work.

Despite reviewing hundreds of pages and thousands of lines of text, many hours passed without the slightest hint of success. Feeling their energies begin to sap, Amelia suggested a different approach.

"Perhaps we should narrow our criteria?"

"In what way?" asked Francis.

"Rather than search through all the criminal cases in the period, we should focus on the more extreme cases first. The hangings and beheadings, even the tortures, then work our way back?"

Francis sorted through the journals on the table, removing a dozen or so from the pile.

"These are the lists of the most notorious prisoners," he said, dividing them between himself and Amelia.

Together they scanned every word, line and paragraph, working through the evening with little progress. Beginning to doubt that the answer was even in the Black Hall, Amelia stepped away from the table.

"What if the name died out under different circumstances or in another country?" she said, "Or if we've somehow missed it, scanning past the entry without realising?"

"You're tired and worried," said Francis gently. "Trust yourself, Amelia. Answers are like mountain peaks. It takes time and effort to reach them."

"And discipline," added Amelia, returning to her seat a little embarrassed.

"If the answers are here, we will find them," said Francis reassuringly, adding to Amelia's admiration.

With the night drawing in, they separated the task into shifts, each taking a turn to sleep while the other continued the search. Amelia took the first shift, searching through a pile of records before restocking the table with journals for Francis to carry on with once her time was up. They continued this way through the night and into the next morning, when Amelia, having all but given up, pulled a bulging journal off one of the remaining shelves and flicked through its pages, only to find it contained the names of all the infamous prisoners' visitors from 1500–1700. It listed the family members of Anne Boleyn, Catherine Howard and Elizabeth Throckmorton—the maid of honour to Queen Elizabeth I, who secretly married Sir Walter Raleigh behind her monarch's back, leading to his imprisonment in the Bloody Tower.

Intrigued, Amelia continued scanning the long rows of names, flicking through page after page until she finally placed her shaking finger on the name she'd been searching for all this time. In front of her, alongside the date December 12th, 1605, was the name Maria Pulleyn.

"Francis," said Amelia, waking him, "I've found it."

"Found what?" asked the groggy curator, slowly sitting up.

"The name," said Amelia, showing Francis the listing. "We were searching for a woman all this time. Her name was Maria Pulleyn. She made a single visit to the Tower in December 1605."

Amelia traced her finger along the page to name of the prisoner Maria Pullyen was listed as visiting.

"She was here to see Guy Fawkes." said Amelia amazed. "Wasn't Guy Fawkes born and educated in York?" she asked, suddenly piecing things together.

"Indeed he was." replied Francis, impressed by her knowledge of the subject. "And, if I remember correctly, a member of his family even held the title of Lord Mayor of York some decades before."

"Do you have a list of marriage certificates here in the Tower?" asked Amelia, thinking aloud. "Preferably in the York area?"

"No, never for the north. But I know someone who does."

Francis carefully placed the records back on the shelves, restoring the Black Hall to its original order, then led Amelia back through the corridors to the White Tower's main office. He picked up the telephone receiver and spoke into the mouthpiece.

"Public Record Office. Chancery Lane."

After a few moments, he heard a voice on the other end of the line.

"Richard. It's Francis from the Tower. I need a favour. Would you be able to investigate something for me? I was hoping you could check your records for a woman named Maria Pulleyn,

1590 to 1605, focussing on the towns and parishes of the city of York."

While they waited, Francis made a pot of tea and retrieved a tin of Huntley & Palmers assorted biscuits from the cupboard. Amelia opened the window to get some much needed air, when she was surprised to see lines of tourists beginning to form outside the tower again. It was a strange sensation, having worked through the night without seeing the change in light. She felt tired but also full of energy. She was so close to finding an essential part of the jigsaw that she could hardly contain herself, let alone service the need for sleep.

Having drunk their tea and had their fill of biscuits, Amelia and Francis were finally disturbed by a faint buzzing sound coming from the telephone receiver and a voice speaking on the other end of the line. Amelia looked at Francis, who quickly took hold of the telephone, placing the receiver close to his ear.

"Hello, Richard," he said, his voice brimming with anxious excitement. "Did you find anything?"

Amelia placed her ear alongside Francis's, touching her cheek to his face.

"It appears Maria Pulleyn was descended from the Pulleyns of Scotton Hall, a small town outside York," said Richard. "She was born in 1573, the second of two girls, and attended the local parish school until the age of fifteen. That's when the records start to get a little hazy. Aside from references to her baptism and the premature death of her older sister, there is very little information about Maria. No records of how, where or when she died. She simply vanished off the face of the earth from around 1588 onwards. There is, however, a rather curious document in the records that is barely even legible, which suggests…"

Richard paused for a moment.

"Yes?" pressed Amelia impatiently. "I mean, carry on," she said softly, trying to mimic Francis's voice.

"Well, I cannot verify its provenance, nor indeed its truthfulness," continued Richard, "and it feels rather odd to say this out loud, but the document seems to suggest that she was married to Guy Fawkes."

Amelia and Francis looked at each other in bewilderment. They could hardly believe what they had just heard.

"Thank you, Richard. That's been most helpful," said Francis, quickly replacing the receiver and finishing the call. "Remind me of those lords' names again," he asked, turning to Amelia.

"Monteagle and Cecil."

"Of course!" exclaimed Francis, kicking himself. "How could I not make the connection? The old Lord Cecil is widely believed to have masterminded the entire gunpowder plot and the arrests to position himself as the King's saviour. And it was Lord Monteagle who exposed the plot after the conspirators sent him a letter warning him not to attend Parliament. It all adds up!"

"Francis, I need you to do something for me," said Amelia, suddenly panicked.

She reached for a piece of paper and a pen and scribbled something down.

"Take this to Downing Street as quickly as you can. Ask for a man named Humphrey and tell him I've sent you. Place this note in his hand, no one else's."

Francis nodded, somewhat confused. Before he could ask why or even say goodbye, Amelia turned on her heels and hurried out, leaving the Tower of London quicker than you could say South Texan Longhorn.

Magic of Misdirection

Felix was still feeling the effects of his exposure to the smoke at Bryant & May when he finally came around. His head was pounding, and there was a burning sensation in his chest and throat. He looked around, trying to gather his bearings, only to discover that he was lying in Alfred's makeshift bed on the floor at Old Pye Street.

"You've been out for ages," said a concerned voice. "I didn't know if I should call for a doctor."

Felix looked up to see Alfred sitting close by. It was clear from his drawn face and tired eyes that he'd been by Felix's side the whole time, keeping a close eye on him.

"I'm okay, thank you, Alfred," said Felix, slowly sitting up. "What happened?"

"You saved them," replied Alfred, "I thought they were all goners. But you got them out. You're a hero."

Felix nodded, acknowledging the compliment. He appreciated the young man's sentiment but did not see himself as a hero or someone to be revered. Yes, he had managed to save the lives of those workers at Bryant & May, having placed himself in great danger, but he was merely balancing the books, making up for past failures, of which there were many.

"What time is it?" he asked.

"Early morning; you slept through a whole day and night."

"Early morning! I need to get to Parliament," said Felix, springing up from the bed.

"Are you sure you're up to it?" asked Alfred, concerned.

"I don't have a choice," croaked Felix. "The vote is today. I must address the Commons and state my case to the members."

Felix hurried out of the oval office and down the long tunnel back to Downing Street. He entered his study to find the morning newspapers on his desk, along with a rather sour note from

Humphrey questioning whether he intended to bother with the parliamentary vote, given his recent habit of disappearing without a trace.

Felix picked up the newspapers and scanned the headlines. The events at the Bryant & May matchmaking factory dominated the front pages. Although there had been significant damage to the buildings, there had been no deaths, only injuries from which the women would thankfully recover. He read some of the workers' accounts, detailing the explosions, the fiery infernos and their miraculous escapes. Fortunately for Felix, there was no mention of him personally, only references to a strange but courageous gentleman entering the building and helping those trapped inside.

There was, however, something else of concern for Felix, given the impending vote. Some newspapers had interviewed union representatives who, having previously agreed to call off their protests, were now urging their fellow workers to march on Parliament, believing the disaster to be caused by more faulty machinery and angry with the government.

Felix's deal with the TUC had only just come into effect, helping him climb a few rungs back up the political ladder. But now he could feel himself tumbling back down it again. Although successfully thwarted, the events at Bryant & May had been enough to re-ignite the social unrest among the workers, making it highly likely he would lose the impending vote and see an end to his time in power.

Felix placed the newspapers back on his desk and reached for his journal. He flicked through the leather-bound book, observing the long paragraphs of information, commentary and conversation he'd jotted down since the abduction of Lord Monteagle. The pieces of this mystery were buried somewhere within these pages, but they felt almost impossible to put together with so much happening and so many moving parts.

Felix approached the study window, gazing out onto the street. He watched the people pass by, blissfully unaware of the events that had consumed his life over the past few weeks. Perhaps the adage was true: ignorance really was bliss. He took a moment to look around the famous Downing Street study, his home and refuge over the past few years, where he had spent many a long night trying to make a meaningful difference. How little the voters knew about the actual work that went on inside this historic house. How fortunate they were.

Felix's eyes fell back upon the journal in his hand, this time not in some vain hope of solving the case, but with a sinking realisation that his fixation with this investigation had cost him his time in office. He should never have allowed himself to get involved in the first place, let alone become so caught up in it. If he had just left it to the proper authorities, as Percy had urged, he wouldn't have been so distracted from his role as prime minister. An honour that was now slipping through his fingers.

Frustrated, Felix tossed the journal aside. He opened the study door and checked the hallway for any signs of Humphrey, then made a quick dash for his bedroom, where he washed and changed in preparation for Parliament and the vote.

Having decided to walk to Westminster, much to Humphrey's consternation, Felix took his favoured route via the park, with its tall canopy of trees, wildlife and beautiful lakes. It was the first time he'd found the picturesque walk lonely since becoming prime minister. He tried to enjoy it, to make the most of each step, aware that it could be his last along this famous route once he was removed from power and his residence at Number 10. However, as usual, his mind was firing in all directions, still trying to find solutions to his problems, even though it all felt hopeless.

As Felix turned into Great George Street, approaching Parliament Square, he heard the raucous sound of shouting and chanting. A large group of protestors had amassed outside the Palace of Westminster. They had turned out in force, just as they had threatened, and were continuing to arrive in great numbers. Some voiced their frustrations, while others carried signs calling for an end to slave labour and the substandard working conditions they were forced to endure under his government.

Although Felix knew the factory fires were criminal acts plotted and carried out by Ezra Fox and his men, it didn't change the fact that his government had failed to improve the lives of ordinary workers. Their inability to reform and modernise these factories had allowed their enemies to capitalise on the growing ill-feeling and stir up anarchy. Rather than becoming the great liberal reformer he aspired to be, Felix had become a largely ineffective prime minister. It was a bitter pill to swallow.

Rather than divert his path and take the back entrance into Parliament to avoid the protestors, Felix floated towards the growing mob like a moth drawn to a flame. He couldn't explain why he'd chosen that route with its apparent dangers. Maybe it was habit, routine, or perhaps something more profound, a need to show himself and make amends for everything that had happened. He entered the crowd, passing through unnoticed amidst the cacophony of noise and animated gestures, until one of the protestors, distracted by his smart suit, realised a gentleman was walking among them.

"It's the prime minister! It's Felix Grey!" he shouted, garnering the attention of those who could hear his voice over the melee.

One by one, the protestors began to turn, nudging the person next to them and pointing at Felix until the entire crowd had been alerted to his presence. Felix continued to walk forward as the shocked protestors began to step aside, creating a narrow pathway for him. They watched his every step in stunned silence. The hush seemed to last an eternity for Felix, as did the long walk towards Parliament's gates. As he drew closer, Felix heard a wave of whispered insults thrown his way. The *how dare yous* and *you've got a nerves*.

Once a few people in the crowd had gathered enough courage to speak their minds, it didn't take long for the rest of the group to turn their anger on Felix. Even the most silent whispers quickly escalated into enraged shouts, and Felix felt a surge of movement at his back as the crowd began to swarm forward, closing off his pathway. They barged and jostled to get within earshot and deliver their furious tirades. Felix fought his way through the crowd, pushing forward, trying to get to the safety of the police line as the protestors continued to shout and bark in his face.

With the crowd squeezing against him, Felix suddenly felt a strong hand grab his collar and extract him from the melee. He turned to see a colossal policeman being marshalled furiously by an animated Percy.

"Make way for the prime minister! Make way, I say!" bellowed Percy as the line of policemen stepped forward, pushing the protestors back.

Percy seized Felix by the arm and pulled him away towards the Houses of Parliament. They entered through the small Gothic doorway to shocked glances from the members who had gathered at the windows to watch the scene developing outside.

"What were you thinking, Felix?" asked Percy, bewildered. "You're lucky they didn't tear you limb from limb!"

"They have every right to feel that way, Thomas," said Felix, trying to understand what had just happened. "Something was telling me that I needed to show myself to them."

"Whatever it was, it was either incredibly brave or downright foolish!"

"Possibly a bit of both," said Felix, taking in the reactions of the watching faces.

"Well, it was always going to take something out of the ordinary to win this blasted vote."

"What is the current state of play?" asked Felix.

"As far as I can tell, Cavendish has healthy support across the house," replied Percy. "However, our whips have been kicking up dust over the past forty-eight hours. The question is, have they done enough?"

"It will all come down to how convincing we both sound when we address the house," said Felix, thinking aloud. "That will be when the members' votes are truly won or lost."

"The final stand!" snarled Percy, shaking his fist.

As the men continued through St. Stephen's Hall towards the House of Commons, the density of members increased, as did the volume of their gossiping. Felix and Percy passed a group of loud parliamentarians nattering away in the Central Lobby, followed by an even louder gaggle in the Commons Corridor, before finally running into an entire herd of people in the Commons Lobby. Through their incessant chitchat, Felix heard a familiar voice. He stepped to one side to see Humphrey conversing with one of the members.

"It's a matter of pride rather than good housekeeping," he said earnestly.

"Humphrey?" called Felix, surprised to see his steward. "What on earth are you doing here?" he asked, stepping away from Percy.

"You forgot your journal, Prime Minister," said Humphrey, handing Felix the leather-bound book he had tossed aside in his study some hours earlier. "Everything you need for today is inside."

"Thank you," said Felix, looking curiously from the journal to Humphrey.

"Now, if you don't mind, I have chores to attend to," said Humphrey. "Number 10 looks like a *bomb* has hit it."

Felix was about to question Humphrey on his odd behaviour and choice of language when the doors to the Commons sprung open, and the members began to stream in. Felix stepped into the crowd and felt himself being carried along with the wave of bodies, eager to get inside and get on with the vote. He cut through the human traffic towards the front bench, sat and opened his journal, finding a note wedged into the middle pages close to the spine. He took the paper out, carefully unfolded it and read the message inside. It was from Amelia, it read:

Felix,

The name Pulleyn is descended from Guy Fawkes and his secret wife, Maria Pulleyn. Monteagle's and Cecil's predecessors betrayed Fawkes and the plotters to the king. The vote of confidence is a ploy. Part of an elaborate plot to blow up Parliament and finish Fawkes' work.

Amelia

Felix read the note in disbelief. He looked around the Commons at his colleagues taking their seats. Every one of their lives was in danger. He wanted to stand on his bench and shout from the top of his lungs. But with the house full of members baying for his blood, Felix knew that any attempt to disrupt the vote would be met with scepticism on both sides of the chamber, slowing down any possibility of an evacuation. It was a delicate balance. He wanted to keep his colleagues safe and prevent the destruction of Parliament but could not afford to arouse suspicion, not while the plotters were potentially watching and waiting to detonate their explosives.

Felix felt a terrible twisting in his stomach. He took several deep breaths, trying to calm his nerves and clear his mind, just as he had done at the George Inn. He needed to think fast if he was going to avoid the most catastrophic disaster of them all. He studied Amelia's note again. She had provided the missing link, the connection to the name, the place, the ancestry and the abductions, Guy Fawkes. Humphrey had even tried to warn him about the chosen weapon sitting in the parliamentary undercrofts, waiting to be detonated, in his own subtle way. All Felix had to do now was piece it all together and uncover the culprit.

Felix cast his mind back to the past few weeks' events. It was clear that whoever had orchestrated the abductions and the factory disasters had meticulously planned them to build up to this moment. He scanned the chamber, studying his fellow members. He felt confident that the mastermind behind everything was a politician or at least someone with a working knowledge of politics. How else could he have managed to manipulate events to such a degree? He would have to have known the minds of the Commons members, the TUC and the working people to have simultaneously caused national riots and forced a vote of no confidence in the government. Only a person with status and knowledge of the parliamentary system could have wielded that level of power.

Felix looked across the table at Barnaby Shaw, engaged in conversation with his leader, Milton Cavendish. Was Shaw the local politician Mrs. Hughes' brother had encountered at the Blossom Street Carriage Works? If so, was he working in his own interest or on his leader's orders? It seemed more than coincidental that Cavendish's attacks had followed so swiftly after each industrial disaster. First at Felix's parliamentary dinner, then in the House of Commons, and finally at the Carlton Club. But then, could he blame the opposition leader for using every opportunity available to capitalise on his opponent's failings? Wasn't it to be expected in the murky world of politics? A few well-timed political attacks certainly didn't implicate him in any criminal activity nor provide any reason to believe he was Mr. G. Pulleyn.

Felix felt his head beginning to spin. There was no definitive proof of either Shaw's or Cavendish's guilt; indeed, the culprit could be anyone in the chamber. He looked around at the rows of seated politicians and the many others who stood by the chamber doors. They all looked identical in their tailored suits, polished shoes and top hats. It was like a great magic trick, hiding the guilty man in a room filled with people who all looked the same. As had been the case so often over the past weeks, Felix once again found himself searching for a needle in a haystack. Only on this occasion, with a ticking bomb in his ear.

If he could not solve the mystery, the least he could do was raise the alarm and give the members a fighting chance of evacuating, even if he knew the vast majority would not survive. He stood up, gesturing towards the Speaker of the House, trying to get his attention, but the Speaker was too distracted by the opposition.

Suddenly a thought occurred to Felix. His time in power had always been like this, fighting to be seen and heard. The only constants in his life were the distractions, the meaningless debates and petty quarrels that diverted his attention away from the real work and his promises to the public. It had been the same with the case. Whoever had concocted this heinous plan had undoubtedly mastered the use of misdirection.

It had begun with the poker match, made to look like a business meeting between gentlemen when, in reality, it was a collection of strangers brought together to arrange the abduction of Lord Monteagle. Then there were the cards left at both abductions with their strange secret society symbols implying masonic involvement to throw the police off the scent. The factory disasters came next, each made to look like faulty machinery to incite the riots, followed by the burglary at the East India Club to cover the hostess's tracks and the murder of the two sailors at Shad Thames to expose the secret detective. Finally, a parliamentary confidence vote to divert the gaze away from a plot to blow up the Houses of Parliament and everyone inside. The instigator of the scheme had even gone to the trouble of amassing demonstrators outside to distract the police. It all slotted together perfectly.

Felix sat back down on his bench. Fortunately, all the major players were still inside the chamber. All he had to do was think of a way to make the mastermind show his hand. He quickly scribbled down two notes, calling for the house clerk. He placed them in the clerk's hand and whispered some instructions in his ear. The clerk had barely set off on his errand when the Speaker stood up, beckoning the chamber to come to order before proceeding with the day's business.

"Let us begin directly with the no-confidence motion. The Leader of the Opposition," he announced, motioning towards Cavendish.

Cavendish rose from his bench to a chorus of cheers.

"I beg to move that this House has no confidence in His Majesty's Government. Although I must say, there isn't much of a government left to have any confidence in," he joked, much to the amusement of the house.

Felix could feel Percy wriggling in his seat with rage. He placed a reassuring hand on his colleague's shoulder, trying to calm him down.

"Political pressure has been mounting for some weeks now," continued Cavendish, "leading to the protests you see outside Parliament today. There is only one plausible solution to these terrible events. The British people must be allowed to have their say. We need a general election!"

Cavendish stepped away from the table to a rapturous round of applause and waving handkerchiefs.

"The Prime Minister," called the Speaker to a muted response.

"Mr. Speaker," began Felix, rising to address the chamber. "It is only right for the opposition to challenge the government of the day. It is also their democratic duty to test the confidence of this House if they believe the circumstances warrant it. I make no complaint about that. Let us proceed with the vote."

Felix's words were greeted with shock and amazement. Never had the house witnessed such a capitulation from a serving prime minister. It was so spectacularly strange that a rare silence fell over the members. Even Percy, with all his bluster and gusto, turned to face Felix, speechless.

Felix, however, kept his eye on the clerk as he handed one of his notes to the Speaker before passing the other across the opposition bench to Shaw.

"The motion is…" began the Speaker, reading Felix's note, "that this House has no confidence in His Majesty's Government. As many as are of that opinion, say aye."

The chamber rang out with the sound of deafening ayes.

The Speaker waited for their yelps to die down before continuing.

"Those of the contrary, say no," he called to the whispered sound of a few loyal nos.

The members watched and waited for the Speaker to announce the result. Usually, with such an overwhelming and undeniable victory, there would be no need to take the motion to a physical vote. However, to everyone's surprise, the Speaker appeared to be stalling.

Choruses of *Come on!* and *The ayes have it!* rang out from the benches. After some confusion, the Speaker finally rose to declare the result.

"Division!" he shouted at the top of his voice to a cacophony of disbelieving boos. "Clear the lobbies!" he continued, undeterred.

The division bell rang out across the chamber, prompting the members to leave their benches and march towards the lobbies to cast their votes.

As they reluctantly rose from their seats and began to exit the chamber, Felix followed, staying close to the migrating herd and keeping a close eye on the Shadow Chancellor, Barnaby Shaw.

The Descendant

Barnaby Shaw left the Commons Chamber with the other disgruntled members. As his colleagues marched towards the voting lobbies to cast their votes, he quietly broke free from the pack, taking a different route through the Central Lobby towards the stone staircase leading to the historic Westminster undercrofts. He glanced over his shoulder, scared of being followed, as he scurried down the stairs towards the infamous dark vaults.

It took a few moments for Shaw's eyes to adjust to the low light. He could make out the undercroft's cracked and uneven floor, worn arches and long wooden beams and taste the polluted Thames on his lips. He scanned the cavernous rooms, trying to get a sense of their scale, but the dark shadows warped and manipulated their shape, giving the impression they were narrow in some areas and broad in others. Shaw plucked up the courage to move deeper into the crypt when he heard something moving in the shadows.

"Who's there?" he called out anxiously.

He edged forward, feeling the stone floor turn to grit under his shoes. He took another step only to find his path blocked by something broad and solid. He felt around in the darkness, his hands landing on a large wooden object, oval-shaped with strips of studded metal running along it. He leant forward, trying to focus on the obstruction, when he was overcome by a sharp dank odour that singed his nostrils. It was so strong that it even overpowered the potent stench of the Thames.

Shaw stepped back, gasping for air, when he heard movement again, coming from somewhere in the undercroft.

"What is the meaning of this?" he snapped into the darkness, a tremble of fear in his voice.

He waited, watching nervously, but again there was no response. He quickly turned, determined to leave, but in his haste, slipped on the grit, landing heavily on the floor. He pushed himself up, only to find he was covered in a dark, grainy substance. He tried to dust himself down, but the grit was too sticky to brush off. Suddenly the smell of burnt air was all over him. Hearing footsteps approaching unquestionably now, he stood up tall, bracing himself, when to his surprise, the plump frame of Thomas Percy emerged.

"What on earth is going on, Thomas?" barked Shaw, relieved to see a familiar face.

"I might ask you the same question," replied Percy.

"Excuse me? You asked to meet here. Although now I see that it was merely for your amusement. A very unsporting reaction to losing your place in government."

"I did not invite you here!" protested Percy.

"You mean to say you never sent me this message?" asked Shaw, reaching into his pocket and removing a note for Percy to see.

"I did not. Why, in heaven's name, would I ask you to meet me here, of all places?"

"But, if not you, then who?"

"It was me," called a voice from behind them.

Both men turned to see Felix emerge from the narrow stairwell carrying a small lantern.

"What is the meaning of this, Prime Minister?" demanded Shaw.

"Yes, what's all this about, Felix?" asked Percy.

"Life can be a rather strange undertaking, wouldn't you agree?" asked Felix, looking around the dark undercroft. "I've always had a bizarre curiosity about other people's lives and what drives them to do what they do. Perhaps that's why I chose a life in public service."

"Have you completely lost your mind?" asked Shaw, beginning to lose his patience.

"Far from it," replied Felix, holding up his journal. "You see, I make a note of all my thoughts in this book to insure against that very thing. It's easy to second-guess oneself in this role, to believe things are one way when they are, in fact, another. Although even my journal doesn't guarantee against tying oneself in mental knots. I used it to note all the information about the missing lords in the naive hope of piecing the puzzle together and finding them. But my inexperience in such matters was abundantly obvious throughout, and regardless of my detailed annotations, the perpetrator always managed to keep a step ahead of me. Well, more than just a step, if I'm honest. Until today, that is."

"What are you suggesting?" asked Shaw.

"That the abductions of the lords and the recent spate of factory disasters were all orchestrated by the same person to destabilise the government and force a vote of no confidence."

"That sounds a little far-fetched, Felix," added Percy apologetically.

"It sounds utterly absurd, Thomas," agreed Felix. "Hence why it took me such a long time to recognise the threat. And why so many people have suffered as a consequence. A mistake I will regret for the rest of my life."

"And what threat is that exactly?" asked Shaw.

"That burnt odour wafting off you is gunpowder. And somewhere in this undercroft are barrels of the stuff, ready to be detonated, just as Guy Fawkes had planned three hundred years ago."

"Guy Fawkes?" chortled Shaw. "You really have lost your mind."

Felix lifted the lantern to reveal a large wooden cask on the floor in front of the men. He moved his light across the room, exposing several more stacked on top of each other.

"How could you?" said Percy, facing Shaw.

"It wasn't me!" protested Shaw. "I had nothing to do with any gunpowder!"

Percy brushed Shaw's arm, lifting his fingers to his nose to smell the gunpowder stuck to the Shadow Chancellor's clothes.

"That was an accident!" squealed Shaw. "I slipped in the darkness. It's all over the floor."

"Barnaby Shaw," began Percy, taking the Shadow Chancellor by the arm, "I arrest you in the name of His Majesty, King Edward VII, on the charge of high treason!"

"This is preposterous!" bellowed Shaw. "I've been framed."

"Lead the way, Felix," said Percy, ignoring Shaw's pleas.

But Felix didn't move. Instead, he remained rooted to the spot, with a look of deep regret and sadness etched on his face.

"It's not Shaw, Thomas," he said, the pain clear in his voice. "It's you."

"Don't be ridiculous, Felix," snorted Percy. "How could you possibly believe I—?…"

"I didn't," interrupted Felix. "I didn't dare to believe it could be you until today. You see, having put it all together, I knew the culprit was likely to be a member of parliament, given his power and influence and his intimate knowledge of the system. All I had to do was draw him out. So, I decided to try some misdirection of my own. I asked the Speaker to call a division and send the members to the voting lobbies. It was the only way to separate Shaw from the others and divert him here to the undercroft. I knew that the culprit, whoever he was, and with his senses on full alert, would have noticed even the smallest threat to his plan, let alone the Shadow Chancellor receiving a curious note in the chamber and suspiciously sneaking away. Driven by the fear of having his plot exposed, I assumed the guilty man would follow to prevent him from raising the alarm. I just didn't expect it to be you, Thomas."

The three men stood in silence for a moment.

"In the end," Percy whispered at last, "it's those who are closest to us who disappoint us the most." He let go of Shaw's arm and quickly pulled a gun out of his pocket. "Keep your hands where I can see them," he shouted, pointing the weapon at Felix and Shaw.

"It's over, Thomas. The Speaker will have evacuated the lobbies by now, as I instructed. There is nothing left to gain from this."

"Oh, there's still plenty to gain, Prime Minister," replied Percy. "I can still raise this House of corruption to the ground in his honour. It's the least I can do."

"But why?" asked Shaw, confused.

"Why?" repeated Percy. "Because, you pompous cretin, it's people like you, the landed, wealthy, privileged power-grabbers, who have kept the British people from fulfilling their true potential all these centuries. This corrupt establishment that only gratifies a chosen few at the expense of millions and worships a monarch like a god is no longer fit for purpose. He knew that three hundred years ago and was punished for trying to bring about real, meaningful change."

"So that's why you orchestrated the murder of so many people?" asked Felix. "To bring about meaningful change?"

"My name is Guy!" shouted Percy. "Guy Pulleyn!"

"That name does not exist, Thomas. It's nothing more than a shadow. A soiled past trying to lurch its way back up from the cesspit of human indecency."

"You will soon regret that comment, Prime Minister," said Percy, hearing a boat approaching.

"The police!" exclaimed Shaw, relieved.

"I think not," replied Percy as a dark barge appeared on the riverside. "You see, the prime minister has a healthy distrust of the police. I can't say I blame him. Never trust a man you cannot buy or scare, and Commissioner Thompson, well, he's boringly honourable. It's these ex-army types; their incorruptibility is of no use to anyone. Although, he did let slip the name of his officer working secretly in the Docklands. That proved very useful in throwing the police off our scent and striking some renewed fear into people. Two birds with one stone, as the expression goes."

Felix felt his stomach lurch. He had misjudged the commissioner and, in doing so, had kept a valuable ally at arm's length this entire time. Had he trusted Thompson from the start, he may have prevented the factory disasters and saved the lives of those poor victims.

"I did warn you," Percy continued. "Do you remember that night, in Downing Street, when Thompson first presented the card to us? I said leave it to the authorities, Felix. Of course, I knew you wouldn't listen. You're the prime minister. You're too high and mighty to listen to your lowly colleagues or the people you are supposed to represent. It's just another example of the entitlement this outdated system confers on a person. Well, not any more."

Percy turned to face a group of burly men approaching from the barge. At their head, marshalling the abducted lords, was the intimidating frame of Ezra Fox.

"You're late!" barked Percy.

"We had some trouble on the river," replied Ezra.

"I thought you owned the river?"

"There were twice as many blue shirts as usual. That's twice as many hands to bribe."

"I'm aware of how bribes work," squawked Percy. "Your failure could've sabotaged the entire plan. Remember who pulled you out of the gutter as a boy and fixed your eye. You'd be nothing without me!"

"It won't happen again," seethed Ezra.

"It had better not. Now tie them up!" ordered Percy.

Ezra and his men rushed forward and took hold of Felix and Shaw, strapping them to the gunpowder barrels alongside the two missing lords.

"It's not too late, Thomas," said Felix, wrestling with his binds.

"You're wrong, Felix," replied Percy. "It's nearly three hundred years too late."

"And what about her? What about Maria Pulleyn? Is this what she would have wanted, too?" asked Felix.

"What do you know about her?" fumed Percy.

"I know that she married Guy Fawkes and that they had a child whose line continues to this day."

"You know nothing. She had to watch her husband, the father of her child, tortured on the rack, day after day, until it broke him.

And even when he could barely lift his arm, he was forced to sign a confession just to end the excruciating brutality. But that was just the beginning for her. Her pain endured. After the execution, she wouldn't dare retain her married name or even her birth name, Pulleyn. Both had become toxic. She had no identity, and neither did her child. She was forced to remarry. Can you imagine the shame? Her new husband agreed to take the boy on if he denied his name. But the boy never forgot his history. No, he passed the dirty family secret on, and it continued to be passed on through the generations until it finally got to me. By then, the family had moved south, adopted a new accent, and become *respectable*. But the injustice never left."

"Injustice?" questioned Felix. "Listen to yourself. He attempted to blow up the Houses of Parliament, to murder hundreds of people."

"How naive you are, Felix. The history books may paint the picture of a heartless monster, but as we know, the victors get to write their narratives, and, as always, they bend the truth to fit their purpose. I think it's high time you all had a little history lesson. But this time, the truth, not that rubbish the establishment feeds our children to keep them complicit in its lies and corruptions."

Percy clicked his fingers, prompting one of Ezra's men to step forward. The man lifted a thick wooden stick in the air and wrapped a piece of cloth around it before drenching it in kerosene. Ezra lit a match, touching it to the soaked cloth, which burst into flames, instantly filling the undercroft with light. Suddenly the colossal mountain of gunpowder-laden barrels stacked under the dark arch became visible for all to see. Felix stared at the barrels in horror. There was enough to blow up the Houses of Parliament many times over. Having lured his enemy to the undercrofts and instructed the Speaker to clear the Commons, Felix had naively believed that he had averted the danger. He hadn't expected to find himself tied to another barrel facing a similar fate to the one he had survived in the George Inn. Having spent all this time scouring London's underworld for the lords, not to mention sacrificing his role as prime minister, he was now about to share in their fate.

Ezra's man handed the torch to Percy, who approached Felix and the men tied to the barrels.

"The gunpowder plot is not quite the story you had handed down to you in your knickerbockers, woollen stockings and Eton collars," he began, crouching down. "No, it's much more calculated than the history books would have you believe. The lords, Robert Cecil and Monteagle, were falling out of favour with King James, so they concocted a most ingenious plan to win him over. First, they found some disgruntled Catholics, active opponents of the Tudor Reformation, and groomed them into believing they'd been chosen to carry out God's work. They then furnished their unwitting recruits with all the resources and religious indoctrination required, even meeting with them secretly to reinforce their grand calling. However, once the plot had been cemented and the wheels were in motion, they betrayed their co-conspirators, catching them in the unholy act and exposing their treasonous plan. They were made to look like heroes, the King's saviours, while my ancestor was labelled one of history's greatest villains and disposed of like a pawn on a chessboard. They destroyed him and his wife and condemned generations of their descendants, each tainted with the mark his name came to bear. A mark that carries to this day, but no further."

Percy stood up and backed away. Ezra stepped forward with a small barrel of gunpowder and used it to run a thick line of the black sand from the bound men across the undercroft to the riverside, where the barge was moored.

"It's time," called Percy, instructing the men to exit. Once they had all cleared the undercroft for the barge, Percy approached the gunpowder trail, hovering his flaming torch over a small pile at the end of the line.

"You don't have to do this, Thomas," implored Felix.

"I'm afraid I do. Goodbye, Felix," said Percy, leaning down to ignite the gunpowder.

His torch had almost touched the black grains when Percy was disturbed by the sound of a rifle being cocked somewhere in the shadows.

"Who's there?" he shouted, pointing his torch into the darkness.

"Step away from the gunpowder, Home Secretary," called a voice in a mock British accent.

"Why don't you come out and show us your face?" said Percy, inching forward to get a better look.

Suddenly a gunshot fired out of the darkness, brushing the wall above Percy's head and causing him to duck for cover.

"I said, step away!" the voice repeated, a hint of an American accent breaking through. "Or I'll shoot you where you stand."

"Is that you, Professor?" mocked Percy. "If you shoot me, I'll happily send us all to kingdom come."

"You're bluffing," replied Amelia, stepping out of the shadows and pointing a long Winchester at Percy. "You wouldn't risk hurting yourself. You prefer to murder innocents instead."

"This is not the Wild West, Professor. We don't bluff here," replied Percy, throwing his torch onto the line of gunpowder, and setting a spark racing along its thick black trail.

Amelia instinctively pulled the trigger, firing her gun at Percy, who dived to one side, barely avoiding the oncoming bullet. She hurried to reload before Ezra and his men, having heard the melee, began to remerge from the barge, but her gun jammed. Outnumbered and outgunned, she leapt towards the arch for cover, as they began to return fire, but was too late and took a bullet in her torso, falling back into the shadows.

"Amelia!" cried Felix.

But there was no response. Only silence.

"Shame," remarked Percy, "an unnecessary sacrifice. Now we've both lost someone to this accursed building."

"You won't get away with this," said Felix, his voice tinged with fury.

"I'm afraid I already have." replied Percy, signalling his men to leave. "Goodbye Felix."

Percy turned and hurried towards the barge. Once on board, Ezra lifted the gangway and the vessel set off down the Thames.

In the silence, Felix watched the spark cut through the dark undercroft, drawing closer to the men and the barrels. He could feel Lord Monteagle shaking furiously beside him and Shaw reaching his leg out, trying to break the line of gunpowder. But none of it mattered. All he could think about was Amelia.

He suddenly heard the slightest sound coming from the shadows.

"Amelia?" he called out hopefully.

"Yes?" she replied.

"Are you okay?"

"I wouldn't say I'm okay, but I'm alive."

"Can you make it to the gunpowder?"

"I can try," she replied, crawling out of the shadows.

Amelia shuffled across the cold stone floor, blood seeping from the wound in her shoulder. She slowly inched forward, groaning with every movement, trying to catch up with the flickering light hurrying along the trail. As she pushed through the pain, closing the distance, she reached for the spark only to come up short and watch it race by her hand. Aware that she would not catch it in time and in excruciating pain, Amelia rolled onto her back and closed her eyes.

"Amelia!?" implored Felix as the two gagged lords groaned and gesticulated at her not to give up.

But the professor remained on her back, incapacitated, and bleeding out on the stone floor as the spark hurried along the trail and past their feet towards the waiting barrels. The men closed their eyes, tensed their bodies, mumbled their prayers, and waited, and waited, and waited, when…nothing happened. The spark hit the barrels at speed and immediately fizzled out. They looked at each other in disbelief.

"What happened?" asked Felix.

"They were empty," groaned Amelia.

"What do you mean, empty?" asked Shaw, still in shock.

"I mean, we emptied their contents hours ago," replied Amelia, barely conscious.

"Why didn't you say?" asked Felix angrily. "And who is *we* exactly?"

"We…is us," replied a voice as two figures in smart suits approached from the riverside entrance.

"Them," added Amelia.

The figures stepped into the light. Felix saw that one was wearing a crow mask, the other an eagle. They were followed by a group of younger, more athletic figures wearing monkey masks. The monkeys swarmed the undercroft. They untied Felix, Shaw and the lords and lifted Amelia off the stone floor, taking her to a waiting boat for medical assistance.

"Prime Minister," bowed the figure in the crow's mask.

"Did you catch them, Percy and his men?" asked Felix.

"No," replied the woman in the eagle mask. "We let them escape."

"What?" said Felix in disbelief. "But if you had time to empty the barrels, surely you had time to plan their capture."

"The Home Secretary and his men are fully exposed now, Prime Minister," said the man in the crow mask. "They have nowhere else to hide, but they do have a further purpose to serve. They've become the bait through which we hope to catch a larger and much more significant fish."

Felix took a moment to study the figure in the crow mask. His mannerisms and tone seemed oddly familiar, as if he'd met him somewhere before. He looked down at the man's clothes, noticing his freshly polished boots and the precisely pressed creases in his trousers: signs of his many years in the British army.

King Edward VII

It had been over a fortnight since Felix had foiled the plot to blow up the Houses of Parliament, but he was still finding it difficult to sleep. He blamed himself for not spotting Percy's betrayal earlier or alerting the police to his investigation sooner. Although having noticed similarities between the commissioner and the masked mason in the parliamentary undercrofts, Felix had begun to wonder if Thompson had known about his investigation this whole time and whether disclosing the information would have made any meaningful difference. Even so, the thought brought Felix little comfort.

After another night of tossing and turning, he was relieved to see the sun finally rise outside and hear the Downing Street staff spring to life. With the vote of confidence lost and a general election looming, Felix had been summoned to Buckingham Palace for an audience with the King. It was like being asked to meet with the hangman in advance of him securing a noose around your neck.

It didn't matter that Felix had exposed his former Home Secretary's plot or that news of his astonishing bravery had dominated the front pages of newspapers worldwide; he was still subject to the democratic laws of the land and a defeat in the House of Commons was still a defeat, regardless of his perceived heroism.

Felix approached the old, cushioned valet stand where Humphrey had assembled a finely pressed suit, polished shoes, a tie and a perfectly folded handkerchief for his jacket pocket. He took a moment to examine the beautifully tailored clothes hanging off the elegant piece of furniture. How he would miss the traditions of the job, he thought. The dazzling pomp and ceremony that made it so uniquely British. Yet, having listened to Percy's tirade about the *entitlement of the few*, he suddenly felt self-aware, almost unworthy of such treatment, even if prime minister. Perhaps his former friend's words had merit, despite his despicable actions.

"It's not wise to keep His Majesty waiting," said Humphrey, entering the room with a tea tray.

Felix smiled, taking hold of his clothes.

"It takes more than just a fine suit and some polished shoes to make a man," he said, reflecting on the past few weeks.

"Indeed, it does," agreed Humphrey, placing the tray to one side. "But this is no ordinary suit. It was given to you by the British people. It is your armour; wear it with pride."

Felix placed a warm hand on his steward's shoulder. "Thank you, Humphrey."

"I didn't say I liked the suit," replied Humphrey. "The colours are a little bold, and the cut is far too modern for my taste."

Felix rolled his eyes in amusement.

"Now, will you be taking the car, or should I prepare the footmen for the long wet walk?" asked Humphrey.

"The car will do nicely, thank you."

Having finished his preparations, Felix descended the long staircase towards the main hallway. To his surprise, his staff had gathered in two lines by the door to form a guard of honour and wish him well. Felix nodded his thanks to each as he passed before stepping through the iconic black door and into his waiting car.

The drive to Buckingham Palace was marked by silence. During his two years in government, Felix's meetings with King Edward VII had always been brief and formal. He could feel a nervous anxiety in his chest and the sweat tingling on his neck. How could he possibly explain the past few weeks' events to his King? He sat back in his seat and closed his eyes, playing everything over in his mind, trying to order his thoughts and prepare his words. Was it better to keep his explanations brief or disclose every detail, regardless of the negative picture it would paint of his time as prime minister?

Felix's car drove past St. James's Park and onto the Mall, following the long road to Buckingham Palace, the King's lavish London residence. Originally known as Buckingham House until King George III purchased the entire plot from the Duke of Buckingham as a private residence for his wife, Queen Charlotte, it had been through several structural enhancements, the last and most significant of which had been to the east wing and the famous central balcony where Queen Victoria had watched her troops depart for the Crimean War, and the landmark Felix now approached.

Having passed through the palace's black iron gates with their royal crests of golden lions, unicorns and cherubs, Felix's car finally stopped in the gravel courtyard, and a royal footman opened the door.

"This way, Prime Minister," he said, ushering Felix through a high-arched passageway towards the Grand Entrance and the palace's main hall.

Felix followed his guide up the winding black-and-gold staircase and across the gallery's scarlet carpet towards the King's audience chamber. The footman knocked twice on the door before opening it and stepping inside.

"The Prime Minister, Your Majesty," Felix heard him say.

Felix waited for the footman to wave him forward before entering the room. The chamber was elaborately decorated and entirely overrun with antique furniture, family portraits and gifts from world leaders. A small ornate lamp lit the area around the King's desk, where thick plumes of smoke spiralled into the air from his cigar.

"Your Highness," bowed Felix.

King Edward VII was a heavy man with warm eyes and a neatly cropped beard shaped into a rounded ducktail at the front of his chin. To Felix's surprise, he was dressed in a casual tweed jacket and wore a Homburg hat rather than the formal suit or naval uniform one would expect for an official meeting with the prime minister. But then, the King was renowned for his love of fashion.

"Please, take a seat, Prime Minister," he said, motioning towards one of the chairs in front of his desk.

Felix crossed the room and sat down.

"It is strange to have to tell one's prime minister that having performed such a heroic service for his country, he will now have to relinquish his position and make way for a general election," said the King.

"Heroic may be a little strong, Your Majesty."

"Nonsense!" countered the King. "If anything, it undervalues your efforts."

"But I—"

"Yes, I know," interjected the King, swatting Felix's doubts away like an irritating fly. "You made mistakes, took your time, made bad choices, and didn't sniff it out earlier. Do you think you're the only leader who ever felt guilty about his decisions? Heaven knows being the prime minister is not an enviable job, like being a King. All that is required is to do your best with the time you are given."

"Thank you, Your Majesty," replied Felix, suddenly feeling reassured.

"Call me Bertie," said the King, looking down at the open diary on his desk. "Now, shall we say November 30th for the general election?" he asked, marking the date. "Roughly six weeks. That should give you enough time to muster the troops and give the opposition a run for their money."

"Me?" replied Felix, amazed.

"But of course." The King smiled. "Many have walked through the doors of Number 10, but few have been curious, benevolent or adventurous enough to truly understand what it is to be the British prime minister."

Felix stared at the King in amazement. Did he know about Old Pye Street, or was his choice of words merely a coincidence?

"Some of us are born to this life," continued the King, "no matter the cost, regardless of our failures and insecurities, and even though we're quite sure to be unloved and misunderstood. That's what it means to serve."

The King stood up and offered Felix his hand. Felix shook it warmly, then turned and departed. He followed the footman through the palace, reflecting on the King's parting words, then stepped out into the large forecourt. He passed back under the arch and across the gravel square, approaching his waiting car, when something in his periphery caught his attention. Felix quickly spun around to see a figure hurtling towards him at speed. Having evaded the royal footmen, a large man in a ragged suit with greying stubble and wild eyes launched himself at Felix's feet as though begging for money.

It took Felix a few moments to recognise him.

"Thomas?!" he said, taken aback by Percy's appearance.

"They're trying to kill me, Felix!" ranted Percy, looking over his shoulder. "I have nowhere else to go. Please, help me! Take me in! I want to be arrested! I confess! I confess to it all and more besides. Please arrest me! I can tell you things about your enemies that will make you—"

Percy was about to deliver the next word when a small wooden dart struck him in the side of his neck, rendering him instantly unconscious. The footmen quickly formed a protective circle around Felix, scanning the gates for any sign of the shooter. But with the palace surrounded by royal parks, it was almost impossible to make out anyone among the dense forest of trees. After a nervous wait and confident that the danger had passed, Felix pushed past the footmen and rushed to his former friend's side, lifting Percy's body to check his pulse, but his heart had stopped. Thomas Percy was dead, poisoned by whatever toxin the wooden dart had injected into his bloodstream.

Felix looked down at his peaceful face. He didn't agree with Percy's twisted beliefs or condone his actions but felt profound grief at seeing his life ended so barbarically. He'd wanted the former Home Secretary to face justice in the courts and for the

British judicial system to decide his punishment. That, after all, was what civilised societies did. The shock of Percy's sudden appearance and the manner of his death left Felix reeling with a renewed sense of injustice and a sinking feeling about what was yet to come.

The Hostess

Given the weather and time of year, Green Park was incredibly busy that afternoon. The cold had done little to dampen the spirits of those who liked to frequent its rugged grounds and abundant wildlife. They had seen everything this park had thrown up over the years, the snow, the sleet, the heavy winds and rain, but few of them had ever witnessed a sight such as Seema Sharma.

They watched in awe as she drifted elegantly through the park in her traditional silk sari, rich with bold and enticing colours. An ornate gold nose stud, matching earrings and rows of gilded bracelets on both arms pointed to her wealth and superior social status, and the tiara in her sleek black hair sparkled with gems from the subcontinent. In one hand, she held the hems of her rich garments, keeping them off the muddy floor, and in the other, a long wooden stick with images of past Indian heroes expertly carved along its frame.

Seema Sharma made her way through the park, stepping out onto Piccadilly. Parked on the roadside next to the construction site of César Ritz's new hotel was a white-and-gold Rolls-Royce V8. It was one of only three ever made and had attracted the attention of several passers-by as it sat idle, waiting for its owner. As she approached the car, Seema Sharma's steward, a tall Indian man in an elegant silk suit with the emblem of the Royal House of Jodhpur on his breast pocket, greeted her.

"Welcome back, Your Highness," he said, opening the car door.

Seema Sharma handed him the blowpipe and stepped into the Rolls-Royce.

"The Indian Embassy, Vinay," she commanded.

Acknowledgements

Writing acknowledgments, it turns out, is harder than writing the book itself! Over the years, I've spoken to so many people about Felix, receiving countless kind words and invaluable tips. If I've missed anyone, please accept my heartfelt apologies.

This book has been a monumental undertaking, much larger than I ever envisioned. Just put one foot in front of the other, I used to naively tell myself, after a few weeks you'll have got somewhere—try a few years, and then some!

During this time, I've bent many ears and leaned heavily on the goodwill of others. To my friends and family who've smiled and nodded as I read endless excerpts to them, pretending to be interested in my ramblings about historical London, secret passages, and fictitious Prime Ministers, I owe a great debt. None deserve thanks more than my amazing wife and daughters, who have heard every line and lived through every corner I've written myself into. They have helped me detach from the occasional stress and solitude of writing and have been the antidote to bad news or terrible writing days.

At the heart of this story is legacy, so I must also acknowledge my family: my parents, my three brothers—Tony, Simon, and Michael—my aunts and uncles, my nieces and nephews, and my many, many cousins, who've all endured a lifetime of my relentless historical enthusiasms. My brothers, and cousin Andrew, were the first to read the book and have always been supportive and encouraging. It's always been our journey.

Thank you to my friend Leon, who went above and beyond by naming his first son Felix. There are friends, and then there are FRIENDS, and I'm fortunate to have many of the latter. They've read early versions of the book, provided invaluable feedback, lifted me through disappointments (there have been many), and helped me celebrate victories. There are too many to name, but they know who they are and they know what they mean to me.

I'd like to extend my gratitude to my agent, Emily Smith, who has been incredibly supportive and always brilliant with advice. It's wonderful to have someone in your corner genuinely excited to see you achieve your dreams. A special thanks also to Sophie Kelleher for being part of this book's journey, along with Matthew Harvey and Fiona Baird. I'm eternally grateful to the team at Neem Tree Press. Working with such a passionate and dedicated group of people who showed immediate love and passion for the book has been a privilege and a joy. I really hope these books make a big splash for us all.

I also want to thank some of my influences: C. J. Sansom, Philippa Gregory, Hilary Mantel, Elif Shafak, The Rest is History Podcast, Legacy Podcast, Historic Royal Palaces, and possibly my biggest influence of all, Corfe Castle. This glorious ruin in Swanage, Dorset, was the site of my first school trip. Its cannon-battered shell and leaning walls made me feel like I'd stepped back in time. I bought a pack of cards from the gift shop featuring every king and queen of England and memorised them all. It became my party trick, a ten-year-old who could name any monarch from any year. Corfe Castle sparked my love for history as a boy, a passion that has only grown with age. This is my chance to say thank you for that gift.

Also, a heartfelt thanks to all of the terrible Prime Ministers who held office over the years. You have driven me to write and craft a politician who the British people can be proud of—someone with integrity and decency, a beacon for future leaders, and a figure who can bring some much-needed hope and honour to such an important and historical role. I couldn't have done it without you.

Most importantly, I want to extend my deepest gratitude to you, the readers. Your support and willingness to embark on this journey with me mean the world. I am excited to take you on more journeys and to write more stories for Felix. Thank you for being part of this adventure.

Author Biography

Mario Theodorou is an award-winning screenwriter, director, and author with an eclectic body of work spanning both comedy and drama. Selected for the BBC Drama Writer's Programme, he was named on the BBC's Hotlist of 200 emerging talents. His original commissions include projects for BBC Drama, BBC Radio 4 and Sky. His short films, *Anonymous*, *Echo* and *The Gifted Hypothesis* have picked up numerous awards, including selections and nominations for multiple Oscar-, BAFTA-, and BIFA-qualifying film festivals, as well as the Best Drama prize at Cannes Shorts. He is also a BAFTA member and serves on the Kingston International Film Festival board.

Read on for an excerpt from the next novel in the series, *Felix Grey and the Seven Assassins*.

Felix Grey and the Seven Assassins

The *Arcadia* cast a vast shadow over the River Thames as it weaved through the Isle of Dogs and past Greenwich on its route to the bustling East India Docks. A marvel of maritime engineering, P&O's new iron and steel titan weighed as much as Blackfriars Bridge, stood as tall as three telephone poles, and carried over five hundred passengers and seven thousand tons of cargo.

Having departed Bombay less than two weeks earlier, the giant steamer had made short work of the Arabian Sea, threaded its way through the Suez Canal, and sped across the Mediterranean all in record time, picking up eager passengers and vital supplies destined for its final stop: London.

However, it wasn't the arrival of the enormous steamship that caught the attention of the dock hands and crane operators and brought their work to a shuddering halt—it was the sudden arrival of the Metropolitan Police. They had turned out in force and were waiting impatiently on the dock for the Arcadia to finally come to a stop. Something had happened on the ship during the long journey from India, something serious enough to require seven police officers, one motorised vehicle, two bicycles, and a huge horse-drawn Black Maria for transporting prisoners.

Having watched the heavy ship crawl to a halt, Police Inspector Ken Jenkins, a stout man with a balding head and cropped moustache, shouted up to the crew to open the hatch. The large metal door had barely touched down on the East India Docks' concrete floor when Jenkins and his constables eagerly leaped on board. While his men spread out to search the ship, Jenkins made his way through the giant steamer toward steerage, where the third-class passengers were being held by the staff in anticipation of his arrival.

"This is all of them, sir," said the waiting steward, waving a hand at the horribly cramped and fed-up passengers. "Well, all of them except for Clifford Bambury, of course."

"Still no sign of him then?" asked Jenkins.

The steward leaned in, keeping his voice low. "We haven't seen or heard of him for nearly two days. We've checked the entire ship and he's nowhere to be found. My guess is that some of this lot may have done for him."

"What are you saying?" asked Jenkins.

"I'm saying that there are a lot of people down here in very tight and uncomfortable conditions. Steerage has a way of getting to folk, you see. Some get irritated by the confinement quicker than others, and a man like Bambury, who was partial to drinking and gambling, could have easily rubbed some of those irritated people the wrong way."

"You believe someone in here has killed him?" asked Jenkins.

"Killed, thrown overboard…there's no better place to hide evidence of a crime than in the deep blue."

Jenkins looked around the room, taking in the clothes and faces of the passengers. He'd never seen such a varied collection of people in one space at the same time.

"A villainous-looking bunch, wouldn't you agree, Captain?" whispered the steward, clearly enjoying the moment.

"It's Inspector. Inspector Jenkins."

"Nice to make your acquaintance, Inspector. I'm David Scarborough, although the crew call me Davy, you know, on account of us being at sea most of the time and Davy Jones."

"And what exactly is your role on the *Arcadia*, Mr. Scarborough?" asked Jenkins.

"I'm the steerage steward. Although, as fate would have it, my father actually wanted me to be a copper, you know, an inspector like you. I've always had a nose for rooting out the wrong'uns."

"How interesting," replied Jenkins dryly, eager to get back to the matter at hand.

"Hold on!" boomed the steward excitedly. "I've had an idea. I could help you, with the questioning. I've spent the last two weeks with this lot, racking up tons of invaluable intelligence. It wouldn't be hard for me to get them to talk."

Jenkins raised his hands to protest when he was interrupted by one of his constables entering the room. The officer approached and quietly whispered something into Jenkins' ear, before receiving instructions from the inspector in return.

"So, are we on then?" pressed the steward. "I could use the first mate's office, or the second's, or, come to think of it, more likely the mess. But don't worry, it'll be quiet now we've made land."

"That won't be necessary," replied Jenkins, motioning towards his officers who had begun rounding up a few male passengers while directing the rest toward the exits. "We'll take a handful down to the station for questioning, for now. We have the full passenger list for the others, should we need to bring any of them in."

"You're letting them all go?" asked the steward, shocked.

"There's no blood, no body, no weapon or witness to any violence…we can't very well detain all these people after two weeks at sea on the slim possibility that a crime has been committed here."

"Slim possibility!" repeated the steward, aghast.

"Who's to say that Mr. Bambury isn't hiding somewhere on this ship right now, determined not to be found? Or that he didn't disembark during one of your stops?"

"He was on the ship after we left Egypt, our final stop. I saw him myself."

"Then who's to say he didn't decide to jump off? You admitted yourself that he was a drunk and a gambler. Perhaps he'd had enough and decided to end his unfortunate life prematurely?"

"I very much doubt it," replied the steward, casting a sneering glance at the passengers as they hastily gathered their things and sped for the doors. "You don't know what it's been like down here. Most of them were barely civilised to begin with. After two weeks at sea, some stopped being human entirely."

Irritated by the steward's vitriolic comment, Jenkins shifted his attention away only to notice an Indian woman leaning forward, clearly eavesdropping on their conversation. As he turned towards her, she quickly averted her gaze, hastily gathering her things and making her way towards the exit with the other passengers.

"You see," continued the steward, observing the woman's odd behaviour. "They're all in on it."

Curious, Jenkins followed after her. "Excuse me," he called out gently, but the woman kept her head down and continued striding forward.

"You there," he called again, quickening his pace, determined to catch her before she reached the door.

"Wait!" he bellowed firmly, reaching out and placing a hand on her shoulder.

The woman turned and looked up at him, her expression guarded. Jenkins took a step back, so as not to frighten her.

"Apologies, I'm Police Inspector Ken Jenkins," he said slowly and clearly, so that she could understand him. "I'd like to ask you some questions."

"You may ask, but I might not have the answers you are seeking," replied the woman in perfect English, her mild Indian accent barely noticeable.

"You speak English?" asked Jenkins.

"I had an English tutor and nanny growing up," she replied calmly.

Jenkins looked her up and down, taking note of her expensive clothes and travel case. "How is it that an Indian woman with such fine belongings and whose family could afford the luxury of an English tutor and nanny is now traveling alone in steerage?"

"My father had his wealth and home taken by the British, like many Indians before and many more after him. We were, however, permitted to keep some of our personal belongings. You British like people to keep up appearances, even when you've taken almost everything from them," she explained.

"Forgive me, it was a poor choice of question," said Jenkins, feeling immediately remorseful.

"Do you mind if I eat while you continue with your questions?" asked the woman. "The long journey and lack of sleep have taken a toll on my energy levels. I get tired very quickly and need a little dose of sugar to revive me."

"Please, do as you must," replied Jenkins.

The woman leaned down and rummaged through her bag, pulling out a small plate wrapped in a pristine white cloth. She carefully untied the knot and removed the cloth, revealing an array of small Indian desserts.

"If I may," continued Jenkins, "did you come across Mr. Clifford Bambury at any time during your journey? Only, I noticed you listening intently to my conversation with the steward before hurriedly departing."

The woman held out the plate towards Jenkins. "Can I tempt you?" she asked.

"No, I really mustn't," replied Jenkins, keen to get an answer to his question.

"You know, in some cultures, it's considered impolite to refuse lovingly prepared food," said the woman. "Especially when asking for something in return. Go on, no one will see; the ship is practically deserted."

Jenkins looked around the ship, surprised at how quickly it had emptied. The cramped and overcrowded space he had entered moments before now seemed open and spacious as his constables led the last of the passengers to the exits.

"That's the lot, Inspector," called one of his men. "Should we hold the vehicles outside for you?"

Jenkins considered the question, then glanced down at the mysterious Indian woman standing in front of him. On the surface, she appeared harmless enough, quite ordinary actually: a single woman, small in stature, traveling alone to a foreign country with a plate of homemade sweets. Yet, there was just something about her that compelled him to want to stay and delve a little deeper.

"No need, Constable," he replied. "You go on ahead. I'll meet you back at the station shortly."

"Very well," replied the constable, leading his fellow officers out.

With the room finally emptied, Jenkins turned back to the woman, who held the plate a little higher. Consenting to the trade, he reached out and took the smallest dessert on offer: a golden-brown ball made of flour, butter, sugar, and cardamom, known as a laddu, and took a small bite.

"Delicious," he said politely, though not entirely convinced by the sweet's unfamiliar taste. "Now that we've honoured your cultural traditions, perhaps you could indulge mine by answering my questions?"

"Very well," replied the woman, lowering the plate.

"Did you come across Mr. Clifford Bambury at any time during your journey?" asked Jenkins again.

"Not until yesterday," replied the woman. "We spent almost two weeks occupying the same space, and I hadn't noticed him once, until yesterday."

Jenkins leaned forward, intrigued by her answer. "And what happened yesterday to suddenly bring him to your attention?"

"To understand that, I need to take you back to the start of our journey," replied the woman, lowering herself into a cross-legged sitting position on the floor.

Curious, Jenkins took a seat opposite her.

"When we first set eyes on the *Arcadia* in Bombay, there was an enormous wave of excitement," she began. "People were in awe of this floating metal city that had come to take them over the wide sea and change their lives forever. We all boarded with such hope and adventure, regardless of our backgrounds or social status.

"For those fortunate enough to travel first class, the journey promised to be an ostentatious display of modern travel. They would luxuriate in spacious cabins with private bathrooms, dine in elegant restaurants offering lavish menus, relax in comfortable lounges, enjoy smoking rooms, peruse libraries, and even stroll on the ship's wide promenades.

"For those in second class, the journey would be a more modest affair, with basic accommodations and fewer luxuries, yet still far beyond anything they had ever seen or experienced before.

"However, for us poorer folk in steerage, the two weeks at sea would prove to be a monumental test of endurance as we grappled with cramped quarters, shared facilities, and the sickness-inducing movements of the ship. Confined to the bowels of the *Arcadia*, we felt every swell of water, every passing current, and every one of the ship's cumbersome manoeuvres with greater stomach-churning intensity than our fellow passengers in first and second class.

"With little else to do aside from clutching our stomachs and dreaming of the English coast, we resorted to guessing the stories of our fellow travellers to pass the time. They hailed from all corners of Asia, the Middle East, and North Africa, a vibrant mix of students, merchants, intellectuals, and workers. They wore a kaleidoscope of clothes, from ornate silk robes to simple linens, every hue and texture, and carried a fascinating array of objects, from practical contraptions for holding spices to precious trinkets that reminded them of distant homes.

"To fill the time, some played exotic instruments like sitars and tabla hand drums, while others prayed and chanted in equally melodic tones to the sound of Arabic tambourines, or played games of logic with stones and dice. A few even managed to smuggle aboard live animals, treasured family pets and auspicious creatures like snakes and small monkeys, to bless the voyage with good fortune and ensure safe passage.

"However, even among such a colourful collection of people, it was a group of seven Indian travellers, four men and three women, sitting cross-legged in a tight circle, that garnered the attention of the curious passengers. Though incredibly alike in appearance, it was their differences that made them stand out in the crowd.

"The first thing anyone with a keen eye noticed was that each of the seven wore differently coloured clothes. Among the three women, one wore a saffron sari elegantly draped around her body, another donned a delicate green sari with a white blouse choli, and the last was dressed in a red and gold shalwar kameez, a long tunic with wide, comfortable trousers.

"Among the men, one wore a dark blue dhoti, an unstitched piece of cloth about five meters long, wrapped around his waist and legs, paired with a long blue kurta tunic. Another man sported a black kurta and turban, while the two remaining men wore pink and yellow dhotis, each with a similarly coloured long coat known as a sherwani, and intricately designed pashmina shawls. Sitting together, they looked like the vibrant rainbows one sees after a heavy downpour followed by piercing sunshine.

"The next curiosity for the eagle-eyed passengers was the markings on each of the seven's bodies. Proudly displayed on their arms, hands, and feet were an array of intricate ink patterns: henna tattoos and colourful mandalas. To most, the designs might have looked similar, but to the trained observer, it was clear that the patterns on each of the seven were entirely unique. As individual as snowflakes in winter, as were the designs on their vast array of jewellery: stunning gold, silver, and iron bracelets, earrings, nose rings, and armlets.

"However, to truly perceptive observers, the most curious thing about the seven was the way they acted towards each other. Despite sitting in a close circle for nearly two weeks, there seemed to be a great distance between them, a cold reluctance to engage or connect. It wouldn't have been an exaggeration to say there was an obvious dislike, even disdain, for one another. Over the course of the journey, few words passed between them, and even fewer signs of friendship.

"During the day, the seven made use of the ship's additional facilities, including the thirdclass deck. However, they never left together or walked the ship in groups. Instead, one would leave for a few hours while the other six waited patiently for their return.

Once back and seated in their position within the circle, another would get up and leave for their daily dose of fresh sea air. This pattern continued all day until each of the seven had taken their allotted time, and evening came back around, confining the steerage passengers to the ship's underbelly once more.

"Even when seated together, they barely took their eyes off one another. It was as though they'd formed the circle specifically to keep watch over each other, the most efficient way to maintain collective vigilance and avoid any blind spots.

"When they ate, they shared food, taking a mouthful from the plate of the person next to them. When they stood up to stretch their limbs, the others watched their every move with growing suspicion. When it was time to use the toilet, they were given a strict ten-minute window in which to return, and even at night, when it was time to sleep, a group of them kept watch, rotating the order every evening to ensure each received their fair share of duty and rest. With more and more passengers becoming aware of the seven and their peculiar behaviour, it wasn't long before the group became the primary topic of conversation in steerage. The odd whispered comment quickly turned into full-blown conversations, and before long, the mysterious seven were all anyone talked about, offering an escape from the hardships and boredom of the long journey.

"Theories about the seven ranged from a radical religious sect sent to impose discipline on London society to a family troupe touring Europe with their traveling show. Some suggested they might be emissaries from the farthest corners of India, sent to negotiate trade with the government, or offspring of India's royal houses sent to marry British nobility and mix the two countries' bloodlines.

"However, it wasn't until drunken wagers were made, prized possessions were staked, and money changed hands that harmless speculations became unhealthy obsessions. Compelled to prove their theories correct and win their bets, passengers set about engaging the seven, determined to uncover the truth.

"At first, they attempted to approach the group's tightly formed circle and engage in polite conversation. But each time someone got close enough to say hello or wish them a good morning, they were met with stern glares or an icy wall of silence. Sometimes, the seven would even turn their gaze to the floor in unison, making it clear they did not wish to be spoken to.

"After several failed attempts over several days to breach the group's stubborn defences, the passengers conspired to approach them one by one during their solitary walks on the ship's deck. They would pop out of doorways or accidentally bump into them, some even feigning falls or dropping items to gain their attention.

"Male passengers attempted to act suave and gentlemanly in front of the three women in the group, hoping to catch their eye, while female passengers tried to use their femininity and seductive charm to attract the four men. However, no matter the timing or tactic, the passengers couldn't break the seven's iron resolve.

"For many, it was an odd and infuriating conundrum. How could these people, who clearly didn't like one another or enjoy each other's company, be so united in protecting the integrity of their group? For those with money on the line, the ongoing mystery was stretching their patience to breaking point. With just under two days left at sea, they had to find a way to break the impasse if they hoped to settle their bets and collect their winnings in time.

"With the passengers at a complete loss on how to proceed, it was Clifford Bambury, a drunk British merchant with a novel but dangerous idea, who found a way to pierce the seven's armour.

"An old sailor with firsthand experience of life at sea and weeks spent in confined spaces like steerage, he had seen and heard it all. Deciding that the only way to get the truth out of the seven was to give them something of equal value in return, he set about trying to uncover the root of their desire to travel to London. If he could find out what motivated them, it would be much easier to get them to talk.

"Having spent most of the journey drinking rum, playing cards, and sleeping, he had cunningly portrayed himself as a harmless sea dog, interested only in gambling and booze—a quiet and reclusive man of no consequence or threat to anyone. Positioned near the seven, he began drunkenly ranting about various topics: the British weather, the economy, the aristocracy, even the king. However, it wasn't until he started ranting about the Prime Minister and his former Home Secretary, Thomas Percy, that Bambury finally struck gold."

"What do you mean? What did he discover?" asked Jenkins, fully engrossed in the tale.

"A chink in their armour," replied the woman. "For nearly two whole weeks no passenger had even managed to make eye contact with one of the seven, but when Bambury mentioned Felix Grey and Thomas Percy, he noticed one of the women flinch and steal a momentary glance at him. He got what he was fishing for—a reaction."

"The next morning, he waited for the woman to take her daily walk and quickly followed after her. Confronting her on the third-class deck he finally uncovered the true reason behind the seven's mysterious journey to London."

"And, what was it?" pressed Jenkins, feeling a sudden wave of dizziness come over him.

"Nobody knows," replied the woman. "Clifford Bambury was never seen again."

"And what about the seven?" asked Jenkins, placing a hand on the ground to steady himself. "What happened to them?"

"They vanished," replied the woman, calmly observing the beads of sweat starting to roll down his forehead. "When the passengers awoke the next morning, there was no sign of them—no circle, no possessions, no colourful clothes or ornate jewellery. They were gone, simply disappeared into thin air.

"That's preposterous," barked Jenkins, suddenly irritated by the woman's story and its unsatisfactory ending. "Even if your story were true, how could you possibly know that level of detail?

How can you be sure that he uncovered the truth about the seven?"

"Now, that's a much better choice of question," replied the woman, methodically packing away the plate of desserts without touching a single one.

Jenkins glanced down at the plate and the white cloth, then noticed the henna tattoos peeking out from under her long sleeves, and finally, the holes in her nose where ornate rings would once have been attached. Suddenly, the realisation set in.

"It was you," he began, his throat tightening. "You're one of the…"

But before he could finish his sentence, the poison in his sweet finally overcame him, and the woman had claimed her second victim of the journey.